D0566317

# Death and a Pot of Chowder

# Also available by Cornelia Kidd (writing as Lea Wait)

## Mainely Needlepoint Mysteries

*Thread the Halls*

*Tightening the Threads*

*Dangling by a Thread*

*Thread and Gone*

*Threads of Evidence*

*Twisted Threads*

## Antique Print Mysteries

*Shadows on a Morning in Maine*

*Shadows on a Maine Christmas*

*Shadows on a Cape Cod Wedding*

*Shadows of a Down East Summer*

*Shadows at the Spring Show*

*Shadows on the Ivy*

*Shadows on the Coast of Maine*

*Shadows at the Fair*

## Also available by Lea Wait

*Pizza to Die For*

*Uncertain Glory*

*Finest Kind*

*Wintering Well*

*Seaward Born*

*Stopping to Home*

# Death and a Pot of Chowder

## A MAINE MURDER MYSTERY

Cornelia Kidd

NEW YORK

This is a work of fiction. All of the names, characters, organizations, places and events portrayed in this novel are either products of the author's imagination or are used fictitiously. Any resemblance to real or actual events, locales, or persons, living or dead, is entirely coincidental.

PUBLISHER'S NOTE: The recipes contained in this book are to be followed exactly as written. The publisher is not responsible for your specific health or allergy needs that may require medical supervision. The publisher is not responsible for any adverse reaction to the recipes contained in this book.



Published in the United States by Crooked Lane Books, an imprint of The Quick Brown Fox & Company LLC.

Crooked Lane Books and its logo are trademarks of The Quick Brown Fox & Company LLC.

Library of Congress Catalog-in-Publication data available upon request.

ISBN (hardcover): 978-1-68331-583-4
ISBN (ePub): 978-1-68331-584-1
ISBN (ePDF): 978-1-68331-585-8

Cover illustration by Teresa Fasolino.
Book design by Jennifer Canzone.

Printed in the United States.

www.crookedlanebooks.com

Crooked Lane Books
34 West 27th St., 10th Floor
New York, NY 10001

First Edition: June 2018

10 9 8 7 6 5 4 3 2 1

For Bob, who believed in me.
And still does.

# Chapter One

"Hospitality is a most excellent virtue; but care must be taken that the love of company, for its own sake, does not become a prevailing passion; for then the habit is no longer hospitality, but dissipation."

—*The Book of Household Management*
by Mrs. Isabella Beeton, London:
Ward, Lock, and Tyler, 1861

I never got letters.

Until now.

Oh, sure, electric and fuel bills addressed to "Mr. and Mrs. Burt Winslow, Island Road, Quarry Island, Maine" arrived regularly. Too many of those. But they hardly count as personal.

And no one I know writes letters with pens anymore. They call, or text, or e-mail.

So when Jake dropped the day's usual pile of hunting magazines and seed catalogs on our kitchen table, I didn't even glance through them.

"The school bus was late again. They should get a new driver. Mrs. Sage is too old." At fourteen, Jake was taller than me, borrowing his dad's razor, and full of opinions. He poured himself a bowl of sweet cereal and drowned it with milk. "I'm starving. And I'm going to be late getting to Maine Chance."

After school and weekends Jake had been helping Luc Burnham get Maine Chance Books, the secondhand bookstore Luc ran out of his ell and barn, ready for summer customers. The two of them spent hours sorting and shelving the hundreds of used books Luc bought at library sales and auctions during the winter. Jake earned enough to buy the video games he preferred to books. He was saving for a new, more powerful, rifle, too, hoping to be a winner in Maine's Moose Permit Lottery this year.

"Don't eat so fast. You'll upset your stomach," I automatically advised him, as I had thousands of times.

"Are you talking to me, or Blue?" Jake grinned and pointed at our old Maine Coon cat, who was scarfing up his dry food as if he were starving.

"Both of you," I answered.

At least Jake didn't choke up hair balls.

On school days, I packed two sandwiches for Jake and two for Burt. Jake ate one of his sandwiches (always bologna and cheese) and an apple on the morning school bus. The only day he stuck around for breakfast was Sunday, when I made blueberry pancakes.

I watched as he gulped his cereal. "Much homework tonight?"

"Nah. Did Algebra in school and read History on the bus.

I'm good." He hugged me quickly, too old to do that anywhere but in the privacy of our kitchen.

"Be home for supper."

The door slammed after him.

Jake got decent grades without much effort. Maybe that would change next year, when he'd take the other school bus, the one that picked up Quarry Island kids and took them over the bridge to the regional high school on the mainland.

I secretly hoped he'd get more interested in books after working with Luc. Jake talked of lobstering, as most island boys did, but I didn't see him taking up the family trade. He'd been in and around boats all his life, but he didn't have the same addiction to the sea that some island boys, like his friend Matt, did.

That was just as well. The Gulf of Maine was warming, driving lobsters into deeper waters farther north. I had nightmares about what would happen if lobstering no longer brought in a profit.

Despite the climate changes, life for most of us on Quarry Island was defined by the sea, as it had been for generations. People joked that islanders had salt water in their veins. We were different, separate, and wary of off-islanders who commented on the beauty of the island, wondered at our isolation, and then left.

Although I'd grown up here, and my husband lobstered, I also had ties to the land. For nine years, I'd kept the books for my stepfather Seth's roofing business and made sure his office ran smoothly. I'd enjoyed working with the roofers, doing the accounts, and generally keeping the office in order. Plus, my paycheck had helped our heads stay above water and provided health insurance. But since Seth's death last year I'd stayed close to home. No other office management jobs were on the island, and I didn't want to be far from home in case Jake or Burt needed me. Occasionally one of the baby quilts or placemats or pillow covers I stitched sold at a craft show or church fair, but quilting didn't seem to be my destiny.

I hadn't had any special training, like Cynthia Snowe, who was a nurse, or her sister, Rose, who was a nurse's assistant. Burt's younger brother, Carl, had dated both Cynthia and Rose (as well as probably every other eligible woman on the island), but in the past year had seemed to settle on Rose, the younger, more eager of the sisters. Both of them had steady incomes. I hoped he'd settle down with Rose. His erratic lifestyle was a constant worry to both Burt and me.

For now, I put all those thoughts aside. I assumed the rest of my day would be like every other day. At six tonight we'd eat the macaroni and cheese casserole I'd made this morning. Then I'd clean the kitchen, Burt would turn on the television to hear the weather forecast and fall asleep watching the evening news, and Jake would disappear to his room to study or, more likely, to play video games.

I bent to stroke Blue, who napped most of the time, but checked in with me occasionally to make sure his Giver of Food didn't forget him. On my dark days, I wondered if Burt and Jake also thought of me as their cook and housekeeper. Some moments I felt that way about myself.

But, don't get me wrong, I loved my husband and son and living on Quarry Island in Maine. Dark days didn't come often. My life was comfortable. Predictable.

We took for granted the smells of pine and wild blueberries and beach roses. The irregular cliffs, sharp ledges leading into the sea, and rounded sea stones. The wildness of nor'easters, and the calm of low tide. Cooking s'mores over fireplaces in the winter and at lobster bakes in summer. Collecting blue and green sea glass and sea pebbles that were pure black or pure white. Hold one in each hand and you got a wish. Every island child knew that, just as everyone on the island knew everyone else, knew where they'd come from, and could probably predict their futures pretty accurately. We weren't all close friends, but we were neighbors. No secret remained hidden for long on Quarry Island.

My family was part of a line of hardy New Englanders who'd sailed here from England or Scotland in the seventeenth or eighteenth century, pushed roots down through the granite core of the island, and remained, held by those roots and by the sea. Sometimes its fierce waves gave. Sometimes they took. Tides ebbed and flowed. They marked the rhythm of our lives, of our ancestors' lives, and, we hoped, the lives of generations following us.

I'd never thought of doing anything but marrying Burt and staying right here.

Mom had told the teenaged me that I lacked imagination; that I should fly away for a while before settling down and lining a nest with my feathers, like a female eider duck. But I was young and stubborn, and then I was pregnant. Burt and I were married when we were both eighteen. Jake came along four months later. No regrets.

Mom had seldom left the island for long, either, so I'd taken her advice with a handful of salt.

I moved the day's mail to the table next to Burt's chair in the living room. The thin blue envelope postmarked in Connecticut and addressed to me, Mrs. Anna Winslow, by hand, slipped from between a hunting supply catalog and this week's *Granite Gazette.*

A birthday card? My thirty-third birthday wasn't for another two months.

I didn't recognize the handwriting. Did any Quarry Island summer folks live in Connecticut? None I could think of. Could someone have heard about my quilting and want to order something? If I sold a whole quilt, I could buy Burt a new chair. The upholstery on his favorite recliner was thin and patched. Even the quilt covering it was beginning to wear through.

I held the envelope. It was fun to dream.

Then I sat at our round pine kitchen table and opened the letter that changed my life.

# Chapter Two

"The beginning of love may be compared to the uncorking of champagne. When the great outburst does come, it is tremendous; but if the effervescence which causes it is very great indeed, it soon exhausts itself."

—*Echoes from the* (London) *Clubs*, March 1868

The note inside wasn't long, but raised a deep-sea of questions.

*Dear Anna,*

*This letter may come as a surprise. I didn't know about you until last week, and you may not know about me.*

*I'm sorry to write that our father, Peter Jordan, died in an accident on the Merritt Parkway three weeks ago, on March 6. I learned he had another daughter when I read his will last week.*

*If you knew Dad, you know he spent most of his money, but we're to divide what's left. His lawyer's going to contact you, but I wanted to write first.*

*I've never had a sister, and I've always wanted to see*

*Maine. I Googled Quarry Island and it doesn't look far from Portland. Could we meet there? Soon? I'm hoping you're as curious about me as I am about you. And I think we have a lot to talk about.*

*Your sister, Izzie (Isabel Jordan)*

I read the letter again. And again.

Then I headed for the secret stash of chocolates I kept in an oatmeal box in the pantry. Some days I craved sweetness. If I didn't hide my supply, Jake and Burt would devour them.

I took two. No. Three.

Of course, I knew I'd had a biological father. I remembered Mom and Seth sitting on my bed one night when I was in kindergarten. I'd expected them to read one of my favorite Dr. Seuss books. Instead, they told me a story about myself.

"Anna, once upon a time you had another father. He was a good person, but he went away before you were even born. The dad you have now loves you very much."

That night I stopped calling Seth "Dad." He'd winced at first, but told me to call him whatever I was comfortable with. He probably thought I'd change my mind and call him Dad again, but I never did.

I never stopped wondering about my real father.

I didn't even know his name. After a while I stopped asking.

Was he Peter Jordan?

Did I have a sister?

Why hadn't Mom told me?

Or was this letter one of those hoaxes they talked about on the news—someone promising money if you sent them some first?

It had to be a hoax.

But she wasn't asking for money.

I read the note over again. Could I really have a sister named Izzie?

I had to know. Now.

I popped another piece of chocolate in my mouth, pulled on my low mud boots and old red cardigan, slipped the letter into my pocket, and headed for the house I'd grown up in, just down the street.

We lived inland, but nowhere on Quarry Island was far from the sea. Today the salt breeze and smell of mudflats at low tide was comforting. My life might have changed, but the island hadn't; the air smelled like home.

Island Road circled Quarry Island. I'd always lived here, in the cluster of homes near the Congregational church, not far from the town wharf where Burt, Carl, and the other lobstermen kept their boats.

Beyond the wharf was the drawbridge connecting us to the mainland. Leaving the island in July or August meant sitting for ten minutes while the bridge opened for sailboats or sightseeing boats. If you needed the bridge to open between November and April you had to call Silas Bean, the bridge tender, at his home and ask him ahead of time. Calling before noon was smartest, before he'd started drinking.

North of the bridge was a small restaurant that closed a few years back.

Only two houses were between mine and the one where I'd grown up.

Dolan and Lucy Martin and their son, Matt, now lived next door in a small colonial cottage with red shutters. Dolan,

Burt, and I had been close friends since junior high, and our sons, Matt and Jake, had been inseparable since they were toddlers. On Quarry Island, most people stayed around after they'd grown up.

Rob Erickson, in the next house, had grown up on the island, but left to become a detective with the Portland Police Department. After his divorce and then his mother's death two years ago, he'd retired and moved home to take care of his father, Gus, whose stroke kept him in a wheelchair. "Born an islander, die an islander," Rob sometimes joked.

The church, Luc Burnham's bookstore, Martha Decker's general store, and Willis Tarbox's gallery and home were across the street. Summer folks gaped at the faded purple paint Willis had used on his house, and the wind-tattered American flag he'd painted on his barn door, but the rest of us hardly noticed. Willis, like us, was part of Quarry Island.

I sniffed the wood smoke pouring out of his chimney. Willis depended on a woodstove to heat his home. We'd converted to oil, but I still loved the smell of a wood fire, and early April temperatures were chilly.

The slate path to my childhood home was damp with melted snow. Bare branches and thorns covered the trellis around the doorway. In late June it would be covered with the fragrant pink sea roses Mom planted years ago.

I walked in without knocking. Only a few summer people locked their doors.

Mom was sitting on the old flowered couch in the living room where she hand-sewed her quilt pieces. The couch was faded, and she kept threatening to make a slipcover for it, but the yellow and green upholstery I'd known as a child was still there. Mom sitting on that couch said "home" to me as much as the scent of apple cranberry pudding wafting from the kitchen. Mom patted the space next to her. "What's wrong, Anna?"

She'd always been able to tell when I was upset.

I blurted out my question. "Who's Peter Jordan, Mom? Is he my father?"

"What did you say?" she asked carefully, putting down the baby blanket she was stitching in the deep blues and greens of Maine's waters and forests.

Mom had always been straight with me, through good times and bad, except on one subject. I'd stopped asking about my father years ago.

The clatter of dishes meant Mamie, my grandmother, was in the kitchen. She'd always lived with Mom, Seth, and me in this small house. I'd asked her, too, about my father. She'd told me he wasn't an islander. He was from away. He wasn't part of our lives, so he wasn't important.

Over the years I'd accepted that he hadn't wanted me, although I'd never understood why. As an adult I'd wondered if it was Mom he was rejecting, not me.

Seth had taken me to father-daughter picnics and dances. He and Mom had both walked me down the aisle when I'd married Burt, the man I'd loved since we'd built a treehouse together when we were in sixth grade.

Islanders married islanders often enough to be joked about. The headstones in the island graveyard almost all belonged to members of six or seven different families. Go back enough years and most islanders were cousins.

Mom and Seth lost two babies when I was young. Maybe because of that, she and I'd always been close. She'd even been the one holding my hand when the midwife delivered Jake. Burt had been too young and too nervous to stay by my side.

I sat next to her and repeated, "Peter Jordan. Was he my father?"

For a moment she didn't say anything. Then she touched my arm gently. "Yes." Her dark blue eyes reminded me of the sea in winter storms. "I never told you because I didn't want you looking for someone who didn't want to be found. I didn't want you to be hurt. I wouldn't even have told you Seth wasn't your real father, but he said too many people on the island knew, and one day someone would tell you. He wanted you to hear it from us."

I ignored her tears. "So, was I Anna Jordan when I was born?" The name sounded strange. Anna Jordan was someone I didn't know.

"For a short time, legally. You're thirty-two now. I hope that's old enough to understand."

Mamie stood in the doorway leading to the kitchen, wiping her hands on her flowered apron. The dish towel in her hand matched her gray hair.

"As soon as Seth and I married, we started calling you Anna Chase." Mom put her hand on mine. "How did you find out about Peter? Who told you?"

I pulled the creased letter out of the pocket in my jeans. "This came in the mail today."

Mom unfolded the paper. Her hands shook as she read the words. I'd already memorized them.

As she read the letter a second time, her eyes filled. "Peter had another child. So you have a half sister." Her voice was almost a whisper. "I wonder if he stayed with her—with this

Izzie's mother—or whether he left her, too." She paused, and looked at me. "She's included her e-mail address. What are you going to do, Anna? Are you going to meet her?"

"I haven't decided. Tell me about Peter Jordan. My father."

She handed the letter back to me. "It was a long time ago. He was from Connecticut. His family rented the Warner cottage one summer. He was tall and handsome and charming, or at least I thought he was. We fell in love. One night we drove to Portland and got married. We were young and it was crazy, but we did it. Then he left."

"Why didn't you go with him?

Mom didn't answer immediately. "He didn't ask me."

"And you were pregnant?"

"I found out a month after he'd gone."

"Did you tell him?"

"As soon as I knew, I wrote to him at his college address. At first he sent a few dollars, but he didn't stay in touch. I signed the divorce papers when his parents' lawyer sent them to me a few months later, but I kept writing to Peter. After a year his letters came back; he must have left that school. The Jordans never came back to Quarry Island. After that, I fell in love with Seth. He was a good husband, and a good father to you."

"He was," I agreed. Stepfather, I added silently. Seth had been kind. But his love hadn't stopped me from wondering about my real father. The man I'd never met, and now never would.

Mom looked toward Mamie. "Peter's dead. He'd married again and had another daughter."

She nodded. "I overheard." She walked toward us. "I knew about his wife, and their daughter."

"What?" Mom sat up straight.

"I kept in touch with Peter's parents for a while." Mamie looked determined. "They deserved to know about their first grandchild."

"You had no right to do that!" Mom's face flushed, the way it always did when she was angry. "Peter was my husband, not yours. My mistake. My life was fine without him."

"I did what I thought was right. For his family and for you, though you didn't know it. I knew someday Anna would want to know. She had that right. I wanted her to be able to find him, if she wanted to."

"It was my right to decide what to tell Anna. Not yours. I married Seth. I gave her a good father."

"True enough. But she wasn't his blood." Mamie looked straight at Mom. "And I never told Anna because of how you felt. You should have been the one to tell her."

The two women who'd raised me—the women I'd loved all my life—glared at each other.

Mamie was even more stubborn than Mom.

"Then you knew about Izzie," I said, breaking the tension by going over to Mamie and handing her the letter.

She glanced at it. "I haven't heard from Peter's family in years. I only knew he had another daughter." She looked up at me. Mamie's head only reached my shoulder. Mom had said Peter Jordan was tall. Maybe he was why I was taller than both Mamie and Mom.

"So. Are you going to meet her?" Mamie asked.

"Don't get too involved, Anna," Mom cautioned. "Don't get your hopes up. She may be your sister, but your family is here on the island. Always has been and always will be. You don't know this woman, or what she may want."

At that moment I decided what I had to do. "I'm not leaving my family here, Mom. But Isabel Jordan's my sister. She's family, too. I'm going to meet her."

# Chapter Three

*"As substitutes for coffee, some use dry brown bread crusts, and roast them; others soak rye grain in rum, and roast it; others roast peas in the same way as coffee. None of these are very good. Where there is a large family of apprentices and workmen, and coffee is very dear, it may be worth-while to use the substitutes, or to mix them half and half with coffee; but, after all, the best economy is to go without."*

—*The Frugal Housewife: Dedicated to Those Who Are Not Ashamed of Economy* by Lydia Maria Child, Boston: Marsh & Capen, 1829

Ten days later, I was on my way to Portland to meet my sister. Connecticut seemed like a world away, but it was only about five hours driving time. Izzie's car had broken down, though, and, impatient to meet me, she'd insisted on coming today anyway. She was taking a bus that arrived a little after two.

What would she think of me, and of Maine?

After trying on three different outfits, I'd decided on my newest jeans and a yellow sweater, the color of daffodils. I'd left my shoulder-length brown hair down, curled it a bit, and even added my favorite earrings with yellow sea glass.

The April air was beginning to freshen on this Saturday. Snow drops and early crocuses were appearing in dooryards and catbirds had returned, but Maine in mud season was still a good two months from looking like the pictures tourists saw on postcards or calendars.

Normally, I didn't notice the dirty patches of unmelted snow lying in the protected shade under trees and in corners of parking lots, or the beer cans and burger wrappers discarded since November and hidden all winter. How would Izzie react to the world I took for granted?

Spring cleanup, preparing the state for summer visitors, would start in a few weeks.

Mamie says we have it easy today. When she was a girl, newly arrived from Quebec so her father could work in the textile mills up to Lewiston, side roads were dirt. Today most are paved, although by April they're temporarily pockmarked with frost heaves and posted with orange signs warning against travel by heavy vehicles.

I steered our old truck around the deepest potholes. Year-rounders had four-wheel drive and knew how to cope. I hadn't seen a car or truck trapped in mud for years.

Did it matter what Izzie thought of Maine? After all, she'd go back to her world and leave me in mine. But I was proud of my state, and wished she could see it at its best.

Would she be as tall as I was? Would she have dark brown

hair like mine? Would she think her ears and nose were too big? Would she love daffodils in spring, and the smell of baking bread?

Mom had shaken her head when I'd asked if she wanted to come with me to meet Izzie. "She's your sister," she'd said. "And besides, you've met summer people. They don't stay. Connecticut thinking is farther than miles from Maine."

"She seems nice," I'd said, already defensive about the sister I didn't know.

"So far you've . . . what? E-mailed each other?"

I'd nodded. "We decided not to exchange pictures or many details about our lives until we met."

Mom had her doubts. I was determined to prove her wrong.

Although, I admitted to myself as the miles to Portland went by, all I knew about Izzie Jordan was that she was my sister and she wanted to meet me.

"You do what you need to do, Anna," Mom had counseled. "Take the day. Don't worry about us on the island. How's Jake getting to Saturday baseball practice?"

"He's staying at the Martin's Friday night. Lucy's going to take both Jake and Matt to practice and bring them home."

"Tell him to come to my house if he wants a hot lunch after practice. I'll be working at the food bank in the morning, but I'll be home before he is, and Mamie'll have a pot of bean soup on the simmer. There'll be plenty for Jake and Matt, too, if they're together."

When were Jake and Matt not together?

And they'd love an excuse to eat at Mom and Mamie's. Mamie's passion was cooking the Quebecois dishes her mother and grandmother had taught her. I'd grown up with two women who were good cooks. Burt had always preferred hamburgers and fried fish and casseroles, so I hadn't focused on learning to cook everything I'd eaten growing up. When his parents were alive, we'd eaten at their house at least once a week, and now we often ate with Mom and Mamie. Since I'd been out of a job I'd taken more time with meals, but my cooking wasn't up to their standards.

I didn't want to admit it, but I was nervous. Maybe my sister and I would have nothing in common but genes.

Maybe we'd become best friends.

But no matter what happened, meeting a sister I'd never known existed was more exciting than anything that had happened to me since Jake was born.

Burt understood that. At first he'd been hesitant about my decision. "You don't know this woman. You don't even know how old she is, or how she was brought up. Just tell that lawyer to send whatever's due to you from your father's will. No matter how much it is, it won't make up for his abandoning you and your mom to manage on your own."

"Izzie has to be younger than me, and she knew our father. She can tell me about him," I'd answered. "I don't even know what he looked like."

Burt shook his head. "What does it matter? He left. When he did that, he gave up all claims to being your father. You're your own person, Anna. What matters is your family here on the island, and that Jake and I love you."

"You grew up with your parents, and a brother. You've always known everything about them. Your father lobstered, and now you and Carl do. You all even look alike!"

"We're not the same. Sure, Carl's my little brother, but he's irresponsible and a pain sometimes. You and Jake are the most important part of my life. I'd rather have you and Jake any day than any of the women Carl comes up with. He squanders money and time, and then complains he can't afford to repair the engine on his *Fair Winds.* I've been helping him set his traps, but he should have put aside money for emergencies."

"Carl's not organized, like you are," I'd reminded him. "And he's been seeing Rose Snowe for a year now."

"And her sister, Cynthia, before that." Burt shook his head. "I've been watching out for Carl since we were kids. He tagged along after me and got us both in trouble. Sure, we share history and heritage. But he's twenty-nine now. He needs to grow up and take responsibility for himself."

"Carl's lucky to have you," I'd agreed. "But Izzie and I share a father, too."

"That may be all you share. You don't even know where she grew up. All you know is her address in Connecticut now. Folks from away move around a lot. She could have been raised in California. Or Texas." He paused. "I know you're excited, Anna, but I don't want you to be disappointed."

"I understand," I'd assured him. And I did. Where you were born and raised was important.

"Are you going to bring her here?"

"I don't know." I didn't tell him I'd already made up the bed in the small guest room I used for my quilting supplies. "When I see her, I'll know. Maybe she'll have to go right back to Connecticut. Maybe she won't want to come here." Maybe she'd look at me and decide I was boring and frumpy and too unsophisticated to be worth bothering about.

Some summer visitors looked right through Mainers who

were waitresses, clerks, and fishermen, seeing them only as providers of services or photo ops. Not all vacationers dismissed the locals who made their vacations possible, but it happened.

"She'd be welcome here, of course," Burt said, putting his arm around me. "She's your sister, so she has to be special. You do what you feel is right. Are you sure you don't want me to go with you? Carl and I were going to work together today, but he could take my *Anna* out by himself." He hesitated. "You've never driven to Portland alone."

Burt always drove when we went any distance. And yes, I was nervous. But I was an adult. I didn't want to admit to my sister that I needed my husband to drive me somewhere.

"I'll be fine," I assured him. "Izzie and I should get to know each other a little, just the two of us at first."

"She's going to love you, Honey," he said. "How could she not?"

I reached up and kissed the end of his nose. Thank goodness Jake had inherited Burt's nose, not my pointed one.

"And she'll love Maine. Why do you think it says 'Vacationland' on our license plates? Everyone loves Maine."

"Not in April they don't," I pointed out.

"So, invite her to come back in July," he said. "Who wants to be in Connecticut in July?"

I shook my head and laughed. No matter how nervous I was, Burt had my back. Did Izzie have a man like him in her life? I hoped so. I couldn't imagine life without Burt.

"See if you can find out how much money that father of yours left you," he'd said as he headed for the door. "We could take a little vacation, if there's enough. You've been wanting to see Boston. We might even take in a Sox game."

"After we pay off our bills," I amended. Our emergency fund was low, as it always was after a winter without lobstering. I dreamed out loud. "And buy a new couch to replace the one that sags. And a new chair for you. And put money aside so Jake can go to college." That last dream was mine alone, seldom-voiced. We had enough to get by, but money was never easy when you depended on tides and traps.

"Sox game would be fun. Jake doesn't need college to learn lobstering." Burt came back, bent over, and kissed me lightly, smiling at my fantasies. "My wife, the heiress."

He picked up the box of ham sandwiches and thermos of hot coffee I'd prepared for him, as I did every day, and was gone, down to the town dock. It was first light. Lobstermen spent long, cold hours on the water. This time of year the bugs (as fishermen called them) were migrating, coming closer to land. Burt and Carl and the other lobstermen were setting traps to follow them.

The storm door banged on his way out.

I spent the next few hours filling time by cleaning the house. About eleven-thirty I finally left home. I waved to Willis, who was checking his mailbox, and drove over the bridge and off-island.

Traffic on Route 1 was heavier than I remembered. I focused on the road and passed two New Brunswick trucks carrying lumber south.

Izzie's note said our dad hadn't left much money. But it was fun to imagine. Like buying a lottery ticket, it was an excuse to dream.

Dad. Peter Jordan. If I'd grown up as Anna Jordan would I have been a different person? Had Izzie always lived with our father? Had his parents told him where I lived, and that I'd married? Had he known he had a grandson? So many questions.

I reached onto the passenger seat, into the sea bag I used as a handbag, and felt for one of the chocolate bars I'd tucked in there this morning.

The chocolate melted in my mouth as I drove off Route 295 into Portland, turned off exit 5, and into the Portland Transportation Center parking lot for trains and Concord buses. Typical Maine economy: Why build two terminals when one would do? I parked in the short-term parking lot.

Izzie'd been on the road for hours. She must be exhausted. Was she as nervous and excited as I was?

I picked up the sheet of poster board Jake had given me. "I've seen it in movies, Mom. If you don't know the person you're meeting you print their name on a card and hold it up, so they can find you." He'd printed "IZZIE JORDAN" with a large red marker on the sign.

I was self-conscious holding it, but Jake was right. One other person waiting for arriving trains and buses was also holding a sign. He was probably a taxi driver meeting a fare, not someone meeting a relative for the first time.

But at least I wasn't alone.

I sat at the end of the row of uncomfortable plastic chairs near the door where bus passengers would arrive. Every time a bus pulled in I stood up. Buses from Boston. Buses from Bangor. Buses from Logan Airport.

I bought two more chocolate bars at the vending machines near the restrooms and ate them both, hardly tasting them. Had Izzie's bus been in an accident? How late could it be?

"That bus is doing fine; it's just delayed in traffic. It should arrive in about fifteen minutes," a friendly woman behind the ticket counter assured me.

Those fifteen minutes were the longest I'd lived through since Matt and Jake had been playing in the quarry, and Jake had fallen and broken his leg. Cell phones only worked intermittently on the island, but thank goodness Matt's had worked that day. He'd called our house, and I'd called 911 before driving to the quarry myself. It had only been fifteen minutes, I was told later, before the ambulance arrived. It had seemed like hours.

At least no one was in pain today. But I couldn't keep still. I paced the small waiting room, grasping my sign.

Finally, "Two fifteen, arriving now," blared over the public-address system. I joined the dozen others who moved toward the glass wall separating the waiting room from where the bus was pulling in, forty minutes late.

Every time a woman started down the stairs from the bus I wondered, was that Izzie? How old was she? Would I recognize her?

I held my sign, and dismissed the young teenager in a ski jacket and shorts and the elderly woman who needed assistance.

One brown-haired woman wearing a red jacket smiled at me, and I went toward her. She shook her head when she saw my sign.

Not Izzie.

I kept scanning the area, looking for my sister. Where was she? Had she missed the bus? Unexpectedly, an elegantly dressed young Asian woman with sleek, cropped black hair stopped in front of me. "Anna?" She wore skinny black pants, a pale blue draped top, a black cape, and three silver earrings in one ear, two in the other. I nodded. Cautiously. My best yellow sweater and newest jeans suddenly felt inadequate.

"I love your sign! I'm your sister! Izzie!"

"Izzie?" I asked, sounding stupid. Who else would it be? But—where was the Izzie I'd pictured? This woman was shorter than I was, and didn't look at all like me.

We both laughed nervously as she reached out and hugged me, but my sign got in the way, keeping us apart.

Then she pulled back. "You didn't expect me to look like this, did you?" She gestured toward her face, smiling.

"I didn't think . . ." I blurted. "I mean, I thought you'd look like me."

She looked at me, pretending to be critical. "I inherited big ears from Dad. You did, too. And we've got the same ugly nose. But my mom was Korean. I suspect yours wasn't?" Izzie smiled, but her eyes had filled with tears when she said the word "Dad."

She was mourning our father. A man I'd never even met. I swallowed a flare of jealousy. "I didn't know. About your mom, I mean."

She laughed again. "I should have warned you. But we agreed not to exchange pictures. I loved the expression on your face when you realized who I was! Here," she took the sign. "Let's ditch that. You found me!" She stuck the poster board behind a trash container. "I'll get my bags and then we can take off. Your last e-mail promised lunch in Portland. I'm starving!"

She headed back to the bus, where she pointed out two enormous red suitcases to the driver.

My sister was half Korean. I couldn't believe it. I'd imagined we'd look like twins. Instead, despite the ears and the nose Izzie had immediately noticed (she must have been imagining what I looked like, too), we didn't look at all alike.

How surprised Jake and Burt—and Mom—would be.

My sister! Life, and I suspected Izzie herself, was full of surprises.

# Chapter Four

> "How to Preserve a Husband: Be careful in your selection; do not choose too young and take only such as have been reared in a good moral atmosphere. Some insist on keeping them in a pickle, while others put them in hot water. This only makes them sour, hard, and sometimes bitter."
>
> —*International Cooking* by Federation of American Women's Clubs Overseas (Copenhagen). Undated

Izzie's suitcases could have held every piece of clothing I owned, with room to spare.

"I always travel with too much. I wasn't sure what Maine weather would be like. And my knife kit takes up a lot of room. I never leave my knives in my apartment."

"Knives?" I asked dubiously. I took the handle of one of her suitcases and led Izzie and her luggage toward my old blue pickup. Burt had knives, of course—knives he used when he was lobstering, or fishing, or hunting. Even Jake had one or two. But why would this elegant young woman in her early twenties (I guessed) travel with knives? For protection?

"I'm a chef," she explained as we reached the parking lot. "Of course, you didn't know. We said we'd wait to talk about our lives until we were together."

What else hadn't she mentioned before today, beside her mom and her profession?

Burt was right; my sister was from another world.

"Then you work at a restaurant?"

"Not yet," she said, climbing into the passenger seat. "I just graduated. CIA."

"What?" I turned my key. "CIA?"

"Culinary Institute of America. Don't worry—I'm not a spy or anything," she assured me. "Lots of people get those two mixed up. I'm looking for a job." She took off her cape and folded it, revealing a tattoo of a crossed knife and fork on her right forearm.

"I see," I said, pulling out of the parking lot. I didn't, actually. But at least she wasn't a spy.

"Getting a decent job in New York City is impossible, and finding an affordable place to live is worse. And I don't want to go back to Connecticut. It's a culinary wasteland. Plus—too many memories are there." Izzie paused. "I've heard Maine's a foodie state, so maybe I'll find a job here. Thought I'd check out Portland restaurants while I'm visiting."

What would Izzie think of the diner where I'd planned we'd eat lunch? Should I have chosen a fancier restaurant in the Old Port section of Portland? I didn't even know which those were, and probably couldn't afford them.

"Your husband's a lobsterman, right? That's what you wrote. How cool to be able to eat lobsters any time you want to!"

That was one of the few details I'd given her. Married to a lobsterman, with a teenaged son. "Fourth generation," I said, with some pride. Burt's father, uncle, grandfather, and great-grandfather had put out traps. Burt and his brother had followed in their footsteps. I didn't point out that we hardly ever ate lobster. They were the economic center of our life, not our favorite food. "Burt's been lobstering since he was twelve."

"That young?" Izzie looked amazed.

"He started with a skiff and a couple of traps then," I explained. "Lots of kids start that way."

"Wow. When I was twelve I didn't even wear a bra," Izzie said. " 'Course I don't always wear one now, either." She looked around as I drove off Route 295 into Portland. "So where are we going for lunch?"

Izzie might be a chef, but this was my state. "I decided somewhere we could talk would be best," I said. "I know a place where you can get breakfast all day." I glanced at Izzie. She didn't look thrilled. "They have seafood, too."

She recovered quickly. "Sounds great."

As I pulled into the parking lot, Izzie gasped. "You didn't tell me it was a retro diner!"

The Miss Portland was painted bright blue, with its name in enormous yellow letters on the side.

"It was built in nineteen forty-nine." I tried to remember what I'd learned the last time Burt and I'd treated ourselves to a meal in Portland.

The Miss Portland was retro (was that good or bad?) and

popular. Several police cars, a half dozen pickups older than the one I was driving, and a couple of dozen cars were in the parking lot this midafternoon.

"Seagulls on the roof! Seagulls everywhere!" Izzie looked from one side of the pickup to the other. I hoped she'd approve of eggs and pancakes for lunch. The Miss Portland probably had crabmeat or lobster benedict too.

My phone buzzed as I pulled my key out of the ignition.

"Excuse me a second." I quickly thought through a mental list of people who might call. Mom and Mamie knew I was meeting Izzie. They wouldn't bother me. Burt was out on the *Anna.* Jake had eaten lunch at Mom and Mamie's after practice and would be at Maine Chance Books, or hanging out somewhere with Matt. When you lived on an island there weren't too many places to go.

Who would be calling?

I pulled my phone out of the canvas bag made of used sails Burt had given me for Christmas.

"Yes?" I said quickly.

"Did you pick up Izzie all right?" Burt's voice was tight.

"No problem. Izzie's with me right now," I said, smiling at her.

"Sorry about the timing. But you need to come home. Now."

"What's happened?" I tried to keep my voice calm. Burt, my steady, understanding Burt, would never ask me to return early unless there was a serious problem. My world focused on his words. "Are you all right?"

"I'm fine," he assured me.

"Then, Jake? Mom? Mamie?" What could have happened since I'd left Quarry Island?

"They're all fine." His voice hesitated. "It's Carl."

"Carl?"

"He didn't want to go out with me this morning. Said he'd tinkered with his engine again last night and hoped he'd fixed it. Wanted to take his *Fair Winds* for a test run."

It wasn't safe for a lobsterman to go out without his sternman, but sometimes Burt and Carl did. They all did.

"Yes?"

"I found the *Fair Winds* adrift off Granite Point. Rolling. He wasn't on board."

Burt couldn't be saying what I thought he was.

"Carl's gone, Anna. I called 911 and towed the *Fair Winds* in. The Marine Patrol and the police are searching, along with Dolan and me and the other guys."

"I'm leaving Portland now," I said. "I'll be home in about ninety minutes."

"Good," said Burt.

"And—I'll be praying."

Burt hung up.

The air seemed twenty degrees colder than it was before my phone rang. The parking lot and the other cars and even my newly found sister were in a haze.

For a moment I went blank.

"What's happened?" asked Izzie. "Who was that?"

"Burt. My husband. He found his brother's boat adrift. Empty. Carl's missing. The Marine Patrol and police are searching, along with the locals."

"Searching?"

I put my key back in the car. "He must have fallen overboard."

"Get out, Anna. We're changing places. I'm driving." Izzie directed. "Head me in the right direction. I'm going to Quarry Island with you."

At first I didn't move. Then I nodded, numbly, and did as she said.

North Atlantic waters were deep and cold. I hugged myself in silence.

"Get back on Route 295 and head north," I directed.

What could have happened?

My brother-in-law wasn't my most reliable relative, but he was close to Burt, and an important part of our lives. We were family.

Burt and Carl had lobstered all their lives. They knew their boats and the waters. They knew when to come in if storms threatened.

No Quarry Island fisherman had been lost at sea since I was five or six. Everyone on the island had been at that funeral. I hadn't known the fisherman whose sternman hadn't been able to haul him up after his foot caught in the trapline that pulled him overboard. But I never forgot his story.

Each spring, Reverend Beaman, Quarry Island's minister, held a blessing of the fleet at the town wharf and the head of the town council read the names of everyone from the island who'd been lost at sea. The first man—a boy, really—he'd been younger than Jake was now—had been hit by a boom and knocked into the rough North Atlantic in 1689.

Two brothers from my family were lost together in an 1848 storm, and three of Burt's ancestors were also on the list. So far no women were listed, but one day they would be. More women fished and lobstered every year.

Every May, I cried during the Quarry Island memorial reading. It was a reminder, as if we needed one, that island life was challenging, and the sea couldn't be trusted.

"Maybe they'll find him," said Izzie. "Maybe he'll be fine, and waiting for you at home."

Izzie didn't know lobsters and ropes and waters. "Maybe."

I wasn't usually the praying sort, but this wasn't a usual day. I kept saying Carl's name, over and over, in my mind. He had to be all right. He had to be.

But I was a lobsterman's wife. I lived on an island. I knew the odds.

They weren't good.

# Chapter Five

"Cure for headache: Sponge the head all over, night and morning, with water as hot as you can bear it, and rub dry with a coarse towel."

—*Peterson's Magazine*, March, 1886.
Peterson's, an American magazine for women, was published from 1842–1898.

"The town wharf's over the bridge, on your left," I instructed as we approached Quarry Island.

Izzie nodded.

Neither Izzie nor I had spoken, except to give or confirm directions, in over an hour. I silently thanked her for sensing, without being told, that I couldn't chat right now.

The drawbridge was down, thank goodness. The wharf parking lot was full: two police cars, multiple trucks, and several cars were parked close together. Carl's shiny red Ford pickup was next to the boathouse, in the space he usually used. He was so proud of that new truck.

"Turn into the field across the street," I said.

Izzie glanced at me. “It’s not a parking lot.”

“People park there when the wharf lot is full,” I explained. “Stop near the street. Farther in will be deep mud. We don’t want to get stuck.”

We headed for the knots of people near or on the wharf. When there was trouble, Quarry Island people gathered.

“Thank you for understanding,” I said to Izzie. “We haven’t had a chance to talk. But you’ll stay with Burt and me at least for tonight, all right?”

“Of course,” she agreed, looking around. “What’s happening?”

“We’ll find out,” I promised both of us as we got to the wharf.

Lucy Martin waved and I headed toward her. “Lucy! I was in Portland when Burt called. I came as fast as I could.”

She was wearing a jacket that almost matched her slacks. Her hair was ruffled by the wind, but her makeup was in place. Appearances meant a lot to Lucy. She looked past me at Izzie, questioningly.

“This is my sister, Izzie Jordan,” I said. “Izzie, my friend and neighbor, Lucy Martin.” Lucy had known I was going to meet my sister today. I didn’t bother to explain how I had an Asian-American sister who dressed like a sophisticated New Yorker. Lucy didn’t ask. Today we were focused on Carl. “Any word?”

She shook her head and pointed at the float where Carl’s *Fair Winds* was tied. “Burt towed his boat in. The search and rescue patrol boats are still looking for Carl. They’ve got helicopters, too, and our guys are all out looking. We don’t know how long Carl was out there before . . .” Lucy’s voice broke.

She and Carl were the same age. They'd played hide-and-seek together when they were children and been close friends ever since. In all the years I'd known her, I'd never seen Lucy cry, not even when her mother died. Today her eyes were red and swollen. Her mascara must have been water proof.

I hugged her. "Carl and Burt have been setting their traps together since Carl's engine went on the fritz. Burt said Carl got it started today."

"Must have," Lucy agreed. "Tide was full early this morning, so it was dead low about noon. By now, currents would have pulled him out to sea."

She carefully avoided saying "his body would have been pulled out."

"Couldn't he swim to shore?" asked Izzie.

Lucy and I looked at each other.

I answered, "He couldn't swim, Izzie. Not more than a few strokes. Most men who work the waters can't."

She looked surprised. "But why?"

"North Atlantic waters are wicked deep and cold, and currents are strong. Fall overboard, and unless someone is there to pull you out, chances are you'll freeze and be pulled under. Knowing how to swim would prolong the pain. Not swimming is an old mariner's tradition."

Lucy's eyes filled.

Izzie pointed to the wharf. "If everyone's out looking for Carl, who's on his boat?"

We turned toward the dock. A man and a woman were on the deck of the *Fair Winds*, taking photographs and examining the starboard gunwale, the upper edge of the side of the boat.

"They've been out there for the past half hour," Lucy

explained. “The man with Officer Heedles is one of the Marine Patrol officers.” Carmela Heedles was from the County Sheriff’s Office. When the law was needed on Quarry Island, she was the one who came. But we were pretty law-abiding. We didn’t see her often.

“I talked to the Marine Patrol dispatcher. It’s still being called a rescue operation,” said Reverend Beaman, joining us along with Willis Tarbox. I quickly introduced them to Izzie.

“Is a rescue operation good?” Izzie asked quietly.

“That means they’re still hoping. Maybe Carl was wearing his life jacket. Maybe he had a raft with him,” Willis explained.

Reverend Beaman’s curly gray hair was almost covered up by her navy seaman’s watch cap, and she was wearing sweatpants and a sweater. She laid it out bluntly. “When there’s no hope, it turns into a recovery. As long as it’s a rescue, there’s hope they might find him alive.”

Lucy’s fists were tight. “He has to be all right. He has to!”

The missing fisherman could have been Lucy’s husband, Dolan. Or my Burt. I squeezed Lucy’s hand. For early April, it was a warm day, but Lucy’s hand was frigid. “Where are the boys?” I asked, looking around.

Lucy’s Matt and my Jake were seldom far apart. “They’re out with Burt, searching,” she said. “They volunteered as soon as they heard.”

I nodded. Fourteen was old enough, and two more sets of eyes would help to glimpse something—someone, I silently corrected myself—between the waves. Island boys were told the dangers of the sea. This afternoon they were getting a hard lesson.

“Hot coffee?”

Luc Burnham, the used bookdealer Jake worked for, was holding a tray of covered take-out cups. Luc was in his late seventies, wore his long gray hair in a braid, and walked with a slight limp he called his "war injury." His worn jeans hung low on his hips, and he wore a plaid flannel shirt over a warm silk tee shirt. Jake once told me he suspected Luc wasn't injured in war; he'd slipped off one of the ladders in his barn when he was shelving books. No one knew for sure. Luc was an off-islander who'd moved to Quarry Island when I was in kindergarten. Along with our small library that depended on donations from summer patrons, his Maine Chance Books was the chief source of books on the island. In summer months, it also drew antiquarian bookdealers and vacationing readers.

"Thank you," I said, reaching for a cup.

Izzie and the reverend took cups, too. Lucy shook her head. Willis stamped his feet, as though to keep them warm. "Just what we need," he said, accepting a cup. "Good of you to think of it."

"They're all black, I'm afraid. I have a large percolator in my barn for customers, but I didn't have enough milk," Luc apologized. He looked at Izzie. "Don't believe we've met."

"Izzie Jordan," she said. "I'm Anna's sister."

Luc looked her up and down. "Nice of you to visit," he said. "Timing was off, though."

Izzie nodded, and Luc moved on to another group of people with his tray.

On the far side of the wharf, I spotted Mom and Mamie talking to Rose and Cynthia Snowe and Rob Erickson and his father, Gus. Gus had been a lobsterman, of course. After his stroke, he'd sold his traps to a younger man. His aging body was a constant frustration to him and he'd taken the death of his wife hard. We'd all been relieved when Rob came home to the island to live with him.

"Izzie, let me introduce you to my mother and grandmother," I said, excusing us and leading Izzie toward another knot of watchers.

"Crime scene guys," Rob Erickson was saying as we got closer. "Checking for blood."

"Blood?" I interrupted before I introduced Izzie. "What blood?"

"I know one of the Marine Patrol guys from my days in Portland homicide," said Rob. "He told me there was blood on the gunwale. Could be Carl hit his head when he went overboard."

I mentally scanned through all the scenarios that would have ended with Carl being in the sea. Why was there blood on the lip of the boat? Or maybe it was on the outside of the gunwale. Rob was right. He could have hit it as he went over the side. I shivered, imagining.

"Mom, Mamie, Rob, Gus, this is my sister, Izzie. She's staying with Burt and me," I added, for Mom's benefit. "Izzie, this is my mother, Mrs. Chase, and her mother, Mrs. Nolin. Rob Erickson and his father, Gus. And Rose and Cynthia Snowe."

Rose nodded, but kept her gray eyes focused on the water. She was wearing pale blue scrubs; she must have come straight from the hospital on the mainland where she and Cynthia both worked. Although Rose had been Carl's girl for the past year or so, I didn't know her as well as I knew Cynthia. Cynthia was closer to my age, Carl had dated her earlier, and she was a close friend of Lucy's. Both Rose and Cynthia worked at the island clinic when they weren't scheduled at the hospital.

They lived in their parents' home on the other side of Quarry Island, near where Burt and Carl had grown up. The sisters' mom and dad wintered in Florida, so Cynthia and Rose just had each other most of the time. On the island, relationships were sometimes confusing, but I hadn't been surprised when Carl dropped Cynthia for Rose. Cynthia was the prettier sister, but she was much more serious about her career, and life in general, than her younger sister. Probably too serious for fun-loving Carl. I suspected Rose saw her future as Carl's wife, not as a health care professional. Every time I'd seen her with Carl she'd clung to him like a barnacle on a wharf piling.

A century ago, Cynthia and Rose, both unmarried and over twenty-five, would have been dubbed spinsters. Despite the times, I suspected some islanders still viewed them that way.

"We got here as soon as we could," said Cynthia. Her long light brown hair was braided and wrapped around her head in an old-fashioned style that suited her. "I was at home. Dr. Neeson called me as soon as he heard. He had a patient to take care of at the clinic, but wanted me to be here in case I could help." She glanced over at Rose. "I called Rose. She headed here after her shift was over."

"Rose is Carl's girl," I explained quietly to Izzie.

Rose stood stalwartly, ignoring everyone around her and staring out to sea.

She'd thought Carl was her future.

I reached over and squeezed her hand. She hardly noticed.

"Pleased to meet you all," said Izzie. "Although not under these circumstances." She gestured toward the dock.

Mamie smiled and hugged Izzie lightly. "And good to meet you, Izzie. We're hoping you'll stay long enough so we can all get to know you."

"I hope so, too," said Izzie.

"Welcome to Quarry Island," said Rob. "This is a time for family to be together."

"You don't look like your father," Mom blurted out, staring at Izzie.

"More like my mother," Izzie answered easily. "But Anna and I have the same ears, and nose. She has beautiful blue eyes, like yours, Mrs. Chase."

*Well done, Izzie.*

"How long has it been?" I asked. "Since Carl was reported missing?"

Rob glanced at his watch. "Burt called in the *Fair Winds* adrift a little after noon. It's past four thirty now."

I nodded. Too much time had passed for a positive outcome. Everyone here knew that, but no one would give up hope this early.

If he wasn't found soon, the search would end, but the waiting would go on. Sometimes a body would show up weeks later. Sometimes never.

"Sun sets a little after seven," Rob pointed out. "The search can go on for another two and a half hours, more or less."

"Can't they search with lights, at night?" Izzie asked.

"Depends," said Rob. "Helicopters may stay out there a while. So will the Marine Patrol. They have strong lights. Smaller boats will come in. And if winds come up strong tonight, they'll suspend the search until daybreak. Can't risk losing someone else."

As if in answer, the flags of Maine and the United States, which had been hanging limply from the pole at the side of the boathouse, billowed out, catching a late afternoon sea breeze.

Izzie shivered.

I couldn't just stand there. "The men searching will be cold and hungry when they dock," I decided. "I'm going home to pull some food together." I turned to Izzie. "We never had lunch, so I'll find us something to eat, too."

"I made bread and soup this morning, and there's fish pie left from last night," Mamie volunteered. "I'll bring it all over to your place in an hour or so."

I nodded. "Thanks. Tell Lucy and Luc and anyone else you see that they and their families are welcome, too. We'll have enough for everyone." I turned to Rose and Cynthia. "I hope you'll both join us."

Cynthia glanced at her sister. "I can't. My shift starts at seven tonight. But I'll try to get Rose to come. She's having a hard time right now."

Rose didn't answer. I'd sometimes wondered what she and Carl had in common other than being unmarried and living on the island.

I nodded. "It's not easy for anyone," I said. My voice sounded shaky, even to me.

"We can't give up hope," Mom reminded me. "Nothing's over if there's still hope."

How often had the words "hope" and "prayers" been repeated on Quarry Island this afternoon?

I wished I were as optimistic. Ever since Burt's call, now hours ago, I'd been sure Carl was lost.

I turned and looked out past the harbor and Granite Point

and its lighthouse, toward the ocean. On a summer's day the water sparkled. At night you could see the shadows of people walking back and forth behind windows lit on the mainland, across the harbor. Today, visibility was limited. One lobster boat was out by the point, so far away I couldn't tell whose it was. Everyone in the area who had a boat was searching. When a neighbor was in trouble, people came.

Izzie and I started back toward the truck.

"I can help with food," Izzie volunteered.

"Thanks," I said. "I hadn't imagined our first afternoon together would be like this."

"I'm fine. I'm just sorry for what happened to Carl," she said.

"It's hard on everyone when there's an accident."

"Looked like everyone on the island was back there. How many people live on Quarry Island anyway?"

I got into the driver's seat this time. "About three hundred, year-round. Four times that in summer."

"They'll search again tomorrow? If they don't find him soon, I mean," she asked.

I nodded. "At least one more day. Tomorrow they'll start looking closer to shore."

Even Izzie, who didn't know about life on the waters, knew if he wasn't found today, Carl wouldn't be found alive on shore tomorrow.

Unless there was a miracle.

# Chapter Six

"Hospitality is an art as well as a virtue."

—*The Epicure's Year Book and Table Companion* by Blanchard Jerrold. London: Bradbury, Evans and Co., 1868

"How far do you live from here?" Izzie asked as we pulled out of the field.

"Walking distance. About a quarter mile," I answered.

Izzie nodded, looking from one side of Island Road to the other. "What a cute, tiny town! Have you always lived here?"

"Since I was born." I pulled into my driveway. "I grew up in the white house with green shutters over there." I pointed. "Mom and Mamie, that's what we call my grandmother, still live there. When Burt and I were first married, we lived with his parents on the other side of the island." I smiled as we got out, and Izzie pulled her suitcases out of the back of the truck. "I was wicked homesick, can you believe?"

"Living on the other side of the island?" asked Izzie.

"True."

"You've never lived alone?"

"Never," I confirmed, as we headed for the kitchen door, the one closest to the driveway. "How about you?"

"Lived with Mom and Dad when I was little. Mom died when I was fourteen."

"I'm sorry," I said, opening the door for her. "Watch out for Blue. He's supposed to be an indoor cat, but sometimes he makes a break for the outdoors."

She nodded, focused on her story, not my cat. "Mom's death was awful. Cancer. She only lived a couple of months after she was diagnosed. After that, I was alone most of the time. Dad traveled a lot on business."

"When you were only fourteen? Didn't you have a relative, or friend, or housekeeper? Someone?"

Izzie shook her head slightly. "Dad said I was old enough to take care of myself. And I guess I was. I did it. But I was by myself a lot in high school. Then I went to CIA and lived there. I still share an apartment in Poughkeepsie, near school."

"Jake's fourteen. I can't imagine him living alone."

Izzie shrugged. "You do what you have to do" She paused. "Your cat's name is Blue? That's unusual."

"He was left on the island by a couple who'd adopted him in Blue Hill, as a living souvenir, before they rented a cottage for a week here. His collar included his name. I guess they changed their minds and didn't want to take him home to Virginia."

"He's beautiful," said Izzie, bending to stroke him. "He was lucky you rescued him."

The living room was dominated by our old couch and three overstuffed armchairs, a flat screen television, which had been our big gift to each other two Christmases ago, and a small bookcase filled with picture books Jake had outgrown. Blue got up from his favorite pillow on the couch, stretched, and looked at Izzie. A new person? Someone who might bring food or attention? Izzie scratched between his ears, and Blue collapsed with joy. All was well.

"Do you have a cat?" I asked. "You've just made a friend for life."

"Once, when I was little, I had a dog named Jack. I loved that dog! But I've been working and studying long hours for years. No time for a pet." She gave Blue another scratch. "Your Blue is the biggest cat I've ever seen."

"Coon cats are pretty good sizes," I agreed. "He weighs about twenty pounds."

She pointed at one of the framed pictures on the wall. "Your wedding picture?"

"Burt and I were both eighteen," I confirmed. We looked awkward, but happy, smiling on the steps of the church across the street. The dress I was wearing was the same one Mom had worn when she'd married Seth. Mamie had lengthened it and taken out the seams to allow for Jake's increasing presence. In those days, I'd felt tall and skinny even when I was pregnant. I wasn't skinny anymore.

"You were glowing," she said. "And that Burt of yours was handsome! I'm looking forward to meeting him." She moved on to the next picture. "And this must be Jake."

"When he was six months old," I agreed. "Burt and I had a horrible time getting him to stop screaming so the photographer could take the picture." I smiled, remembering.

"And Christmas," she said, looking closely at a group shot.

"Mom and Seth, my stepfather, and Mamie," I pointed. "And Burt and Jake and me." I hesitated. "And Carl. He's younger than Burt."

Saying Carl's name brought the day back.

"So you're not going to move back to Connecticut?" I asked, trying to change the subject.

"The house Dad and I used to live in has a big mortgage. I can't take it on, so it'll have to be sold." Izzie looked as though she might burst into tears. "Not that I want to live in Connecticut again. But it was home."

"Izzie!" I put my arms around her and we hugged each other, thinking of our dad, and Carl, and the strangeness of life. "I'm so sorry. And glad you came here, even with what's happening."

"I'm glad, too," she said. "Your family seems so close." She looked around the room. "And your home is cozy. It looks loved."

"We are close," I agreed. "But we squabble, too."

"That sounds normal. You're lucky."

I thought of how I'd felt when I'd first read Izzie's letter. "You were lucky, too. You got to know our dad."

She nodded.

"Let me show you your room. You've had a long day. You could wash up, or change," I suggested.

"I'm not exactly dressed for here," Izzie said, smiling. "I was so nervous when I was deciding what to put on this morning. I didn't know what to wear. But I brought jeans and sweatshirts, too."

"Wear whatever you're comfortable in. While you're settling in I'll get out cheese and crackers and see what else we can come up with to serve if people stop in."

I picked up one of Izzie's suitcases and walked up the stairs to the second floor ahead of her, hoping she'd find our tiny guest room adequate. "Let me know if my quilting supplies get in your way. Clean sheets are on the bed and you can use the small pine bureau and the closet. If you need anything else, let me know." I pointed to the bathroom. "We all share a bath. I'll get you towels. Your room is the second on the left."

I opened the door of the old wardrobe in the hallway where I kept extra towels and sheets, and Izzie went on down the hall.

"This is perfect," she called back. "Did you make the quilt on the bed?"

I joined her, handing her two blue flowered towels and a facecloth. "It was one of my first efforts. My mom's an expert quilter. I'm still learning."

The quilt on the bed was a patchwork of my old clothes along with Jake's and Burt's. Lots of jeans and plaid flannel shirts. I'd tried to arrange the reds, whites, and blues in a flag pattern, but it hadn't entirely worked.

"I love it," said Izzie, sitting on the bed and stroking the fabrics. "It's warm and cozy and perfect for this room. I didn't know people still made quilts."

"A lot do, here. I'm glad you like it." I flushed. My quilt wasn't the best, but it was nice to hear it complimented.

Then she glanced at the bookcase in the corner. Two shelves held pins, needles, threads, and scissors. The other shelves were full of books I'd loved as a child, but Jake had discarded or dismissed. "Now I know we *are* sisters," Izzie exclaimed. "You have all my favorites! *Little Women* and *An Old-Fashioned Girl* and *Rebecca of Sunnybrook Farm* and a whole shelf of Nancy Drews and . . . you have *Anne of Green Gables*! I love that book! My copy is worn out, but I still have it!"

"That one was my mother's," I admitted. "I remember her reading it to me. My copy's pretty well-read, too."

"Then we must be," Izzie grinned as we said it together, "Kindred spirits!"

In the Anne of Green Gables series, Anne was always looking for people she called "kindred spirits," who shared her enthusiasm for life and curiosity about it. I'd hoped to share Anne with my daughter someday, but life had brought me Jake instead. I loved Jake dearly, but it would have been fun to have had a daughter.

Or a sister.

"I wonder what else we have in common." Izzie said.

"I suspect we may find out," I said. If we'd both loved the same books, we must have a lot to share. "Now, you unpack and get settled. When you're ready, come back downstairs."

With only three rooms on the first floor and three plus the bathroom on the second, she wouldn't get lost.

"I will. And I'd like to contribute something to dinner."

"It's not going to be fancy," I warned her. "I made mac and cheese casserole this morning, and you heard Mamie. She's bringing anadama bread, bean soup, and fish pie."

"Anadama bread?" Izzie asked.

"Simple yeast bread made of wheat flour, cornmeal, and molasses. Legend says it got its name when a Maine man came home from the sea and found his wife missing and no bread in his kitchen. Angrily, he threw all the ingredients he could find together, cussing 'Anna, damn her!' and made his own bread."

"Is that a true story?"

"I don't think anyone knows. But I've heard it a thousand times, especially since my name is Anna. And the bread is good. Mamie's the expert cook in our family." I started to leave, and then turned. "Until now. We've never had a CIA graduate in the family before."

I arranged cheeses and crackers on a board, and put my casserole in the oven on low heat before reaching for a chocolate.

Izzie seemed to be making herself at home. I wasn't nervous about her anymore; I hadn't had time to be. Carl's accident had changed everything.

I put my brass kettle on to boil, sat at the kitchen table, and ate a cracker. And then another. I wasn't hungry, but eating was automatic. I felt as though I was watching myself from a distance.

Even focusing on simple tasks was hard. I kept thinking of Carl.

Had he tripped? The deck of a lobster boat was often slippery with bait or salt water. But if he'd lost his balance, wouldn't he have fallen inside the boat? Like Burt, Carl was a little under six feet tall.

I hoped Rose would join us for supper, talk a little, and eat something. To have hopes for a future and then . . . She shouldn't be alone tonight.

The afternoon sun was fading rapidly. I said a silent prayer that Carl would be found quickly. And, if he were dead, that

Burt and the boys wouldn't be the ones to find him. Recovering the body of your brother or uncle would be awful.

Izzie had to grow up when she was fourteen. I wanted Jake and Matt to be children a little longer.

Carl had been tinkering with his boat's engine, got it going this morning, and decided to test it out. That made sense.

Whatever happened after that didn't make sense.

# Chapter Seven

"Under ordinary circumstances, a woman whose husband enjoys a moderate income has no need to do much in the way of cooking; but as most of the domestics to be obtained know very little about this very important branch of household economy, it is absolutely necessary that the mistress of a family should herself be able to give the most particular directions on the subject."

—*Advice to Young Ladies on their Duties and Conduct in Life* by T.S. Arthur. Philadelphia: J.W. Bradley, 1860

Izzie joined me a few minutes later. She put a black roll of fabric on the back of the kitchen counter as I poured us each pottery mugs of tea.

"What's that?" I asked.

"My knife kit," she answered, joining me at the table. "I want to help you while I'm here, and I'm spoiled. My knives are sharper than most people's, and the perfect sizes for kitchen tasks. Is it okay if I use them? It shouldn't get in anyone's way."

"Of course," I said, smiling to myself. Izzie was the first person I'd ever met who brought her knives with her when she visited.

I sipped my tea, and noticed Izzie hadn't touched hers. "Would you prefer coffee? I should have asked you before."

"I drink both. No problem," she said, picking up her mug and sipping a little. "How many people will be here for dinner? I know your grandmother said she'd bring food, but you all have so much on your minds. I can't help find Carl, but I can cook."

"I put my casserole in the oven, and Mamie's going to bring soup and fish pie. I don't know how much more we'll need. We'll somehow find enough food for whoever shows up." I always did.

"Fish pie?" asked Izzie, looking puzzled.

"It's got salmon, potatoes, spices, and other stuff," I said vaguely. "Everything's baked in a pie shell. Wait. You'll find out. It's delicious."

"I can't wait to taste it," Izzie agreed.

"Mamie grew up eating a little differently than most Mainers. She's from Quebec. Mamie's an abbreviation for mémère—grandmother. I couldn't pronounce the French when I was little."

"Quebec! Fantastic! I've heard they have delicious food up there—a combination of New England and French."

"Ask her about it some time. I've always taken what she cooks for granted. I should pay more attention."

"Do you think she'd share some of her recipes?"

"She'd probably love to, if she has recipes. She usually cooks without them." Izzie was so enthusiastic about facts that I took for granted, I couldn't help getting excited, too.

Izzie popped a piece of cheese into her mouth and got up. "Mind if I look in your refrigerator?"

"Go ahead," I said. "I suspect family and neighbors will be in and out tonight, so if you see something you could cook, that would be great." People would be in and out tomorrow, too, I added to myself. If Carl was found, however he was found, friends and neighbors would descend on us.

"I see brown eggs, milk, and there's cheese on the table. And you have asparagus and mushrooms."

"I got those at the mainland grocery yesterday," I agreed.

"Bacon or sausage? Tofu?"

"There's a little bacon behind the eggs," I said. "No sausage or tofu." What did tofu taste like, anyway? I'd seen it in stores but never tried it.

She found a few slices of bacon. "What about potatoes? Onions?"

"In the pantry," I said, becoming intrigued with whatever she was doing. "The door on your left. Burt built shelves in that closet for canned goods and I keep some vegetables and fruit in there, too. Are you going to scramble eggs with vegetables?"

"Something like that," Izzie answered, putting a large onion and two potatoes on the table. "If you have a frying pan or skillet that can go in the oven I can make a frittata."

"A what?" I asked.

"Frittata. It's good, and easy, and quick to make," said Izzie. "And different from what you and . . . Mamie, you call her? . . . made."

"Go right ahead," I said, pulling out a deep frying pan I hadn't used in years. "Will this do?"

"Perfect," she agreed. "I know this is an awful day for you

and for everyone here. I didn't know Carl, but he was a member of your family, so he was sort of a member of my family, too."

My eyes started stinging. I'd rather talk about Mamie's food than about Carl.

"It's all right," I said. "Go ahead and make your—frittata, you called it?"

She lifted two of my other frying pans off the wall where I'd hung them, put bacon in one and turned the burner under it to low, unrolled her knife kit, selected a medium-sized knife, and began chopping vegetables.

Her knife was true and fast. I watched her hands for a couple of minutes, fascinated. "Have you always cooked?" I asked.

She nodded. "When I was little there weren't any Korean restaurants nearby, and Mom missed Korean cooking, so she did it herself. We'd have chop chae—that's a vegetable and noodle dish with beef—one night, then spaghetti and meatballs the next. The first thing I learned to make was kimchi. We always had that in the house."

"What's kimchi?"

"Pickled cabbage, with garlic and hot pepper. A Korean condiment, or side dish. It doesn't need cooking . . . just chopping. Mom taught me how to make it before she let me use the stove. After she died, I kept cooking. When I cooked, especially when I made a dish she'd loved, it made me feel close to her."

Izzie wiped a tear from her face. Maybe she was crying because she was dicing onions. Or maybe not. "And, I'll admit, I love to eat," she continued. "If I'd left cooking up to Dad, we would have existed on take-out burgers and pizza. I worked in a local restaurant on weekends when I was in high school.

While other kids thought about colleges, I looked at cooking school catalogs."

When I'd been a senior in high school I'd shopped for maternity clothes at a thrift shop in Camden.

"What was he like? Our father? If you can talk about him."

She nodded as she cooked the chopped potatoes, onions, asparagus, and mushrooms. "When it first happened, when the police showed up at my door and told me about the accident, I didn't want to believe he was gone. It all happened so fast, and there was no one else to make funeral arrangements, or talk to the lawyers. I had to do it all." She glanced at me. "This might not be the right time to talk about that."

I was struggling to focus on Izzie, when half of my mind was with Carl. Burt and I would have to take care of those things if Carl was . . .

"You're right. Another time," I agreed.

"I brought a few pictures of Dad," said Izzie. "They're in my suitcase. I didn't know if you had any."

"I don't. I didn't know anything about him until I got your letter," I said. "All I knew was Mom had been married for a short time when she was young."

"So he wasn't here on Quarry Island long." She picked up pieces of parmesan and asiago from the table and started grating them.

"He left when Mom was only a month or two pregnant. Mom married again when I was still little, so I grew up with a stepfather."

"Was he a good man?" Izzie asked. "Your stepfather?" She'd stopped stirring the vegetables and was beating eggs with the whisk I'd bought at a yard sale last summer. I'd never used it.

Then she added seasonings. I watched, fascinated. She could still be making scrambled eggs, as far as I could tell.

"Seth? Yes, he was a good father to me," I said. "But I always wanted to know about my biological dad."

"So you didn't know about me."

"Nothing."

"I didn't know about you, either, until his lawyer told me. But Dad had your name—your married name—and your address. It was all in his will. So he'd kept track of you, at least a little."

"I wonder whether he ever would have come here, to meet me. Mom never talked about him. If he hadn't died, and you hadn't written to me, I might never have even known his name."

"Or I, yours," said Izzie. She put the vegetable mixture into the deep frying pan, sprinkled the grated cheeses on top, covered everything with the beaten eggs, and put the whole pan in the oven.

"I always wanted a brother or sister," I said. When Mom lost her babies, I'd been old enough to be disappointed that I wouldn't be a big sister.

"Me, too," Izzie said. "I always wanted a little sister. But an older sister is exciting, too!" She joined me at the pine table where I'd been nibbling crackers with brie and cheddar. Izzie had hardly eaten anything.

"How long will your—frittata—take to cook?" I asked.

"Fifteen or twenty minutes," she said. "It'll be ready about the same time as your casserole. But it doesn't have to be served hot."

"After they're both cooked we could leave everything in the oven on low until someone comes," I suggested.

"Good thought," she said, sitting next to me.

"I'm not sure it's polite to ask . . . but how much money did our father leave us?" I couldn't help wondering about that, and Izzie might know.

She shook her head. "We won't know exactly until the insurance comes in, the house is sold, the debts settled, and all his investments are sorted out. His lawyer is handling that. You and I'll split whatever's left." She smiled. "We won't be millionaires. The lawyer estimated there'd only be two or three hundred thousand left."

I gasped. "We'd each inherit over a hundred thousand dollars?"

"Dad didn't want to leave us a fortune. He wrote in his will that he wanted to leave us each other."

I was glad we'd found each other, too. But a hundred thousand dollars? For Burt and me, that *was* a fortune.

# Chapter Eight

"If your husband brings home company when you are unprepared, rennet pudding may be made at five minutes' notice, provided you keep a piece of calf's rennet soaking in a bottle of wine. One glass of this wine to a quart of milk will make a sort of cold custard. Sweetened with white sugar and spiced with nutmeg, it is very good. It should be eaten immediately; in a few hours it begins to curdle."

—*The Frugal Housewife: Dedicated to Those who are not ashamed of Economy*, by Lydia Maria Child. Boston, 1833

No calls must mean no news. I pulled out my stash of disposable plates, knives, and forks. With a crowd to feed, they'd make cleanup easier.

I didn't want to be left with a sink full of dishes to wash when my mind was occupied. Right now, my mind was overflowing.

Carl, missing. Izzie, here. A father who might have left me a small fortune.

Izzie was making herself at home, organizing the dining room table for a buffet and chattering about how lovely Maine was. I didn't interrupt her.

Blue sensed his quiet world was going to be disturbed. He'd disappeared, probably to his favorite hiding spot under the quilt and between the pillows on Burt's and my bed.

The sun was going down quickly. Outside, wheeling gulls were crying. Did they know something? Some islanders swore gulls could tell people apart. I wished we spoke the same language. Gulls might be the only witnesses to whatever happened to Carl.

Gulls knew immediately if Burt or Carl threw the herrings they used for bait overboard—the gulls' version of a buffet dinner—or if someone sitting on the wharf or at the little pebble beach near the lighthouse was eating a sandwich. Any food they could see was fair game.

When I was a teenager, I'd packed a wicker picnic basket with chocolate chip cookies and potato chips and sandwiches for Burt and me and another couple. We'd left the basket above the high tide mark and gone for a quick swim before lunch. When we turned back to the beach, a dozen gulls were feasting. They'd turned the basket over and torn through the wrap I'd used to cover the food.

That was the last time I'd left food unattended outside.

Mamie was the first to arrive. "Hello?" she called. She was holding the same picnic basket I'd been remembering. "Is there space in your oven to warm up the pie?"

"Just enough," I said, holding the pie out so Izzie could see it. "Salmon and potato, like I said." I turned to Mamie. "Izzie's a chef. She's made us a frittata, and she's been asking about your Quebecois recipes." I rearranged the oven to hold my casserole, Izzie's frittata, and Mamie's pie while Mamie poured her soup into the large pot I most often used for chowder or pasta. "We've turned the oven to warm. Will that be all right? And what about your bread?"

"Bread can be room temperature," she declared. "A warm oven will be good for everything else." She turned to Izzie. "Your dad's parents wrote to me when you were born. They were thrilled. I'm the only one here who knew about you."

"So you were in touch with Dad?" Izzie asked.

"Only a little through your grandparents, and I didn't hear much after that," Mamie admitted. "I kept writing to them, though, for maybe ten years. Until their letters came back, 'forwarding order expired.' I wanted them to know their granddaughter in Maine was doing fine. I hoped they'd pass that on to their son."

"So he wasn't totally out of touch," Izzie said, turning toward me.

"He didn't contact my mom, or me," I reminded her.

"Or even me," put in Mamie. "It was his mother who wrote every year or two, and that stopped after you were born, Izzie. So you're a chef?" she said, changing the subject. "I'd love to talk recipes with you another day. I don't do fancy cooking, but mine is a little different than most Mainers' because I was born in Quebec City."

"Mamie, you came to Maine when you were four years old!" I smiled.

"True enough. But my mother never changed the way she'd learn to cook in French Canada. I learned from her."

Izzie didn't let on that I'd already told her Mamie's history.

"I'd love to talk food," she said. "And I'm glad you were in touch with my grandparents. I never knew them. They moved to Florida when I was little, and we didn't visit. And my mother's family died before I was born."

"That's sad," said Mamie, opening the cabinet where she knew I kept wine. "Families should be in touch. Anyone else ready for a glass of wine?"

"I'm in," Izzie agreed quickly.

I should have offered her some earlier, I realized. Tea wasn't comforting to everyone. "I'll have a glass, too, Mamie. Is Mom coming?"

Mamie poured us each a glass from my box of chardonnay. "I don't know. I left the wharf before she did, and I haven't heard from her." She raised her glass to Izzie's and mine. "To better days. And to family."

"To family," Izzie and I repeated in unison.

The front door banged open. "Any news?" asked Rob Erickson. "Dad was getting tired, so I took him home. For now, he's happy with his bourbon and CNN and some hummus and crackers. I promised to let him know as soon as I heard anything."

"Nothing yet," I answered. "Glass of wine?"

"Absolutely," he answered, handing me a bottle of red. "My contribution." Rob was tall, and his years as a detective on the Portland Police force had kept him in shape. He still jogged past our house every morning, although he didn't look like a cop anymore. His hair was grayer and longer than it had been when he was on duty, and his plaid flannel shirt and worn jeans were more island than city. He was a good neighbor, and kept an eye on what was happening on Quarry Island. Once a detective, always a detective, he'd once said.

He ducked a little as he came into the kitchen. Low ceilings kept warmth inside in winter, but were a challenge to those over six feet tall. He helped himself to a glass of wine, and sniffed the air. "I smell good cooking."

"Something from each of us," Mamie said. "After everyone gets here we'll eat."

"Must admit, Dad and I don't eat as well as you ladies do," he added.

"Izzie just graduated from the Culinary Institute," I put in.

"A CIA graduate?" he said appreciatively, looking at Izzie. "I've eaten some good meals in that restaurant the students run. Had to go down to Sing Sing a couple of times. I always tried to time it so I could stop in Hyde Park on my way back."

"You *must* have liked our restaurant," said Izzie. "Sing Sing's more than an hour from CIA."

Rob shrugged. "A man'll do a lot for good cooking. Hope you're staying on the island long enough to show us what you learned."

"Us!" I grinned, but wasn't surprised. Rob had a way of stopping in right about mealtime. I suspected he'd lived on takeout in Portland after his divorce. Burt and I usually found enough on our table to share with him, as well as a portion for him to take home to his dad. He returned the favor by helping with the *Anna* when an extra hand was needed, and last spring he'd rototilled my vegetable plot and I'd shared the resulting tomatoes, zucchini, and lettuce. He was a good neighbor, although I suspected he was lonely. Rob was young enough to have interests besides painting his house and doing his father's laundry.

We heard voices outside, the door opened again, and our house filled.

Burt looked exhausted. He ignored everyone else and came and held me for a minute. He smelled of lobster and bait and the sea. He smelled wonderful.

"Any word?" I asked quietly.

He shook his head. "Marine Patrol's still looking, but they told the rest of us to go home for the night. If he's not found by morning, we'll go back out."

Dolan Martin collapsed on one of the living room chairs, and Lucy found a Shipyard beer for him in the fridge. Willis Tarbox added a six-pack of Gritty McDuff's to our supply, and quietly put a sketch of Carl looking out to sea on our mantel.

"Thank you for bringing that, Willis," I said, giving him a quick hug.

"Seemed the right day to pass it on to you folks," Willis answered. "Been thinking I'd do a painting of Carl one of these days, but never have. The sketch is all I have of him."

"It's perfect," I assured him.

It was. But it reminded me of funerals, when people brought old pictures of the deceased to share. This wasn't a funeral. Not yet.

Matt and Jake were helping themselves to the crackers and cheeses, which Izzie had moved to the dining room table. Matt was gangly; Jake was shorter, but wiry. Both of them were always hungry.

Matt shoved Jake as he reached for an extra slice of cheese. Jake responded by taking two crackers off Matt's plate. Both of their heads were down. I couldn't see whether they were teasing each other, or something more.

"How'd the boys do today?" I asked Burt quietly as he reached into the refrigerator for his own beer.

"Pretty well," he said, keeping his voice low, too. "They were more uptight and scared than they wanted each other to know. Showed lots of bravado at first, then didn't talk much, not even to each other, and stood on opposite sides of the boat the rest of the time we were searching. Both of them were clearly relieved when I said it was time to come in."

I nodded, glancing into the dining room. The cheeses and crackers were disappearing. "Plus, I can see they were starving."

"They'd both eaten lunch at your mom's. When they heard about Carl they came right to the wharf and volunteered to help."

"Good for them," I said. "But I'm not surprised."

I sent a proud glance in Jake's direction. No matter what his future would be, he was an island boy, for sure. In a crisis, he showed up.

Izzie was checking the food in the oven.

"Izzie, you haven't met my husband or son yet. This is Burt," I said, turning him toward her. "And, Jake?" I called, "Come meet your Aunt Izzie."

Burt swallowed his surprise, but Jake didn't. "Are you Chinese?" he asked, joining us in the kitchen.

"Half Korean," Izzie said, comfortably. "I like the sound of Aunt Izzie. I've never been anyone's aunt before."

Jake grinned. "Good to meet you. Whatever's in that oven smells good."

"It's about ready to eat," she confirmed, taking the three dishes out.

"Put them on top of these," I directed, putting wooden trivets on the dining table. "Folks," I announced in the door to the living room. "Come and get some supper. Mamie's brought her potato and salmon pie and anadama bread, there's a macaroni and cheese casserole, and Izzie's made a frittata for us, which smells delicious. A pot of Mamie's bean soup is on the stove and mugs are on the kitchen table. Make yourselves at home."

Rose hadn't come, at least not yet. Maybe she wanted to be alone. Some folks were like that. Or maybe she had another obligation. Cynthia was working tonight. Hospital staff had funny hours, so far as I was concerned. I couldn't count the number of times we'd told Carl to bring Rose over to our place for supper, and Rose had to work.

Jake and Matt, not surprisingly, filled their plates and headed to Jake's room. Just as well. They'd heard enough grownup talk today.

Izzie and I waited until everyone else had taken their suppers. I made sure a piece of Mamie's fish pie was left for Izzie, and saved myself a helping of her frittata. "Delicious," I told her as soon as I'd tasted it. "I hope you'll give me the recipe."

She finished her fish pie quickly, sending positive glances toward Mamie.

The gathering was quieter than when neighbors usually visited. A wake without a body. Dolan and Burt talked about where they'd each searched for Carl, and Mamie tried to soothe Lucy. After a glass or two of wine, Lucy finally stopped dabbing her eyes with the tissues she'd stuffed in the sleeve of her orange sweater, and started telling stories of escapades she and Carl had shared as children.

Behind our conversations, we could hear the sounds of gunshots and car crashes from the video games Matt and Jake were playing upstairs.

Everyone stopped talking when we heard a knock on the door.

People on the island didn't knock. They walked in.

I glanced at Burt. He swallowed deeply and went to see who it was, although we all had already guessed. I followed him.

Officer Carmela Heedles and a Marine Patrol officer were standing at the door.

The officers exchanged glances. They weren't smiling.

Burt spoke first. "You found him?" His voice was low and slightly quavering.

"Sorry to have to bring you bad news," said Officer Heedles. "He was about three miles out, off Granite Point, near Maiden Island."

"Drowned," Burt said, almost to himself.

I shuddered to hear it said out loud.

"Officially, the medical examiner has to determine that," the officer said.

"Medical examiner? Why does Augusta have to be involved?" Burt asked.

"It's the law. Unattended death," she explained. "Really sorry about your brother, Burt. Knew him a lot of years, and he got himself in some trouble, but never anything serious. A good guy."

Had Carl dated Carmela once? I couldn't remember. But, then, he'd dated practically every appropriately aged female on the island and the nearby mainland.

"But you found him three miles out. What could it be but a drowning?"

The two officers exchanged glances. "We'll get him up to Augusta tonight. You should hear from the state police tomorrow or Monday."

Rob Erickson stood up. "You've brought in the state police?"

"Had to, Rob," said the Marine Patrol guy. "You know what has to be done in these cases."

Rob shook his head. "Yup. Just wicked sorry. Carl was a friend of mine."

# Chapter Nine

"Oyster Over-Eating: When too many oysters have been eaten, and they lie cold and heavy upon the stomach, drink a half-pint of hot milk and it will dissolve the oysters into a cream jelly that can be quickly digested."

—*Old Doctor Carlin's Recipes: A Complete Collection of Recipes on Every Known Subject* by Doctor William Carlin. Boston, Massachusetts: The Locker Publishing Company, 1881

"I'm sorry, Burt," said Rob. "Carl was a good man. If I can help with anything, let me know."

Burt stood there, frozen.

Lucy was sobbing again.

"We need to tell the boys," I said. "And call Rose."

"I'll get Jake and Matt," said Izzie.

In a few minutes, the three of them were back. Izzie let us talk while she cleaned up empty plates and cups.

"Boys, I'm afraid the Marine Patrol found him," Burt told them.

"Then Uncle Carl . . ." Jake made him say it.

"He's dead, Jake. They found him three miles out."

Dolan stood, reached for Lucy's hand, and pulled her up after him. "It's time for us to go home. We've had a long day, and are so sorry it ended like this. Matt, c'mon. We need to leave. The Winslows should have some privacy."

Matt hesitated, looking at Jake.

"You can see Jake tomorrow. Thanks for the food, Anna, and nice to meet you, Izzie. We'll see you all tomorrow in church. If we can help with anything, let us know." The Martins knew Burt and I didn't go to services every week—we were more Christmas and Easter congregants. But they also knew us well enough to know we'd be attending tomorrow.

"We all could use a prayer or two today," I agreed, and Burt nodded as the Martins left.

In tomorrow's sermon Reverend Beaman would be talking not only to her regular congregation, but to everyone on the island who'd known Carl. His death was a painful reminder to our whole community that we could never underestimate the treacherous waters surrounding us.

Mamie and Izzie took over the kitchen, putting leftovers away. "If there's enough food left, make up a plate for Gus," I said. "We'll send it home with Rob. Mom didn't come tonight, and you brought your food here, Mamie. Do you have enough for her at home?" I often slipped and called their house "home." Burt teased me about it sometimes. But I really did have two homes.

"Don't you worry about your mom. Maybe she wanted a little quiet time. We have plenty of food over to the house."

Mamie handed me a tissue and I realized I was crying. "You take care of yourself, and your men tonight, Anna. Don't be worrying about the rest of the world."

I nodded. "I'll call Rose first. One of us needs to do that."

Izzie had already filled a plate for Gus, and handed it to Rob. "For your dad," she said.

"Thank you. Both of you," Rob said, looking from one of us to another. "Right now, you all need to get some rest. The next few days won't be easy."

"Thanks for your help," said Burt, as Rob and Mamie left.

Jake had already retreated into his bedroom and shut the door.

"He needs to digest today in his own way," Izzie said.

Was she remembering when she'd been fourteen and her mother had died?

I dialed Rose. She answered right away.

"Rose, this is Anna."

"Yes?" Her voice quavered.

"I'm so sorry, but we just heard. The Marine Patrol found Carl's body."

At first Rose was silent. Then she started to sob.

"I knew you'd want to hear as soon as we did."

Rose stumbled through, "Thank you for calling. I knew he might be gone. I just didn't want to believe it."

"Are you all right? Is someone with you?" I asked. She didn't sound all right.

"How would you feel if the love of your life died? I'll never be all right again!"

Carl had so many women in his life over the years I hadn't

taken any of them seriously. I'd never know how Carl felt about Rose, but clearly she'd cared about him. "I'm so sorry, Rose. Will we see you in church tomorrow?"

"I don't know," she said, her sobs overpowering her words. "I need to be alone."

She hung up, and I put the phone down.

"Not an easy call?" asked Izzie.

I shook my head. "She's taking it badly."

"Some people react immediately. Some people take longer," Izzie said. "You and Burt seem amazingly calm. To lose a brother must be very hard."

It wasn't easy to lose a brother-in-law, either. But I knew my Burt. He'd react later. When his parents died he'd held his grief inside, eating at him until, unseen, it turned to anger and was released in an explosion that blew the hurt out. It would take time, but I suspected the same would happen now. I'd coped with the shrapnel then, and I could again. "This has been a horrible day. But I'm glad you were here." My words were automatic, under the circumstances. But I meant them. I was glad Izzie was here on Quarry Island.

"I'm going to take a hot shower," said Burt, looking at the two of us. "And then see if I can sleep. Rob was right. Tomorrow won't be easy."

"I'll be up in a few minutes," I assured him.

"What *will* happen tomorrow?" Izzie asked a few minutes later as we sat in the living room sipping small glasses of cooking sherry. It seemed an appropriate way to end the day.

"Church is in the morning," I said. "Nine o'clock. I expect most people on the island will be there. You can come with us or stay here or go for a walk . . . whatever you'd like."

"I'm not very religious," Izzie said. "The last time I was in church was for Dad's funeral. I'm not ready to be reminded of that. I'll explore the island a little."

"That's fine. I understand. I expect people will be stopping in here during the afternoon. And after we hear officially from Augusta, we'll have to plan a funeral." Carl's death still seemed unreal. Two days ago, he'd been sitting at our kitchen table devouring cheeseburgers and macaroni salad. Now he was gone. "This must not be easy for you: going through another death so soon. If you want to go to Portland or even go home, I'll understand."

"If you don't mind my being here," said Izzie, "I'd like to stay. I can be an extra pair of hands if you need them. And I need to move on and accept Dad's death. Seeing you and Burt accepting Carl's may help me deal with my own loss."

Neither Burt nor I were accepting Carl's death right now. But we were dealing with it. What other choice was there? Maybe that's what Izzie meant.

We sat for a few minutes in silence. I'd planned to ask Izzie so many questions today. But it wasn't the right time to start sharing confidences. Izzie put down her empty glass. "I'll go on to bed. I was up before dawn this morning."

"Of course," I agreed. "I'll be going upstairs myself in a few minutes. We've hardly had a chance to talk. But I *am* glad you're here. I hope you'll stay with us, at least for the week."

Izzie bent over and hugged me. "I'd like to. As long as I won't be in the way."

"You won't," I assured her. "You're family. Family is never in the way."

She raised her eyebrows. "Really?"

"Well, hardly ever!" I smiled back. It was good to smile. I hadn't done that a lot today.

I poured myself a little more sherry and some for Burt, and took our glasses upstairs.

Sunday would be another long day.

* * *

And it was.

To begin with, Jake refused to go to church. Instead, he insisted on going to the bookstore to work. "Mr. Burnham doesn't go to church," he pointed out, which was true. "And I missed an afternoon's work yesterday."

"Jake, this won't be a regular church service. Reverend Beaman will be talking about Uncle Carl, and those who loved him."

Jake shook his head stubbornly. "I get it, Mom. And I don't want everyone crying and telling me they're sorry."

"Leave him alone, Anna," said Burt.

I finally agreed. Jake had had a harrowing day Saturday, and his swollen eyes said he was grieving. I'd heard wild, discordant sounds coming from his room late last night and wondered at his choice of music. Maybe he was covering the sound of crying. I'd left our door ajar, in case he wanted to talk, but he'd stayed in his own room. After a while I'd knocked lightly, and then peeked in. He'd been asleep despite the noise, curled up the way he'd slept when he was a baby.

"You do what you need to do, then, Jake. Everyone knows you and your uncle were close." Maybe Izzie was right. Jake needed time by himself, or with someone who wasn't mourning every moment.

Burt hadn't slept much, but he'd stayed on his side of our bed. He hadn't wanted my comfort. He'd been lost in his own thoughts and, probably, memories. He'd talk when he was ready.

Izzie'd slept in. She hadn't known Carl; and although I was pretty sure by now everyone knew my sister was visiting, her presence would draw attention away from Carl's death. She'd be here for a few days; there'd be plenty of time for her to meet people.

In the meantime, we'd all have to absorb Carl's death before normal life could begin again. A new normal. Our lives would never again be the way they were when Carl was alive.

How different had Izzie's life been before her father was killed?

I didn't feel up to making our usual Sunday morning blueberry pancakes. All I could do that was usual for a Sunday morning was feed Blue. He purred his appreciation.

I pulled a brown flowered skirt out of the back of my closet, added a dark sweater, and let my hair hang down the way Burt liked it, instead of pulling it back in a ponytail as I did most days. Burt found a navy sport jacket that came close to fitting even when he put it on over a sweater.

We held hands as we walked across the street to the church and sat in our usual pew, fourth from the front on the right. Burt's family had claimed that pew over a hundred years ago. The town considered it ours. When I was in church, I felt all those I'd loved and those they'd loved were somehow still here, watching and supporting us. Burt and my great-grandparents on both sides had been married here, as Burt and I had been. Their children had been christened here, like Jake, and their funerals had been held here.

Carl's would be, too.

Daffodils were my favorite flower; their bright yellow color after the dark days of winter always promised spring. The daffodils on the altar this morning reminded me that from now on, early April would also be a time for remembrance of loss.

Many people stopped to pay their respects and murmur words of condolence. I focused on smiling and saying "thank you," wishing Reverend Beaman would start the service so we'd be left alone.

During the service, my mind drifted. I stared at the pine pews, their seats covered with the red velvet cushions Mom had helped make twenty years before. All those years of sun streaming through the tall, clear windows on both sides of the aisle had faded the once-crimson fabric to a pale rose. Nothing lasted forever.

I wiped away tears as Burt and I joined in singing *Amazing Grace* and *I Would Be True,* both familiarly off-tune, and listened to a sermon with references to Noah and Jonah and the deep seas we must confront in life. Jake had been right. I wasn't the only one crying.

After the service Burt toughed it out, facing our friends and neighbors and accepting condolences, but his face was pale and stiff, and his hand shook so much that he spilled his coffee on the Ladies Auxiliary's pink floral tablecloth.

His mother and father were gone, and now he'd lost his only brother. Just imagining losing Mom or Mamie made me cry.

He and I stayed as long as we could after the service and then walked home to brace ourselves for what we assumed would come next: baked bean casseroles and coffee cakes and more condolences.

Instead, a tall, dark-haired man was waiting on our front porch.

"Burt Winslow?" he asked, pulling out an identification badge. "Detective Jonas Preston, Maine State Police, homicide division. I'd like to talk with you."

"Homicide?" I asked, the word slipping out of my mouth before I could stop it. "Carl was murdered?" My whole world had gone out of focus. Carl's death had been nightmarish enough. But . . . murder?

"Afraid so," said Preston. He turned to Burt. "Sorry to bother you on a Sunday morning, but you may have been the last person to speak to your brother."

Burt opened our door, and showed the trooper in. "Are you working with Carmela Heedles? She usually handles police matters around here."

"Officer Heedles is with the County Sheriff's Office," explained Detective Preston. "Homicides are handled by the state police."

"I'd like my wife to stay with me." Burt reached for my hand. "Anna and I don't have secrets from each other."

Detective Preston hesitated a minute. "I'll need to talk with both of you again, separately. But for now, she can stay." He glanced at me dismissively.

"Would you like coffee? I can heat some I brewed earlier this morning," I suggested.

No matter his mission, the detective was our guest.

Izzie wasn't home, but she'd done some cooking before she left. A plate of fresh warm muffins was on the kitchen table.

"Thank you. Coffee would be good," Detective Preston agreed.

Burt took off his jacket, and he and Preston sat at the kitchen table. They helped themselves to muffins as I began heating coffee. Their muffins disappeared before the coffee was hot. "Hope you don't mind my recording our talk, Mr. Winslow." Preston placed a small recorder in the center of the table. "For the record."

I took a muffin myself. It was lemony and nutty and had a sweet glaze, but I could hardly swallow.

"I have nothing to hide," Burt answered. "You can record. But why are you here from the homicide division? My brother drowned yesterday. Drowning isn't homicide. You can't arrest the North Atlantic." He smiled nervously.

Preston switched on his recorder as I put three mugs of coffee on the table and slipped into the chair next to Burt so our knees touched. He needed to know I was with him, no matter what. As always, for always.

The detective's voice was calm, but straightforward, and probably for the recorder. "We heard from Augusta this morning. The state medical examiner's ruled Carl Winslow's death a homicide. He didn't drown."

"But—how?" Burt ran his fingers through his thinning hair, the way he always did when he was confused. "Who?"

"We're trying to find out," said the detective. "For the record, Carl Winslow was your brother. Correct?"

"Yes," Burt answered. He broke off a piece of muffin and crumbled it on his napkin. "Younger brother. Three years younger."

This wasn't Burt's first experience with the police. Before we were married, he and Dolan had borrowed another friend's boat and taken it to a fisherman's festival down the coast. An overzealous harbor patrolman there had stopped them later that night after they'd left the festival and were headed back for the boat.

After checking the boat's registration, he'd arrested them for theft. He hadn't bothered to listen to their protests, to check with the boat's owner, or to call their frantic parents. The officer had assumed they'd stolen the boat. After all, the boys were young and islanders.

They'd spent the night in jail.

On Quarry Island, even as a boy, Burt had been respected and trusted. That night he'd been treated as though he had no value.

It all got straightened out, but it had been the worst night of his life. Since then Burt had never felt comfortable with the police. But, fairly or unfairly, I knew from television programs that when someone had been murdered, families and close friends were always the first suspects.

Burt shouldn't be defensive. He needed to stay cool, collected. I put my hand on his knee, hoping he'd take it as a calming familiar gesture.

"When did you last see your brother, Mr. Winslow? And where?"

Burt frowned. "Yesterday morning. Early. About seven thirty, on the town wharf. I thought he'd be sterning for me. He's been doing that since the engine on his boat died, a month ago."

"Did he go with you?"

"You know the answer to that!"

*Keep calm*, I told him mentally. *Stay in control.*

"I know this is tough. But I need to hear your story," Preston said.

"No, Carl didn't go with me. He told me he'd stayed up late the night before, tinkering with his boat's engine, and he'd finally fixed it that morning. He wanted to take her out."

"Did you argue?"

Burt glanced at me. "I'd counted on his help. Without him the day's work would take twice as long, and I didn't have time to find anyone else to stern."

Preston let that go by. Had Carl and Burt had a major argument? He hadn't told me. But it wouldn't have been the first time the brothers had disagreed. Loudly.

"What did you do then?"

Blue came out from behind the couch, where he'd been hiding, and jumped onto my lap. Maybe he sensed I needed comforting.

"I don't like fishing by myself; it's harder and it isn't safe. But I had to check my traps and set some. So, I took off."

"You went out in your boat."

"Right."

"What was Carl doing when you left?"

"Standing on the wharf. I assumed he was going to work his traps in his *Fair Winds*."

"And that was the last time you saw him?"

Burt swallowed deeply, and picked up his coffee cup with both hands. "Yes."

Preston didn't speak for what seemed like minutes. Was he waiting for Burt or me to say something? Then, "Burt, did your brother have any enemies?"

"Enemies? No! I mean, he wasn't a perfect person. But everyone loved Carl." He looked at the trooper. "How was he killed?"

Jonas Preston shook his head. "I'm not going to say right now. I wanted to talk with you first, since you saw him yesterday morning. I'm also going to talk with the rest of your family and with his friends. With everyone who knew him well. I'm hoping that will lead to finding out who killed him, and why."

"He didn't deserve to die."

"We all have to die sometime, Mr. Winslow," said Preston, standing up. "But no one deserves to be murdered. I'll stay in touch. I'll have more questions to ask both of you as soon as I know more."

He was going to question me. My chest tightened. Would he want to talk with Jake, too? Jake was just a boy. He wouldn't know anything.

"I'm not going anywhere," said Burt, standing. "When can we bring Carl back to Quarry Island?"

Preston shook his head. "That's up to the medical examiner. I'll be in touch." He pulled a card out of his pocket and handed it to Burt. "If you think of anything that might help us find out who killed your brother, let me know." Then, he looked at me. "Mind if I take another muffin? Those were wicked good."

I passed him the plate. Like a little boy grabbing cookies without permission, he took two. "I hope you find whoever killed Carl, quickly." *And that you leave us alone.*

"I do, too," said Preston, leaving, and shutting the front door.

Burt was silent for a few seconds. Then, he turned to me. "Was what I said all right, Anna?"

"It was fine," I assured him. "Remember, when Preston questions you again, he isn't accusing you of anything. He doesn't know you or Carl. He's gathering information.

"Sure," Burt said facetiously. "Cops are always fair."

"We don't know Preston. He may be." I hoped so, at least.

"Carl wasn't perfect. I told him that."

"You did." I agreed, putting my arms around Burt. Through the soft, brown wool sweater I'd knit for him last year, I could hear his heart beating faster than usual. "He said he was going to talk to others on the island. Let them be the ones who tell him about Carl. There aren't any secrets on Quarry Island." Yesterday I'd said that to Izzie.

Yesterday could have been years ago.

"But there are, Anna," Burt said, burying his face in my hair. "Everyone has secrets."

# Chapter Ten

"How to make essence of bitter almonds: Mix one dram essential oil of bitter almonds with seven drams proof spirit. Use for flavoring custards, but must be employed with great caution, as about ten or twelve drops are poisonous."

—*Old Doctor Carlin's Recipes: A Complete Collection of Recipes on Every Known Subject* by Doctor William Carlin. Boston, Massachusetts: The Locker Publishing Company, 1881

We'd only had a few minutes alone to digest the news when Rob Erickson—still dressed in the jacket and slacks he'd worn to church—arrived at our door, looking over his shoulder at Detective Preston, who'd headed his car down Island Road.

"Sorry to bother you on a day like this," he said, closing our door behind him. "But I saw Jonas Preston leave here."

"Do you know him?" Burt asked, sitting on the edge of his favorite chair.

"I sometimes ran into him when I was a detective. In

Portland we did our own murder investigations, same as they do in Bangor. But state police have responsibility for homicides in the rest of the state. We worked with them." He paused. "That's why he was here, wasn't it? They've ruled Carl's death a homicide."

"Yes," I said softly.

"I'm retired. I don't have any law enforcement authority. But I know what happens in murder investigations. If I can help in any way, I'm here for you."

"Thanks, Rob. Appreciated," said Burt, pointing at the couch. "I should feel angry, or sad, but right now I'm numb."

Rob nodded, sitting. "I'm not surprised. Preston questioned you?"

"He asked where I'd seen Carl last, and what we'd talked about." Burt shook his head. "He actually asked me whether Carl had any enemies."

"That's by the book," Rob assured us. "First he'll talk to the family and call for a crime scene unit to look at Carl's boat and apartment. Those guys will check Carl's computer and bank records, and whatever else he may have left that might help lead them to his killer."

"But . . . a crime scene? I don't know how Carl was killed," I shuddered as I said the words, "but he must have been on the *Fair Winds.* What could they find in his apartment that would help?"

"They'll look for names of friends. Appointment calendars. His computer. Anything that would tell them who he was close to, or who he had problems with."

"What can we do, Rob?" Burt asked. "Of course, we want to know whoever killed Carl, but we're still coping with his death. We're in over our heads. What should we be thinking about?"

"Murder is messy," Rob agreed. "And, bluntly, investigating it can be complicated. The detectives will ask a lot of questions and dredge up history. They may find out things you don't want to know, or that you don't want anyone else to know. And after they find whoever killed Carl, the trial could take months or even years. You need to stay calm and cooperate with whatever you're asked. That won't be easy." He turned to me. "Has he questioned you yet, Anna? Or Jake?"

"Does he have to question Jake, too?" I blurted. "Jake's a child!"

"Jake has the right to have one of you with him during the interview. But, yes, I'm sure he'll want to question Jake."

I wanted chocolate. A whole box of it. A homicide detective was going to interview my son?

Izzie bounced in the front door at just that moment. She wasn't wearing makeup, but her cheeks were pink from the early April morning chill. She was wearing jeans and a green CIA sweatshirt, her dark cropped hair was windblown, and her arms were full of old books. She might have been a student heading for the campus coffee shop between classes.

She didn't know Carl had been murdered.

"You're home! Sorry I didn't get back sooner. I walked to the wharf, and then I decided to visit that used bookstore where you told me Jake worked—the Maine Chance?"

Rob stood up.

"Hi, Rob!" Izzie dumped her books onto the table where I usually piled our mail and turned from one of us to another. "I love that Luc Burnham! What a dear old man. And he has the most fantastic collection of cookbooks. I couldn't resist buying a few really old ones, like from the eighteen hundreds." She turned to look at each of us. "I'm sorry. I got carried away. The day is so beautiful, and I was so happy. I didn't think. You're all in mourning, and I came in here and emoted all over the place."

"Come and join us, Izzie." She'd have to know what was happening. "Thank you for baking the muffins. They were delicious. And, yes, we were talking about Carl. When you were at Maine Chance did you happen to ask Jake how long he'd be working this afternoon?"

"Jake? I didn't see Jake." Izzie plopped down in one of our armchairs, and Rob sat again. "I assumed he was in church with you. Luc was the only one at the bookstore."

Izzie was already on a first name basis with Jake's boss. I felt awkward calling him anything but Mr. Burnham, the name I'd called him since I was a child.

"Jake said he was going to Maine Chance to work today. I excused him from church so he could do that." I looked over at Burt. "Where do you think he is?"

"Probably somewhere with Matt Martin, as usual. Matt wasn't in church this morning either."

"You're right," I agreed. "But I don't like Jake telling us he'll be in one place, and then going to another. Especially with everything that's happening. I want to talk to him before the police do."

"The police? Why would the police want to talk to Jake?" Izzie asked. "Is he in trouble?"

"They're talking to everyone in the family," Burt explained quietly. "They've declared Carl's death a homicide."

"No! And here I came in here chattering about some old

books," Izzie looked at each of us in horror. "What are we going to do?"

*We*. I appreciated that.

"Rob, do we need a lawyer?" Burt asked.

Rob hesitated. "Calling in a lawyer right now might look as though you were trying to hide something. That you didn't want to cooperate." He looked from Burt to me and back again. "But if either of you *do* have anything to hide, I'd advise you to find someone who could represent you. Soon."

"So, unless Preston or one of the others comes to arrest me, I don't need a lawyer. But if I should, do you know any good ones that don't cost a fortune?"

Burt was serious; he must have been remembering that day he'd been accused and arrested without proof. He needed to relax. No one had accused him of anything, but I knew him. He was already thinking he was a suspect.

"Burt, you don't have to worry. You didn't do anything wrong. You don't need a lawyer," I assured him.

"Anna's right. Don't worry about lawyering up. There's no cause now," Rob agreed.

"But what if the police find out something that they think gives me a motive to hurt Carl? I want to be ready for anything."

Did Burt know something he wasn't telling us? He'd always been nervous about police.

But his only problem with them had been when he was a teenager. He was thirty-two now.

"Let's hope you don't have to worry about that," said Rob. "But I'll check around and get back to you. I should be able to come up with a name or two."

"Thank you. That would mean a lot. Rob, I'm sure you were a good detective. But even you know cops sometimes get carried away. I want to be prepared, no matter what happens." Burt seemed to have shrunk. His strong body was now melded with his chair, and his voice kept getting weaker.

"Burt, I know this is awful, but you have to relax. You're acting as though you're a suspect. Rob said the police always question the family of the victim first. That's all that's happened," I reminded him.

"Wicked straight." Those words were a little stronger. Burt was pulling himself together. He turned to me. "I didn't do anything wrong, Anna. But I don't know what the police think. If they take me away, ask Dolan to see about my traps. I haven't set all of them yet, but he knows where they are. He can find someone to help him. Tell him, though, if I'm gone more than a week, to just pull them. No way he can handle both of ours."

"Burt! Stop it! They're not going to arrest you." I said. "You're not a teenager away from home. There's no reason to think you'll be accused of anything." Was Burt overreacting because he hadn't accepted Carl's death? Or . . . could he know something he hadn't told the police or me?

"Better to be prepared for the worst." Burt moved to the edge of his chair. "I want Jake to stay in school. I don't want him taking on my traps until at least summer vacation."

I wanted to kick Burt under the table and tell him to shut up. The more he talked, the guiltier he sounded. I was sure he hadn't hurt Carl; his defenses were just up because of that long-ago night he'd spent in jail. Then I thought of something the detective had said.

"Detective Preston asked Burt about his arguing with Carl

yesterday," I said to Rob. "How do you think he knew they'd argued?"

Rob paused, and then answered. "I told one of the Marine Patrol officers yesterday that I'd heard them yelling at each other down at the wharf."

"What? You told them? You said you wanted to help us!" Burt's words were like daggers.

"I do," said Rob. "But I won't lie. I was out jogging earlier than usual yesterday morning. Dad had a bad night. Neither of us were sleeping, so I went out to get fresh air. I overhead the two of you. I didn't know what it was about, but sounds carry over water. When the officer asked if anyone had seen or heard from Carl yesterday, I told him."

"No wonder they came to see me first," said Burt, his face contorted. "They *do* suspect I killed Carl!"

"Did you, Burt?" Rob asked calmly. "Did you kill your brother?"

My whole body tightened, waiting for Burt's answer.

"No! Of course not!"

Thank goodness. I hadn't thought he was guilty, but I was still relieved to hear him say it.

Rob nodded. "Then that's what you have to tell them, when the police question you again. Be straight, and don't assume they're out to get you. They'll question you. But their job is to find whoever killed Carl, not to accuse you. If you talk to them the way you've been talking to us, they *may* think you're guilty."

I couldn't let them think that. "What if we figure out who killed Carl ourselves?" I said. "Then we could tell the police, and no one would suspect Burt of anything."

Rob swallowed hard. "As a former detective, I can't endorse

that. You don't know what you might be getting involved with. It could even be dangerous."

"But . . . ?" I said, sensing he hadn't finished his thought.

"If you think of something that could help Detective Preston or his team, let them know." He looked from one of us to the other. "I'll keep my ears open, too. Quarry Island isn't a big place. If someone here killed Carl, sooner or later we'll know who."

"The sooner the better," said Burt.

Rob Erickson stood up and turned to Izzie, who'd been quiet all this time. "I'm glad you're here for Anna and her family, Izzie." he said. "I have to get Dad's lunch and settle him in for the afternoon. If I can help, give me a call."

Burt got up as Rob left. "I need to get out myself. I'm going to take a short walk. I'll be back."

The door closed.

"I'm here for you both. I am," Izzie repeated. "What can I do to help?"

The living room air felt thick, and heavy. "First, we can eat the rest of those delicious muffins you made before everyone in the neighborhood descends upon us and devours them," I decided, standing up. "And then, you can help me figure out who killed Carl."

I wasn't a detective, but I knew the islanders. If it was one of us, maybe I could put the pieces together faster than the police could.

But first I was going to eat chocolate. If ever there was a day for chocolate, this was it.

# Chapter Eleven

"We would have the housewife employ a German or Irish girl and give her two dollars a week for going through the daily drudgery of the kitchen, in order that she may earn twice as much, with ten times the ease, comfort, and recreation to herself by employing the time thus rescued from the broom, the dustpan, and the washtub, in attention to her cows, her hens, and her bees."

—*The Philosophy of Housekeeping: A Scientific and Practical Manual* by Joseph B. Lyman and Laura E. Lyman. Hartford, Connecticut: S.M. Betts & Company, 1869

Dolan and Lucy Martin were the first to arrive with food that afternoon. "It's tuna noodle casserole," Lucy explained. "Nothing fancy, but it'll go down easy. I made one for us and one for you, with extra mushrooms and onions, the way you like it." She put her dish on our kitchen counter and hugged me. "I don't know how you're coping. I couldn't sleep all night, thinking of poor Carl, out there, floundering in the water. I know it's selfish, but I kept wondering what I'd do if it had been Dolan. Being married to a fisherman isn't easy."

"I know," I said, hugging her back. "I thought the same about Burt."

"Don't be saying things like that. It'll bring bad luck," said Dolan, joining us in the kitchen and also giving me a hug. "But it's going to seem mighty quiet without Carl around. He kept things lively."

"He did that," I agreed. "For sure."

Word got around quickly on Quarry Island, but Lucy and Dolan must not have heard Carl had been murdered. I hesitated. Should I tell them? Or did the police want to keep that information quiet for now?

"Fishermen?" asked Izzie. "I thought they were lobstermen."

"They fish the waters—for lobsters or fish," I explained. "Fishermen do both, and shrimp, too, in that season. Folks here use both words. And, yes—Carl and Burt and Dolan all lobster." I'd spoken of Carl as though he were still alive, but I didn't correct myself. Part of me still couldn't believe he was gone.

"Izzie, I'm so glad you're here with your sister," said Lucy. "Having another woman around must be such a help to Anna. And I ran into Rob Erickson earlier. He told me you're a cook."

"Chef," Izzie corrected, quietly.

"She made that egg dish we had last night," I pointed out. "The frittata."

"That was tasty," Lucy admitted.

"Thank you," said Izzie.

"It might have been even better with more bacon," Lucy added.

"More bacon would have meant more salt," said Dolan. "I think Izzie did just fine with those eggs. You should write it down for Lucy, Izzie."

"Do either of you know where the boys are?" I interrupted. "I texted Jake half an hour ago, and he hasn't answered."

"He was over at our place first thing this morning, said he wasn't going to church, that he had to talk to Matt. He looked pretty upset, so I didn't make a point of them attending services. The two of them took off on their bikes. I don't know where they headed, but Matt was home by the time we got back from church," said Lucy, looking at Dolan for confirmation. "I assumed Jake went home. He didn't?"

"No. He didn't," I said.

"I'm sure he's fine," said Lucy. "He's had a lot to absorb. Fourteen is a hard age. Matt's been a real pain in the you-know-what recently. Doesn't answer questions, keeps to himself, and when he does say something, he yells it. I guess it's teenage hormones. Whatever it is, it's been driving me crazy."

"Jake has been on edge, too," I admitted. "Maybe you're right. Hormones, or spring. But I need to get hold of him." I wanted to make sure Burt and I were the ones to tell Jake his uncle had been murdered. "Excuse me a minute." I went outside the back door and texted Jake again. Sometimes cell phone reception on the island was stronger outdoors.

When I returned to the kitchen, Izzie was showing Lucy the cookbooks she'd bought, and Dolan had retreated to the living room with a cup of coffee and a muffin.

"And see? This one was published in 1869. It has recipes for curing headaches and female troubles, along with advice on how to hire a cook and maid," she was saying.

"Really?" said Lucy, glancing at one of the worn leather-bound books. "I suppose that's fun to read, if you have the time. It's not exactly useful information today. Those people didn't have computers or television to teach them what they needed to know."

"What cookbooks do you use?" Izzie asked.

"Fannie Farmer and Marjorie Standish. If it isn't in one of those books I figure my family wouldn't eat it."

Izzie's eyes opened wide. I suspected she had dozens of cookbooks.

"Fannie Farmer's *The Boston Cooking-school Cook Book*'s a classic," said Lucy. "I have my grandmother's copy with all her notes in it."

"That sounds like a treasure. I don't know Marjorie Standish," Izzie continued.

"Her book is the classic bible for Maine cooking," Lucy said. "*Cooking Down East.* I can't imagine living without it."

"I have copies of both," I said, joining the conversation. I hadn't heard from Jake yet. I wanted to call Mom and Mamie. Maybe they'd seen him. "Izzie, you're welcome to look at any of my cookbooks, but I'm afraid I don't have many. What I know how to cook I learned from my mother and grandmother." I hadn't learned that much, I admitted to myself, having seen Izzie with her knives. My cooking (and knife work) was strictly amateur.

Izzie nodded. "I learned to cook from my mother, too. She didn't have any Korean cookbooks, but she did have a Betty Crocker that she checked sometimes for American food."

"Did it take long for you to learn English?" asked Lucy. "You don't have any accent!"

"I was born in Connecticut," replied Izzie, more calmly than I would have. "I only know a few Korean words. My mother was born in this country, too, although I do have distant relatives I've never met in Korea."

"Oh," said Lucy. She looked at the cell phone in my hand. "Shall I ask Matt if he knows where Jake is?"

"Thank you," I said. Lucy's cell phone provider sometimes worked when mine didn't.

"I'm sure he's fine," she said, as she texted Matt. "Those two know every inch of the island."

"I'm surprised they took their bikes in mud season," I said.

"They probably stayed on Island Road," she nodded. "It's the walkways and side roads that are messy. And they weren't gone for long. Matt was watching TV when we got back from church."

Almost immediately, she heard back from Matt. "He says he doesn't know where Jake is." She hesitated, reading the text again. "And he doesn't care. Did those boys have a fight of some sort?"

"I don't know," I said. "That doesn't happen often. But thanks for checking with him." Now I was really starting to worry about Jake.

"Why don't you make a few phone calls, Anna?" said Izzie. "See if you can find him. Lucy and I'll join Dolan in the living room. He's alone in there."

I nodded, relieved to have Izzie taking over my social obligations for a few minutes. "Thank you. I'm sure Jake's fine, but I'd like to know where he is."

Izzie herded Lucy to the living room, and I called my mother. "Mom? Is Jake over there?"

"He just got here, Anna. He didn't want people seeing him, and he knew you'd have company today."

"He isn't usually that shy," I said.

The phone went silent for a moment. Then I heard Jake's voice. "Mom, I'm a little messed up. I didn't want Dad to see me like this, with Uncle Carl dead and all."

"Messed up? What happened?"

"Mamie says I'm going to have a super dark black eye," Jake said. He sounded proud. "The cut on my lip is already clotting. She put ice on it."

"Did you have an accident with your bike?" He hadn't fallen off his bicycle in years, but it was April. He could have hit a frost heave or pothole.

"No. Matt and I had a . . . disagreement."

"You and Matt were fighting?" They argued, and they got into trouble sometimes. Usually trouble that involved dirt or water or both. I didn't remember them ever having a real fistfight.

"We had to, Mom. It was important."

I usually tried not to interfere with Jake's relationships with his friends, but that was a strange answer. "Jake, nothing is important enough to fight about. Do you want to talk about it?"

"No! It's private. It's between Matt and me."

"Okay," I sighed. "But you and Matt have to settle whatever it is. We have enough problems right now."

"I know, Mom! I'm not stupid."

"And right now, you need to get yourself home. Come in the kitchen door if you want to, and go up the back staircase to your room. The only people here now are Matt's parents, but other people may be coming."

"Can I stay here for lunch first? Mamie's made seafood chowder."

Mamie's chowder was one of Jake's favorites. "Eat, and then come home," I said. "No more arguments. Or fighting."

Lunch! I hadn't even thought about that. But we hadn't eaten all of Izzie's muffins and we also had Lucy's tuna casserole. No one would starve, even if other friends stopped in.

As if on cue, our front door opened and I heard new voices, including Burt's.

Thank goodness he was back. The sympathy open house had begun. I hoped whoever it was had brought more food. I couldn't focus on cooking right now. And maybe not for a while. At least none of these people knew Carl had been murdered. Not yet. Although someone, probably right here on Quarry Island, did know. His murderer knew.

No matter what Rob had advised, I was determined to find out who that was. Who it was who was hurting my family.

My hands were cold as Izzie handed me a pan of lasagna. "Martha-someone brought this. Are you all right?" she asked. "You look pale. Did you find Jake?"

"Jake's fine. He'll be home in a few minutes," I assured her, not answering her first question. "That must have been Martha Decker. She runs the general store. I'll put her lasagna in the refrigerator. If we get too much food we may have to freeze some."

"Not a problem," said Izzie. "I love that you have so many people who care about you and your family. And that you have a freezer."

"And that our winter venison's gone," I agreed. "But it's *our* family," I added firmly. "Your family now, too."

"I'm going to help you find out what happened to Carl,"

she said softly. "I'm listening to what everyone says. Maybe the murderer will stop in. Visiting the bereaved family would be a good cover, don't you think?"

"You and I must watch the same crime shows," I said. "But you're right. I had the same idea. We might come up with information that will help the police."

In the meantime, I put Martha's lasagna away and prepared to be comforted by my neighbors.

Although Izzie was right. One of them might be a murderer.

# Chapter Twelve

"Rules Recommended to Servants: Never tell the affairs of the family you belong to; for that is a sort of treachery, and often makes mischief; but keep their secrets, and have none of your own."

—*The Gentleman's Magazine*, London, October 1777

"Jake, your father and I need to talk with you." He'd stayed at Mom's longer than I'd expected, and tried to sneak up the back stairway when he finally got home. I'd stopped him and gestured that he should join Burt and me in the living room. On the way there, I'd handed him one of the ice bags I kept in the freezer. All our company had left.

I tried not to stare at his purpling cheek and swollen eye. The ice bag might help a little, but he was going to be colorful for days. Had Matt looked like that, too? His mother hadn't mentioned it. They were old enough so they should be able to settle whatever problem they had without Burt and my help. Fighting was never an answer.

But I bit my tongue. Burt and I had more important issues on our minds than the boys' quarrel.

Neighbors had come and gone all afternoon. I was exhausted by everything I'd had to say, and everything I couldn't say. I'd gratefully turned the kitchen and all the donated food over to Izzie, who'd miraculously found bowls for salads and freezer wrap for multiple baked bean casseroles, macaroni and cheeses, and spaghettis, and tin boxes for the cookies and brownies. She'd emptied a bag of chocolate covered blueberries into a bowl, and I'd already been nibbling. She'd also sliced two of the donated cakes and one apple pie, and served them, along with many cups of coffee. Two large bottles of wine were now empty, and two six-packs of Moxie, and I was pretty sure we were out of beer.

After everyone had left, Izzie'd excused herself and taken her newly purchased recipe books to her room, leaving Burt and me to talk with Jake alone. I looked questioningly at Burt and gestured at Jake's swollen face.

Burt just shrugged, focused on what had happened to his brother. "We need to talk about your uncle."

"Dad, I know about Uncle Carl. You told me last night," Jake said impatiently.

"But you weren't here this morning when we learned more," said Burt, gently.

"What more is there?"

Jake was taller than I was, but he was still young. I hated him having to face what had happened. He slumped into one of the armchairs.

"Uncle Carl's dead. He's gone. What more is there to say?

If you're going to warn me about the dangers of lobstering, I've already got it."

"That isn't it," said Burt. "Slow down and listen, Jake. Your uncle Carl didn't drown. He was killed."

Jake's eyes opened wide. "What do you mean? How?" He leaned forward, listening.

"We don't know. But a homicide detective from the state police was here today. He's going to be talking to all of us and to our friends in the next few days."

"I don't want to talk to him!" said Jake, standing up. "I have nothing to say!"

"Your mom or I will be with you when you're interviewed," said Burt. "You don't have to worry. Give the detective simple answers, and tell the truth. That's all."

Jake looked from Burt to me and back again. "Simple answers?"

"Right," I said. "Whatever he asks, you answer. But don't add anything, or guess."

"Your uncle and I argued yesterday morning, down at the wharf," said Burt "The police already know that."

"You argued? Again?" Jake's voice rose. "Why yesterday, Dad?"

"I wish it hadn't happened." Burt flushed and his voice broke. "But it did. And someone outside the family might believe I hurt Carl, because of the problems he and I were having."

"And the cops are going to ask me about that?"

"We don't know," I said. "It's possible."

He shook his head. "I'm not going to do it. I don't want to answer any questions. I'm not going to talk to the police! You can't make me." He stormed upstairs and slammed his bedroom door.

Burt ran his fingers through his hair as he looked after Jake. "He's going to have to do it."

"Maybe tomorrow he'll be calmer. He's still young. Carl's death upset him, of course, and then he and Matt got into a fight. It's been a hard day for him."

"It hasn't exactly been easy for any of us," said Burt, bluntly. "At his age I was out lobstering on my own, saving for a bigger boat. Planning my future. He isn't a little boy anymore, Anna. It's time he grew up."

I nodded. "I know. But we should cut him a little slack right now."

"Let's leave him alone tonight," said Burt, standing. "I'm too tired to cope with him, anyway. Besides, maybe he'll think on the whole situation and tomorrow he'll accept what he's expected to do. I'm going to get a couple of those brownies someone brought and a glass of milk and go to bed. I didn't get much sleep last night, and I'll have to take the *Anna* out in the morning. Lobsters don't stop for murder."

# Chapter Thirteen

"Kissing don't last: cookery do."
—*The Ordeal of Richard Feverel* (1859)
by George Meredith

Night passed, dawn came, and it didn't bring the police.

At five in the morning, Burt texted Dolan Martin and asked for help. "I haven't been out since Saturday. My traps need checking. I should pull Carl's, too, and I'm missing a sternman."

Dolan stopped in a few minutes later, dressed in the warm layered clothing he wore under the usual waterproof bib pants, jacket, and boots the men kept on their boats. Dolan was taller and wider than Burt. Despite his dark beard, he'd always reminded me a little of Santa Claus. "I was just heading for the wharf when I got your text, Burt."

"Thanks for stopping." Burt pulled on his one of his oldest sweaters. "Hoped you'd be able to help. Circumstances aren't good, and I could use an extra pair of hands."

"Sure thing. No problem. Alex Tompkins is sterning for

me these days. He works afternoons at the hardware store over on the mainland. With the two of us working together, we can check most of my pots before noon. After that, be happy to help with Carl's." He hesitated. "Still can't believe he's gone."

Burt nodded. "Wicked hard. But his traps got to be pulled, and I got no one to stern. Could really use your help."

"You have it. Heading down?"

"Just that." Burt turned and held me for a minute. "With Dolan's help, I'll be out for the day. If you hear of any developments, call me." He turned to Dolan. "Let's go. Tonight I'll see if I can find someone to stern for me regular."

I hated to see Burt going out by himself, even just in the morning, when we didn't know what had happened to Carl. But fishermen don't take days off. I'd known that forever.

Burt turned back just before he reached the door. "Send Jake on to school. Better than his sitting around here thinking about what happened. Life has to go on." He and Dolan headed out.

I poured myself another mug of coffee and fixed Jake's lunch, adding three of the molasses cookies someone had brought yesterday. I didn't even remember who'd brought what. The refrigerator and freezer were full of everything from baked beans to chicken. I hoped Izzie'd written down who'd brought food so I could send short notes, but I suspected she hadn't. She didn't know most of our neighbors. And anyway, I'd thanked everyone who'd been here. No one had come empty-handed.

Had word already gotten around that Carl had been killed?

And how could someone kill him when he'd been alone on the *Fair Winds*? Had someone in another boat come aboard, or alongside?

No explanation I could imagine made sense.

This wasn't July, when folks from both the islands and the mainland were out on the waters in everything from kayaks and sailboats to the occasional yacht or cruise ship touring the coastline. In summer, keeping an eye out for recreational boaters, some of whom didn't pay strict attention to boating regulations or didn't know the currents or tidal patterns, was something all locals did. You never knew what crazy thing an amateur sailor might do.

But this time of year everyone on the water knew everyone else, and recognized their boats.

I shivered. Burt would be alone on the *Anna* this morning. Carl had been alone on his *Fair Winds*.

I finished my coffee, fed Blue, ate two molasses cookies and then a piece of chocolate, and went to make sure Jake was up. He'd slept through his alarm too many mornings. Sometimes I suspected he did it intentionally, depending on me to wake him.

I knocked on his door. "Jake? Time to get up. School bus in half an hour."

I waited to hear his usual groans and protests.

No response.

The joys of motherhood. "Jake, if you don't get up this minute I'm going to come in and pull those covers off you! It's Monday morning!" The threat of my entering his sanctuary usually brought him stumbling to the door on his way to the bathroom.

Not this morning.

At fourteen, he didn't want Burt or me in his room. We'd decided to let him have his privacy, unless the room started smelling. "Boys will be boys," Burt would say. "Carl and I hated when our mom came in and rearranged our room when we were in school. She sometimes threw out treasures or washed clothes we were intentionally messing up. As long as the kid doesn't have rats in his room, or burn the place down, why not let him have it the way he wants it?" We kept his bedroom door closed.

"Jake!" I called again. I was probably waking Izzie, but I couldn't help that. "Last warning! I'm coming in!" Had he fallen asleep last night with his headphones on? Between his alarm and my yelling, he'd normally wake up anyway.

Silence.

Suddenly, I felt a chill. Was something wrong? Was Jake sick? This wasn't normal behavior.

I pushed open the door. Piles of dirty and clean clothes were intermixed on the floor, empty bags of chips he must have bought for himself overflowed from the waste basket, stacks of papers had fallen from the desk I'd gotten for him at a yard sale. A few stuffed animals left over from his younger days still crowded the bookcase near his bureau, along with action figures and matchbox cars he'd collected years ago. His poster of Tom Brady hung askew over his rumpled bed.

Which was empty.

Jake was gone.

# Chapter Fourteen

"Cut your sandwiches in half, each half in quarters, and each quarter diagonally. Trim off all protruding edges of filling. Cover the sandwiches with a cloth wet with a very weak solution of brandy and water and pack them in a tin box until ready for use."

—*Mrs. Seely's Cook-Book: A Manual of French and American Cookery, with Chapters on Domestic Servants, Their Rights and Duties, and Many Other Details of Household Management* by Lida Seely. New York: 1902

Where was Jake? My chest tightened. I looked around his room once more. Had I somehow missed seeing him? I pulled open his closet door and narrowly avoided being hit by his ice hockey stick falling from the shelf above where his clothes should have been hanging. Most were piled on the floor. An old *Playboy* centerfold hung inside the door. Maine Chance Books carried old magazines. He'd probably gotten it there. This morning, it wasn't important.

What was important was that Jake wasn't here, at home, where he should be.

Panicky, I pulled out my phone and called him. Maybe he was . . . I had no idea.

No answer.

Izzie appeared in the doorway. Her short black hair was sticking up in the back, and she was wearing a knee-length black tee shirt with "this IS my sexy nightgown" emblazoned in red on the front.

"I heard you yelling. Is everything all right?" she asked, her voice muffled with sleep.

"Jake's missing," I said. "I came to wake him up for school and he wasn't in his bed."

I felt tears welling up in my eyes. Too much had happened in the past few days. I couldn't deal with anything more.

"In the shower? Gone for an early walk?"

"Bathroom's clear. And he's never gotten up early for a walk alone in his life."

"Is all his stuff here? What he would take to school? His tablet?"

I glanced over the room. "His backpack is gone. He has a laptop, not a tablet. The state gives them to all seventh and eighth graders."

"Nice, but . . ." Izzie pointed to the edge of something almost hidden by the rumpled blankets on Jake's bed.

I pulled the blankets back. She'd been right. It was a tablet. Where had that come from? Maybe borrowed from a friend? Did Matt have one?

"Could he have gone to school early?"

"His school's on the other side of the island. He takes the

school bus." I glanced at his alarm clock. "I've been up for a couple of hours. I haven't seen him."

Izzie frowned. "His friend Matt lives nearby, right?"

"Next door."

"Then maybe he's with Matt. At fourteen, friends are important."

"Maybe," I said. Jake and Matt had argued—fought—about something yesterday. He hadn't said what. Could he have left late last night, after the rest of us were in bed, or before dawn this morning? Gone to see Matt, to patch up whatever they'd fought about? Boys might be boys, but those two were too old for fists. One of them could end up with more than a black eye.

I was desperate. "Dolan's out on his boat. I'll call Lucy and see."

Before I had a chance to call, I heard the kitchen door open. "Mom! It's me!" Jake's voice from the kitchen. "I'm taking my lunch. See you this afternoon!"

The door banged shut before I could reply. Izzie and I both stepped over the pile of blankets under Jake's bedroom window and looked out. Jake was running toward the bus stop in front of the church. Almost immediately, the yellow Quarry Island school bus appeared. We watched him get in before it pulled away.

"I have no idea where he was, or what he was doing," I said.

"But he's okay," said Izzie. "Burt's out on his boat?"

I nodded. "He left a while ago."

"Then we have some time on our own this morning," she said. "Let me get some clothes on and then we can decide what to do."

She headed for the bathroom.

I picked up the tablet. Jake's room was his private place. He'd be furious that Izzie and I had gone into it. But a tablet was an expensive piece of equipment. I'd have to ask him about it.

I felt as though I'd already survived a long day. I was tempted to head back to bed for a nap. Instead, I put the tablet on the kitchen counter, heated more coffee, and opened the kitchen door, inhaling the chilly April air and watching a murder of crows calling to each other between two spruce trees in the woods behind our home.

When we'd been kids, Dolan had rescued a baby crow that had fallen out of his nest and fed him with an eyedropper. For years, that crow sat on Dolan's shoulder and came when he called. Dolan swore he understood everything he was told. Once, Blackie—that's what Dolan named him—had flown in the window of the schoolroom where Dolan was sitting and landed on his head.

We'd all envied Dolan that crow, until one day he'd flown away and hadn't returned.

Dolan still talked about Blackie sometimes.

Crows were smart. But if those crows in our woods knew what had happened to Carl, or why Jake hadn't been in his room this morning, they weren't telling me.

I turned back to the kitchen, the room where I'd spent most of my time, alone, since the roofing business closed. This morning I wasn't alone, I reminded myself. My sister was here.

She'd pulled on jeans and the CIA sweatshirt she'd been wearing yesterday, and her hair was still wet from the shower. "I couldn't get to sleep right away last night, so I read some of those old cookbooks," she said a few minutes later, sipping the coffee I'd poured for her. "They're amazing. I wish I'd had them when I was at CIA. I could have written papers on the sociology of nineteenth century household management. Or had fun trying out the recipes, maybe updating them."

"I don't have any cookbooks that old," I told her. "But I do have a couple of Maine cookbooks from the nineteen twenties and thirties I've bought a yard sales. The sort church women published as fundraisers. The recipes are for the same food we eat today—cakes and pies and pancakes and puddings and chowders. But it's amazing how instructions and ingredients have changed over the years."

Izzie nodded. "And how exact we insist recipes be today. If you were baking bread in a fireplace bake oven or wood stove, cooking time depended on outside temperatures and humidity—even the kind of wood you were burning. Women put their hands in the heat, felt how hot the oven was, and estimated how long the bread would take to bake. Baking—all cooking—took more experience and creativity than it does today."

"Thank goodness for oven settings and thermometers," I put in.

"I'd still like to try some of the old recipes I found," said Izzie. "We could do that together."

How long would Izzie stay?

She kept talking about old recipes for home brews and remedies, but I didn't pay close attention.

What had happened to Carl? Would Burt be all right? Where had Jake been this morning? Would that homicide investigator—Preston—be back to ask more questions today? Who was he talking to now? What had they told him?

"Have you had breakfast?" Izzie asked. Her question broke through my swirling thoughts.

"Coffee. And molasses cookies," I admitted.

She hesitated. "We should have some protein, especially since you're stressed out. A little cheese was left. What about cheese with crackers, or eggs?"

I wasn't hungry, but she was right. "A cheese omelet?" I suggested.

"Coming up." Izzie jumped up, gulped a little of her cold coffee, and selected a frying pan, eggs, and cheese. She'd already figured out where to find everything in my kitchen.

"You don't have an omelet pan," she said, almost to herself. "But this pan's the right size."

I got up and put two plates and forks on the table. "You don't have to cook every meal," I said.

"Feeding people makes me feel I'm contributing a little. I'm a houseguest, and you have a lot on your mind. That can't be easy."

I started to protest, when she gestured "time out."

"No arguments. We may be sisters, but we hardly know each other, and your family is coping with a nightmare. By all rights you should kick me out." She glanced at me. "I'd understand if you did. But as long as I'm here I want to help any way I can. And I suspect you wouldn't eat a healthy breakfast today if I didn't cook one for you."

Chocolate was healthy, wasn't it? I couldn't help smiling. "Someday you'll make a great mom," I said.

She looked startled. "Maybe. But not soon. I have a lot I want to do before that." She added grated cheddar to the cooking eggs, and expertly flipped them. "When you were my age, what were your dreams? What did you want to do with your life?"

That took me by surprise. I'd always lived day by day. Dreams? "How old are you?" She'd never said.

"Twenty-three," she said, cutting the omelet and putting half on my plate and half on hers.

"I'm thirty-two. Nine years difference." I took a bite. "This is delicious! What did you add besides the cheese?"

"A touch of cayenne," she said. "And a little salt and cracked black pepper. That's all. That's why I love omelets. You can add meats, veggies, herbs—whatever you have on hand. So—what were your dreams? What were you passionate about? Or, even better—what do you want now?"

Izzie had been right. I needed to eat. "I don't remember any big dreams or passions outside of being married and making a home for Burt and Jake," I finally admitted. "When I was your age Burt and I had just bought this house. Jake wasn't in school yet, so I was taking care of him, and painting and papering and making curtains." I thought back. "After that I started working for Seth."

When I was a child, I'd wanted fancy dresses for my bride doll. Trips to the movie theater on the mainland, instead of waiting for the latest films to be on tapes or television. A shiny, new bicycle, instead of the dented one Seth had bought for me at a yard sale. But none of those things had been passions. My life might have sounded dull, but I'd been content. When I'd grown up I'd loved working for Seth, keeping the books, and being married and a mother, and I was proud of our little house.

"But now your house is comfortable, and Jake's in school, so you have more time," Izzie continued. "Time to do something for yourself, not just for Burt and Jake."

"Right now, I'm what Mom calls 'betwixt and between.'

I've been doing small quilting projects—you saw my materials in the room you're using. I make pillows and baby quilts. There aren't a lot of jobs on Quarry Island, especially in winter."

"But what do you dream of doing?" said Izzie, looking at me as though there were a crystal ball between us. "If you could do anything in the world, anywhere, what would it be?"

Saturday, Burt and I had fantasized about buying new furniture, and visiting Boston. Those were dreams. But I suspected Izzie was thinking of bigger goals. "I'd love to have enough money so Jake could go to college. I'm hoping he'll want to. And I've never traveled far from the island. That might be fun." Life was as it was. Why dream of impossibilities? "What about you? What do want to do with your life?"

"So many things," Izzie said. "I want to visit South Korea and find my relatives there, and try scuba diving, and write a cookbook, and fall in love, and dance under the stars in Paris! Most of all, I want my own restaurant. Not a fancy place. A place where people feel comfortable meeting friends and eating delicious food."

"You've made a start. You learned all about cooking in school," I encouraged.

"Some, sure," said Izzie. "It was a beginning. But I'd love to experiment. To invent my own recipes. My dream restaurant isn't a place where people have never heard of what's on the menu, or that serves tiny portions of exquisite tasting dishes that cost a fortune. Plenty of restaurants like that already exist. And I don't want a place that serves one kind of food, like pizza, or Asian, or seafood. My restaurant will have a small, diverse menu."

Izzie was looking off into the air, seeing dreams I couldn't imagine. What must it be like to have a passion, as she'd put it, for creating something?

"What I love about cooking is seeing how flavors and textures and colors interact. I like playing with recipes, and making people happy about the food they're eating. Creating something both spicy and soothing, or sweet and salty. Something memorable. Something people wouldn't cook for themselves. Eating out should be a little exciting. A little different."

"Some restaurants in Maine serve lobster macaroni and cheese," I said, trying to understand what she was getting at. Burt and I only ate out on special occasions. When we did, we chose a place Burt could order a huge cheeseburger and a draft, and I could indulge my periodic longing for scallops—a seafood Burt didn't care for. Jake, Burt, and I sometimes went to a pizza place on the mainland with Carl and the Martins to celebrate a success, like the boys winning a Little League game.

"And I'd want to charge prices families could afford."

I shook my head. "Sounds perfect. But impossible."

"Nothing is impossible," Izzie declared. "Dreams come true."

I looked at her doubtfully. "Maybe some dreams." Izzie was so excited about possibilities in her life. Had I ever felt that way?

"Of course, you have to work hard to make them happen," Izzie said, drinking the last of her coffee. Her face lit up when she talked. Her excitement was contagious.

"I'll cheer you on! So where is this dream restaurant going to be?"

"I'm still working that out. Not in a big city like New York, at least not at first. Rents are too high, and pressure's too great. I know I'm young. I can cook, and I've taken classes in restaurant management, but I've never organized a staff or run a business. I have a lot to learn. And I don't want to go back to Connecticut. It's time for me to start over in a new place. That's why I was thinking of looking for a job at one of the restaurants in Portland. Get some experience, build up my bank account, and then decide."

"Does it cost a lot to open a restaurant?" I asked. Izzie and I were going to inherit money. Maybe that would help her.

"It varies a lot. Where the place is, renting or buying, equipping the place, having enough cash to open and carry the expenses of staff and food and liquor until you're in the black."

"It sounds complicated. And running your restaurant wouldn't be as creative as the cooking you're talking about. I know—I took care of the accounts for that roofing business. It wasn't exactly like a restaurant, but we did have to please customers, keep inventory records, and balance the books." I sat back, remembering. I'd liked being in charge, and Seth had let me manage everything in the office while he supervised the outside jobs. I missed working.

Izzie smiled. "I'll have to learn all that." She picked up our empty plates and went to the sink to rinse them off.

"What about a family? Don't you want to get married and have children?" I called after her.

"I'd like to have a man in my life, of course. Maybe even children someday. But families—even one man—take a lot of time. Right now, I want to concentrate on my dreams before I start trying to fit someone else and their dreams into mine."

Izzie'd already figured out what she wanted to do with her life. I'd never thought far beyond what I had now. What would the rest of my life be like? Suddenly the years stretched ahead of me.

"I envy you, though," Izzie said, looking around. "You have a husband who loves you, a son who seems like a normal teenager, family nearby, and you live in a beautiful place. Not many people have all that." She paused. "Dad was busy with business and with his own friends, but he was my family: someone to call when I broke up with a boyfriend or aced an exam. I had a home to go to for Thanksgiving and Christmas. Now I have friends, of course, but they're busy with their own lives and families."

The way Izzie saw her world fascinated me. "We have very different lives, but I'm glad we found each other."

"Me, too," said Izzie, putting her hand on top of mine. "But you already have a full life. We don't know yet if our lives will fit together."

"True. But I'm hopeful," I agreed. Living in a close-knit community meant you had support—like from those who'd brought food and condolences yesterday. My life was centered around the people I loved. I'd never thought of doing anything independently. Would I ever find something I loved doing as much as Izzie loved cooking? It was a new question, but I sensed the answer was important.

As Izzie put our dishes in the dishwasher, I noted that no one had called or stopped in this morning, which was unusual for after a death.

"Do you have to stay here this morning? Is that detective coming back?"

"He may, but he has both my cell and my home telephone numbers. Other people do, too. Some may stop in today to pay condolence visits. But," I admitted, "I'm not looking forward to that. They're being kind, but with all the questions about Carl's death, I know they'll be pumping me for answers I don't have. Or don't want to talk about."

"Last night you said you wanted to solve Carl's murder," she reminded me.

"I still do. But I haven't figured out how," I admitted.

"I'll help! It'll be like putting a complicated recipe together," she suggested.

"You're right," I said, smiling. Izzie could connect anything to food. "But I need a little more time. Distance."

"Then let's get out. Go for a walk," she said. "Or a drive. I'd like to see more of the island. And we wouldn't be too far away, if someone needed you."

No matter where you were on the island, you were never far away. "A good idea," I said. "But I'd like to stop at the Martins' house first to see if Lucy knows what Jake was up to this morning. Or why he and Matt fought yesterday."

"They're next door. Right?"

"Right. Between our house and the Ericksons.' "

"Rob Erickson is the retired detective who's taking care of his father? He seemed nice. And good-looking. For someone his age," she added. "I mean—he must be in his forties, right?"

Rob *was* good-looking. Our island had only a few unmarried residents. Carl had been one. Rose and Cynthia Snowe weren't married. But nearly everyone else on the island who wasn't married was either under eighteen or over sixty-five. Maine had the oldest population in the union. Quarry Island was no exception.

"His house is the one with the buoy tree, right? Does Rob collect buoys?"

I shook my head. "Those are his dad's. They're all red and yellow striped: Gus' colors. He hung them there when he gave up lobstering."

"Would you mind if I went with you to the Martins'?" Izzie asked.

"Of course not. Come on," I said, getting up. "We've been friends since we were kids."

Izzie shook her head in amazement. "I'm not in touch with anyone I went to elementary school with. Here it sounds as though friends really are forever."

"Womb to tomb," I agreed soberly as we headed out the door.

# Chapter Fifteen

"Cookie Recipe: Mix together one pound of powdered loaf-sugar, one pound of flour, and a half-teaspoonful of carbonate of soda; rub in a quarter pound of butter; make into a soft paste, with three eggs, a dessertspoonful of cream or milk, and essence of almond to taste; roll out an inch thick, and cut into biscuits with a wineglass. Bake ten minutes in a moderate oven. They must be kept in a dry place, and will continue good for three months."

—*Peterson's Magazine*, January 1886

Early April was way too soon to garden, but the ground was beginning to warm. It used to be traditional in Maine to plant gardens over Memorial Day weekend, but weather had changed since then. Many islanders now put crops, like peas that could stand cooler nights, in earlier.

Below winter debris and mud, mint and chives and early tulips were sprouting in my garden. Tiny spikes that in a month would be dandelions were beneath the withered grasses of our lawn. Soon I'd be pulling weeds and planting lettuce and zucchini and parsley seeds and tomato and pepper seedlings. Today, a pair of robins pushed aside brown leaves and lunched on early worms. Life and death, everywhere.

"In New York, trees are budding, and others are in bloom," said Izzie, as we walked toward the Martins' house, stopping to watch chipmunks skittering in and out of the low stone wall that separated our homes.

"Trees here won't be really green for about six more weeks. We still have crocuses blooming. Daffodils are just starting to flower." Several naturalized clumps flourished next to our mailbox, which Jake had painted red as a Mother's Day gift to me three years ago. "Let's take the path to avoid the mud."

When the boys had been small, racing between our houses, Dolan and Burt had dug out the path they'd worn in the grass, opened a space in the stone wall, and designed a walkway intended to keep mud out of both our homes. They'd poured cement and then, when it was still wet, covered the path with tumbled sea stones from the beach near Heron Point. The path was well constructed and attractive, but treacherous for anyone in high heels. Lucy'd broken more than one pair on it. My heels were only for weddings and funerals.

Funerals. When could we have Carl's funeral? How long would the medical examiner need his body? I shuddered, thinking of what was happening to it. To him.

Izzie hugged herself. "It's chilly," she admitted. "But I like smelling the salt air."

"I do, too," I agreed.

I dropped the brass pineapple knocker on the Martins' door, and walked in. "Lucy!" I called from the living room. "It's me. Izzie's with me."

Lucy didn't answer. She might be in the shower or on the telephone, but I was almost as at home here as I was in my own house. I led Izzie through Lucy's tidy living room decorated in blues and grays. She'd commissioned Mom to make the quilt thrown over the back of the couch in shades to match the room. Lucy studied *Elle Décor* and *Maine Home and Design* the way Izzie read gourmet cookbooks. She'd saved and done without until she could afford exactly what she'd wanted.

I wasn't as patient with my home. I'd been happy with furniture friends had discarded, or we'd inherited from Burt's parents, or we'd found at auctions or flea markets. My house was cozy and lived-in. Lucy's was lovely and immaculate. A Hollywood movie could have been shot in her living room.

Izzie was looking at the framed sketches above the couch.

"An artist visiting the island a few years back did those. He donated them to a library fundraiser before he left, and Lucy convinced Dolan to buy them for her."

"I recognize the bridge and the church. What are the other scenes?"

"The quarry—there *is* a quarry on Quarry Island, and a gravel pit," I assured her. "Granite Point Lighthouse," I pointed. "And the beach below it."

"I'm looking forward to seeing all of the island," said Izzie. "And that painting?"

Above the Martins' fireplace was an oil painting of what Lucy had told me was a giant wave. I couldn't tell. The swirls of blue and gray and green and white dominated the room. "Willis Tarbox, who lives across the street, did that one. Dolan bartered a pair of lobsters every Sunday for six months for it."

"Interesting," said Izzie, staring at it. "Willis is the man who brought the sketch of Carl to you yesterday, right?

"Right. Let me find Lucy."

I left Izzie looking at the painting and then glancing at the titles in the Martins' bookcase.

"Lucy?" I called upstairs. "It's Anna."

"Just a minute, Anna," she called back. A few minutes later she appeared, wearing a white nightgown embroidered with blue flowers and a blue silk robe, its sash knotted around her thin waist. Not exactly like the flannel granny gowns I wore most of the year. "Afraid I slept in. How're you doing? Izzie, good to see you again. Coffee, anyone? I need coffee."

"Are you feeling all right?" I asked. Usually Lucy was perky and organized. Not this morning.

"I'm fine. Fine," she said, heading for her kitchen. Dirty dishes were piled on the counter. She poured water into her coffee maker. "Didn't sleep last night, that's all. I kept remembering all the happy times with Carl. He and I playing George and Martha Washington in the third grade play. The year the school baseball team lost every game. Taking Jake and Matt to see the Sea Dogs in Portland. I can't believe he's gone. Why was he out in that boat when the engine wasn't working right? He had all that sweepstakes money. Why didn't he stop tinkering and just buy a new engine?"

Didn't Lucy know Carl was broke? Engines cost as much as a car. She must have forgotten he'd spent that money he'd won.

It didn't matter now.

She stood, looking out her kitchen window. Then she turned toward Izzie and me. "Coffee? And how's Burt doing?"

"We don't need coffee; we had a couple of cups at my house," I answered. "Burt's coping. He's out on the *Anna* this morning. Dolan's going to help him pull some of Carl's traps this afternoon." Since Lucy had been asleep, I suspected Dolan hadn't told her he was helping out. "Thanks for the tuna casserole. We'll have it for dinner tonight. I wondered if you knew what the boys were up to."

Lucy's eyes were puffy. "The boys? Aren't they in school?"

"I saw Jake get on the bus this morning. But he and Matt had a fight yesterday, and Jake went out very early this morning, or maybe even late last night. I thought he might be with Matt."

"Sorry, Anna. When I couldn't sleep, I took a couple of over-the-counter sleeping pills. They knocked me out. Matt must have gotten himself off to school, thank goodness." She poured coffee beans into her grinder and turned it on.

I waited until the noise stopped. I hated being the one to tell her, but Lucy was a close friend. She was grieving. And Detective Preston might show up on her doorstep any time. "Lucy, yesterday the police gave us more information about Carl."

She turned around. "What about Carl?"

"He didn't drown."

"What?" Lucy's face froze. "Then what happened to him?"

"The medical examiner said he was killed. The state police plan to talk to people on the island who knew him. You and he were close friends, so I wanted to warn you. Detective Preston may stop in to see you sometime today."

"To question me?" Lucy looked stunned. She grabbed onto the back of one of her kitchen chairs and held on. "Carl, murdered? Who would do such a thing?"

I shook my head. "Whoever it was, I hope Preston and the other detectives figure it out soon."

"When I saw Carl on Friday he seemed good. Getting his act together. He was happy. Optimistic. It's so awful," said Lucy, her eyes filling with tears. She grabbed a tissue from a box on the table and blew her nose loudly. "Ever since we heard he was missing, I haven't been able to think of anything else. And now—murdered!"

She pulled her robe tighter around her and sat at her kitchen table.

"It's rough for all of us," I agreed. "His death hasn't fully sunk in yet. I've just been doing what needs to be done. One hour at a time."

"And you have Izzie with you," Lucy pointed out. "That's good. Enjoying your visit, Izzie?"

Izzie had been hanging back, letting Lucy and I talk. She hesitated. "Maine's a beautiful place. But I'm sorry I came at such a difficult time for all of you."

"I'm going to take Izzie for a drive around the island," I said. "I'm sorry to have woken you. But I wanted to warn you about Detective Preston, and check in about Jake." That part had been a bust. If she knew more about what was going on with the boys, she hadn't told me.

"What will he ask? What would I know that would help?"

"I have no idea," I said. "He thinks one of us may know something that will help him piece it all together." I didn't mention that Izzie and I were going to do some sleuthing of our own. That was our secret. "He'll be back to question Jake and me later, too. Until we know what happened to Carl, I suspect we'll be seeing a lot of Detective Preston."

Izzie moved toward the door.

"We'll take off. Thank you again for the food you brought yesterday," I said.

Lucy nodded, but didn't stand.

"Nice to see you again, Lucy," said Izzie. "You have a lovely home."

"Thank you," said Lucy. "Enjoy your drive."

"She seemed really upset," Izzie pointed out on our way back to my house. "You said she was a good friend of Carl's?"

"They were in the same class at school. They even dated for a short time early in high school. They still did things together that they both enjoyed and Dolan hated, like going to concerts in Portland. Carl was close to Matt, too. He'd take Matt and Jake to movies on the mainland, or we'd all barbecue together." I glanced at my phone. "No one's called yet. Shall we drive around the island now?" Maybe if I kept talking to Izzie, nothing bad would happen.

"I'd love that," said Izzie, and we headed toward the barn, where our truck was parked.

Before we got there, Detective Preston pulled his car into our drive, blocking the barn door.

Jake was in his back seat.

# Chapter Sixteen

"Have a bottle full of brandy, with as large a mouth as any bottle you have, into which cut your lemon and orange peel when they are fresh and sweet. This brandy gives a delicious flavor to all sorts of pies, puddings, and cake."

—*The Frugal Housewife: Dedicated to Those Who Are Not Ashamed of Economy* by Lydia Maria Child. Boston: Marsh & Capen, 1829

"Mrs. Winslow?" Detective Preston got out of his car, and gestured that Jake should too. "I picked Jake up at school. I'd like you to be with him when I question him. Then I'd like to talk with you, alone."

"Mom, he had the principal call me down to the office," Jake complained. "Everyone at school's going to think I did something awful. He pulled me out of Math!" Jake sent an "I can't tell you how much I hate you" glance at Detective Preston.

"Sorry I embarrassed you, Jake. But I know you want us

to find out what happened to your uncle Carl," Preston replied. I suspected he'd heard worse from others he'd questioned.

"That's your job. I don't know anything about it!"

"You might know something you don't think is important, but that would help the investigation."

"Why don't we all go inside?" I suggested.

"Thank you, Mrs. Winslow."

They all followed me into the house. Anyone driving by would think I'd just invited friends in for morning coffee.

We ended up in the kitchen. Guests spent more time in my kitchen than in the living room.

"Miss Jordan? Would you excuse us?" said Detective Preston, looking at Izzie.

She knocked on the table as she went by, wishing me luck. "I'll be in my room, after you've finished talking."

"Coffee?" I offered the detective. "Or, Jake, cocoa?"

Jake was staring at the tablet I'd left on the counter. Then he looked at me. He was clearly angry. But he knew this wasn't the time to discuss it.

Cocoa was one of his favorites. I didn't make it often. We looked at each other. He understood it was a bribe. "Sure, Mom."

The two of them sat at the kitchen table while I fixed the drinks. *Steady, Anna*, I told myself. I'd known the detective wanted to talk with Jake, but that had been theoretical. This was real. Detective Preston was sitting in my kitchen with a tape recorder in the center of the table, about to interview my fourteen-year-old son.

At least it was me, not Burt, here with Jake. I might not

look it, but compared to how I knew Burt was feeling, I was the calm parent.

I finally got two full mugs on the table, with napkins. I didn't dare have another cup of coffee myself; I'd spill it. I desperately wanted something to hold, though, so my hands wouldn't shake. I folded them, as I'd been taught in Sunday school.

I hadn't sat like that since I was four.

"Jake, how well did you know your uncle Carl?"

Jake glanced at me, but answered. "Pretty well. He's always been around. Sometimes he'd take Matt and me places. Or he did stuff with Mom and Dad and me."

Detective Preston looked at his notes. "Jake, is your friend Matt, Matthew Martin?"

Jake nodded.

"Please answer out loud," Preston reminded him. "For the recorder."

"Yeah. Matt's my friend." Jake's lips were pursed, the way they always were when he was upset. "Matthew Martin."

"Did you have any problems with your uncle?"

Jake glanced at me. "No. He was pretty cool."

"What about other people? Did your uncle ever argue with other people?"

Jake bit his lip. "Sure. Everyone argues sometimes."

"What did your uncle argue about?"

"Money, mostly. He won a lot of money in the state lottery a couple of years ago, but he didn't want people to know he'd spent it all. The engine on his boat was messed up. He tried to borrow money to get it fixed."

I bit my lip. Jake was telling the truth, as I'd told him to. But Burt hadn't told Detective Preston any of that.

"Who did your uncle Carl ask for money?"

"Probably a lot of people. I know he asked my dad. Matt's dad, too."

Carl had asked Dolan for money? I clenched my hands. That was embarrassing. Lucy must not have known. She'd thought Carl still had his lottery winnings.

"Did your dad loan him the money?"

"No. Dad said Uncle Carl didn't know how to handle money, and we didn't have enough to squander on him." Jake's voice went down. "They argued about it a lot."

"Was anyone else angry with your uncle?"

Jake squirmed in his seat. Then, looking at the recorder, he said quietly. "Maybe."

"What do you mean?" asked Detective Preston.

"Like, he did funny things. Like he hid beer in his glove compartment."

"Did he ever give you beer?"

Jake glanced at me and then looked down.

"It's all right," I said, although it wasn't all right at all. "Tell the truth, Jake."

"Yeah. He gave Matt and me beer once in a while. It was a secret. He knew Dad and Mom would be pissed . . . would be wicked angry . . . if they knew."

"Did he ever do anything else that was a secret?"

"Like what?" Jake looked defensive.

"Like, touching you in places he shouldn't. Like taking drugs or giving any to you. Anything like that?"

"No! Never!" Jake's voice was clear. "Nothing like any of

that! Sometimes he told us about his girlfriends. He used to give Matt and me advice about girls."

"Do you have a girlfriend, Jake?"

"Nah. Not yet."

The detective smiled. "You have plenty of time for that. So, your uncle Carl had a lot of girlfriends?"

"He used to. Not so much now. He sees Rose Snowe a lot, though. And maybe other people."

How much did Jake know about Carl's girls? Carl had always been a big talker.

Detective Preston glanced at his notes, as though he was about finished. Thank goodness.

"One more thing, Jake. Do you have a gun?"

Could Carl have been shot while he was on his boat? I hadn't let myself think about exactly how he'd died.

"I have a .22. I go hunting with my dad, and sometimes with Uncle Carl."

"So, your uncle and your dad also have rifles."

"Sure."

"Could you bring me your .22, Jake?"

Jake glanced at me. I nodded, and he headed for his bedroom.

Detective Preston smiled. "He's doing fine, Mrs. Winslow. I don't have many more questions for him."

Jake was back in a few minutes, carrying his rifle case. Detective Preston reached out, and Jake handed it to him.

"I'm going to need to borrow your gun for a little while, Jake. I'll get it back to you as soon as I can. Have you used it recently?"

The detective's tone was casual, but his question wasn't. Could he think Jake had shot his uncle? I bit my tongue.

"I haven't gone hunting since deer season last fall," said Jake. "But sometimes I practice up at the gravel pit, at the old quarry."

"How recently did you do that?

"Last Wednesday, after school." Jake shot me a glance. He'd told me he'd worked for Luc every day after school last week. "When can I have my rifle back?"

"As soon as the lab finishes with it. Thank you for talking to me. I don't have any more questions now, but I'd like to talk with your mother. I visited Luc Burnham earlier this morning. He said you were a big help to him at Maine Chance Books. He's expecting you to go over there to work after we finish talking."

He'd talked with Mr. Burnham today? It must have been very early. What had Luc told him? Luc knew Jake well, but he didn't know Carl as well as many others on the island did. Carl hadn't been a reader.

Detective Preston was being thorough.

Jake stood up, and looked at me for confirmation. "I don't have to go back to school today?"

I shook my head. "Go on over and help Mr. Burnham. Be home for supper, though."

He hesitated, looked at me and at the tablet one more time, and left the house. I was proud of him. I'd tell him that, too. As far as I knew, he'd been honest. Honesty was more important than his taking an afternoon of shooting practice at the gravel pit when he'd told me he was working. Or even drinking a forbidden beer. He wouldn't have been the first fourteen-year-old to do that.

Growing up wasn't easy for teenagers or their parents.

"Mrs. Winslow, you heard what Jake said. Several other

people also told me your brother-in-law was having financial problems. Others have said he had plenty of money. Can you explain that?"

What did this have to do with Carl's death? But if the detective already knew the town gossip, he might as well hear the truth from me. "Carl and Burt inherited their family home after their mother died. Carl was still living there back then, but he and Burt had to sell the property. Their parents had mortgaged it heavily; there wasn't a lot of equity in the place. Burt and I put our share into upgrading equipment on our lobster boat. I don't know exactly what Carl did with his share. He's never been good with money." I suspected he'd spent it on beer and the women he was seeing at the time, but I didn't know for sure and it couldn't be important now.

"You said Carl was living at home before that."

"With his mother. His father had died earlier. Since his mother's death he's been living in the Vandergriffs' carriage house. Do you know them?"

Preston shook his head.

"Rich summer folks from Maryland. A few years back they built a big house—lots of glass and patios and a pool—over on Cormorant Cove. They call their barn a carriage house; their cars are in it in the summer, and their boats in winter. Carl lived in their caretaker's apartment on the second floor. He looks—looked—after their house and grounds."

Detective Preston nodded. "Okay. And he lobstered."

"He bought a boat ten years ago and fixed it up. It's had a lot of problems, and most of his income went into keeping it up. The people around here who said he was rich know he won $200,000 in the state lottery two years ago. A good percentage of that went to taxes, and he used the rest to buy a new truck and a few traps. I'm not sure what else he did with it. The money disappeared quickly, but people still think of him as the guy who won the lottery." Like Lucy, they assumed Carl was rich. Or at least richer than they were.

"Your son said his uncle was trying to borrow money."

"Carl's engine was in bad shape. He kept trying to fix it, but it wasn't reliable. For the past month, he'd been going out with Burt to set and check both their traps."

"He asked Burt to loan him money?"

"Yes. But lobstering hasn't been good, and I stopped working last year. We even had to drop Burt's life insurance policy. Commercial fishing is a high-risk profession; health and life insurance cost a fortune. One of the advantages of my working for my stepfather was we'd been able to get group health insurance. Now we have to pay for it on our own."

Detective Preston looked at me. "Why did you stop working, if you were having financial challenges?"

What did all this have to do with Carl's death?

"My stepfather died. His business closed."

"What about Carl? Did he have life insurance?"

Life insurance might be a motive for some murders. But not in Carl's case. "Not that I know of." He probably hadn't even bothered to make out a will.

"So, you and your family are living on a reduced income."

"Right." I paused. "To help Carl we would have had to use the savings we have for emergencies, or borrow money. Burt was afraid we wouldn't be repaid."

"Rob Erickson said your husband and his brother were arguing—loudly—at the town wharf Saturday morning."

"I wasn't there. I don't know. But their relationship has been strained recently." I hated telling this stranger our family problems, but I'd rather he heard them from me than from a helpful neighbor. We had nothing to hide. "Detective Preston, my husband loved his brother. But Carl was angry we weren't loaning him the money he needed."

"Your son said Carl also asked Dolan Martin for money."

"I heard. I didn't know that." What else didn't I know?

"Who else would Carl have gone to for money?"

I shook my head. "I don't know. He had friends, but none of them had much cash." I tried to explain. "Carl was twenty-nine. But he was the younger brother, and he had a long boyhood. His friends settled down, or left the island. He'd lucked out, with his small inheritance, and then with his lottery winnings. He was a good-looking guy. He could be charming. He had an active social life, especially when he was younger. But recently he seemed to be growing up. He was finally beginning to think about his future. The problem was, he wanted everything Burt and I'd worked years to put together—and he wanted it now. He was impatient with the tides, and with himself. And with us."

"Jake said your husband had a rifle."

"He's hunted since he was a boy. Helps fill our freezer in winter."

"Would you get his rifle for me?"

I didn't move. "My husband would never have hurt his brother. Yes, they argued. Even yelled at each other. But they were family. They loved each other."

"It's a technicality. You've probably guessed from what I asked Jake: Carl was shot. We need to rule people out."

"As far as I know Burt hasn't even opened his gun case in months. It's under our bed. I'll get the rifle."

I glanced at the clock next to our bed. Almost noon. The whole morning had disappeared. Burt should be home in a few hours, thank goodness. I didn't want to cope with any more questions. I got on my hands and knees and pulled the heavy case out from under our queen-sized bed. It wasn't locked. People always said guns should be locked away, but Burt had never seen a need. No one went into our bedroom but us, and it wasn't as though he had a loaded handgun in a dresser drawer. Although occasionally, he listened to the news and muttered about getting one someday.

I opened the case.

It was empty.

# Chapter Seventeen

"To make Browned Cod's Head: Boil the head of a large cod. Take off the skin; set it before a brisk fire; dredge it with flour, and baste it with butter. When it begins to froth, sprinkle fine breadcrumbs over it and continue basting until it is well frothed and a fine brown, and serve it garnished with slices of lemon and sauce to taste."

—*Peterson's Magazine*, January 1869

"I don't know where his gun is," I told Detective Preston. "But Burt must. He always cleans his rifle and puts it in that case after he uses it. I haven't seen it in months. Jake was right. They haven't been hunting since last fall."

"Are you sure you looked everywhere?"

"Everywhere in our room. I don't know where else to look. All the years we've been married, Detective—near fifteen now—he's always treated his gun the same way. But when he comes in I'll ask him about it."

Detective Preston stood up. "No need. I'm going to visit

your neighbors, and I'll be back to talk with your husband later today. I'll ask him myself."

"Is there anything else I can help with?"

"Not at the moment. But I'm sure we'll be in touch." He stood up. "Thanks for the coffee and your patience, Mrs. Winslow."

Where was Burt's rifle?

I called him as soon as Detective Preston left the house. Thank goodness his cell phone now worked when he wasn't too far out on the *Anna*.

"Detective Preston was here. He talked to Jake and then to me."

"How did Jake do?"

"He was a trooper. Did just fine. Preston asked both Jake and me about Carl's finances. He already knew most of it. I hadn't known Carl had tried to borrow money from Dolan."

Burt was quiet. All I could hear was the sound of the *Anna*'s engine. "I didn't know that, either."

"And, Burt? Preston told me Carl was shot."

"Shot? When he was out lobstering?"

"I know. It sounds crazy. Preston took Jake's rifle to test it. He wanted yours, too."

"What is he doing? Checking every rifle on the island?" Burt sighed. "So, you gave it to him?"

"I tried. But I went to get it wasn't in its case."

"Of course it is, Anna. Where else would it be?"

"I have no idea. That's why I'm calling. Are you sure you put it away there last fall?"

"Where else would I put it? Cleaned it and put it away, as always."

"It's not there, Burt. Maybe you left it in the barn?"

"I'll think, Anna." He sounded as puzzled as I felt. "I'll check other places when I get home. But right now I don't know where else to look."

"How're you doing otherwise? I've been thinking of you all day."

"Dolan's with me. I'm all right."

"Are you sure?"

"We're pulling Carl's traps. Every time we bring one on board I feel guilty about the arguments we've had recently. I can't believe he's gone, Anna."

"Me, either," I agreed. "Take care of yourself. I'm glad Dolan's there to help. Come in as soon as you can. If I'm not here it's because I've promised to take Izzie on a tour of the island. We won't be long. Probably we'll be home before you are."

It was hard to hear Burt above the roar of his boat's engine, screeching gulls, and the moaning of the sea. "Love you," I said.

"Love you, Lady," he said back. "See you soon."

I wished he were home now, not leaving me to cope with Jake's morning disappearance and the detective's questions and the missing rifle.

As I hung up, a text came in. Mom and Mamie were inviting Izzie and me to come over for lunch.

I put the phone down as Izzie peeked around the staircase. "Is the detective gone?"

"A few minutes ago. I was coming upstairs up to tell you," I said. "Jake's gone to work at the bookstore, and Mom and Mamie invited us to have lunch at their house. Are you okay to do that? We can take our island tour after lunch. Maybe we could stop and see if Rose is at home. She might know something about Carl."

"Sounds good," said Izzie, coming downstairs. "Especially the lunch part. I'd like to know them better. They're family, too."

My family. My mother and grandmother.

But Izzie didn't have anyone. And families stretched.

I'd often heard people say, "When one person in a family dies, another takes their place." They usually meant a baby was born. Carl was gone; maybe Izzie was here to expand our family in a new direction.

Life was unpredictable. Certainly, it had been in the past week.

"Your mom and grandmother live in the house you grew up in, right?" Izzie asked as we walked past the Martins' house, where I suspected Detective Preston was now talking to Lucy. His car was in her driveway.

"I lived there until I married Burt."

Mamie had come to Quarry Island to this house when she'd married. She'd had Mom, her husband had died, Mom had me, and then Mom married Seth. Years later, I'd married Burt and had Jake, and Seth had died. That little house had been the center of our lives all those years. The place we'd celebrated birthdays, Christmases, weddings, and births. And mourned losses.

"I like that your home is still here. You can return to the past whenever you want to," said Izzie as we opened the door.

Not exactly. Every day, every year, life changed. You could never go back. Not even to last week.

Mamie greeted us, squeezing Izzie's hand in one of hers and mine in her other. Mamie always smelled a little of the lavender she grew in the summertime and tucked in her bureau drawers every fall. Whenever I was nervous or upset, I took a long bath scented with lavender bubble bath. Lavender made the world simpler.

"I'm so glad you both came. These are hard days, but you being here, Izzie, gives us something positive to think about," said Mamie as she led us into the living room.

"Thank you, Mrs. Nolin. I appreciate that," said Izzie. Izzie was shorter than I was, but she towered over Mamie's withered, almost childlike figure. "It's kind of you to welcome me."

Mamie nodded. "Your father and grandparents were good people, all of them. Your father was just too young to settle down when he fathered Anna."

"Anna told me you were born in Canada," said Izzie. "And that you're a fabulous cook."

"Fabulous, did she say?" Mamie winked at me. "Seems to me I've spent my life in the kitchen. Ingredients in Maine are similar to those in Quebec, but my mother put a French twist on them. I try to follow her lead. What you'll eat in this house is a little different from what you'll taste in other Maine homes, although a lot of us Quebecoise live here now."

"Where's Mom?" I asked.

"She went upstairs for a minute," said Mamie. "Why don't you both come and have a glass of wine before lunch?"

She led us to the dining room, where she'd set the table for four people, complete with tablecloth and napkins and a bottle of chilled white wine.

"Elegant, Mamie!" I said, impressed. We usually ate in the kitchen.

"It's a special occasion. The first time Izzie's eaten here," she explained. "I wanted it to be welcoming. Why don't you pour us each a glass of wine? I'll see to the food."

"She's sweet," Izzie whispered to me as I poured. Then in her normal voice she added, "Something in the kitchen smells delicious."

"I hope so," Mamie called back. "We're having a simple lunch. A salad with beets, apples, celery, and nuts, the way my mother used to make it, and salmon mousse. Nothing fancy. And I made one of Anna's favorites for dessert: my apple cranberry pudding."

"Yum," I agreed.

"I love this," said Izzie. "Trying new dishes. Can I help you in any way, Mrs. Nolin?"

"You can help me put the food on the table," said Mamie. "And you can call me Mamie. Everyone does."

"I'll see what's keeping Mom," I said, going up the stairs to where the bedrooms were.

Mom was in my old room. The yellow rose-patterned wallpaper I'd chosen when I was ten was still on the walls, although one winter the roof had leaked, and now there was a water stain in one corner.

My bride doll was sitting on the bed, her legs stretched out on the pink, red, and white heart-patterned quilt Mom had made for me years before, worn thin where I'd sat, supposedly studying, while I was in junior high and high school. Now they called it middle school and high school, but Jake was sitting in the same classrooms where I'd daydreamed and paid less attention to my studies than I should have.

This house hadn't changed since I was a teenager. Had I changed? Izzie's questions about what I wanted in life had made me think. I was grown now. A wife. A mother. But part of me was still that little girl who'd loved her bride doll.

My little sister dreamed of owning her own restaurant. She planned to put off being a wife and mother until . . . someday. She had more than one dream.

Dreams risked disappointment if they didn't come true. But dreams were also exciting.

Was it time to move beyond the bride doll I'd loved as a child? Not discard her, but maybe find something more to love?

I shook my head. Izzie's arrival and Carl's death had both come so suddenly. My world had been comfortable, where I belonged. I'd been like a mussel, glued to the rocks I'd always clung to.

Now, everything had changed. I'd been tossed into the waves to survive. Would I find a new rock to cling to? Or be found by a laughing gull and dropped onto a ledge, smashed, and devoured.

"Anna? Are you all right?" Mom turned toward me from where she'd been sitting, in the armchair by the window. "You look as though you're on another planet."

"I'm fine," I assured her, although I wasn't sure I was. "Why don't you come downstairs? I poured wine, and Mamie and Izzie are serving lunch."

"She doesn't look like you, does she?" Mom asked. "I thought she'd look like you."

"I look like you," I said. "I have brown hair and blue eyes like yours."

"How are you two getting on?"

"I like her. She's younger than me, of course, and, Mom, she has so many dreams. She wants to have her own restaurant."

"Her father had big dreams, too. Has she said anything about him?"

"Not much. That he worked hard, and traveled a lot on business. Her mother died when she was fourteen. She pretty much ran his house after that."

"He didn't have enough sense to hire a housekeeper?" Mom shook her head. "Sounds like she raised herself. That must have been rough." She paused. "Funny. Peter's been dead to me for thirty-three years, but I always expected him to show up eventually, even out of curiosity. Now he never will. But he's sent us his daughter."

I nodded. "I'm sorry I never met him. But I was lucky to have you and Mamie. And Seth. And then Burt, of course."

"How is Burt managing? With Carl's death, I mean."

I hesitated. "Has Detective Preston been here yet?"

"Detective? Why would a detective come here?" Mom asked, frowning.

"Because the medical examiner ruled Carl's death a murder."

"Oh, no," Mom stood up and wrapped her arms around me. "I didn't know. His drowning was hard enough." She held me at arm's length and looked at me. "How're you coping, Anna? Carl dead, and Izzie here . . . you must be going mad."

"Some moments," I agreed. "But Izzie's not a problem. She's been a help. She seems to know when I need company and when she should disappear. She's even been doing a lot of the cooking. She seems to fit right in."

"I hope so, Anna. For your sake. But be careful. I thought her father fit right in, too, and then he left, and never came back."

"That was a long time ago. And that was him, not Izzie."

Mom nodded. "I just don't want you to be hurt."

"Like you were?" I asked quietly.

"Like we were," she answered. She straightened her shoulders, as though she was a soldier preparing for duty. "Let's have lunch. I suspect Mamie's outdone herself, as usual."

"You're right," I answered. "And Izzie's already asked for her recipes."

Mom gave me another quick hug. As we headed downstairs I asked, "Did you happen to see Jake early this morning?"

"Early? You mean, before school?" Mom frowned. "Why? Is he all right? He looked wicked awful yesterday after that fight. I patched him up as best I could before he headed home."

"He's bruised, but fine," I assured her. "He went to school and stayed until Detective Preston brought him home to question him. But he was up very early this morning, and out of the house. He's never done that before. I think something between him and Matt isn't right."

"Sorry I can't help you. Jake wasn't here," said Mom. "You're right. Getting up early in the morning doesn't sound like Jake."

"I'll talk to him when he gets home. He's at the bookstore now, so maybe if he has a problem he'll talk with Luc. I think he does that sometimes."

"Kids his age like to share with an adult who isn't their parent," Mom confirmed. "Remember when you used to tell all your secrets to Miss Baylor, that young teacher who was also your Girl Scout leader?"

I winced. "I was eight then, Mom!"

I'd confided in Miss Baylor that I wanted Santa to give me a trip to Disney World. Miss Baylor had told Mom, and I'd been humiliated when Mom explained what had happened, and that Santa couldn't afford a trip to Florida.

I hadn't trusted Miss Baylor—or Santa—after that.

If Jake had any secrets now, they were more serious than mine had been. I hoped if he told someone it would help resolve any problems between him and Matt. With Carl's murder, Jake would need his friend.

We all needed friends. Especially now.

# Chapter Eighteen

"The host who has compelled a guest to ask him for anything, is almost a dishonored man."

—*The Epicure's Year Book and Table Companion* by Blanchard Jerrold, Bradbury and Evans, 1868

"This is fantastic," said Izzie, after Mamie had toasted Izzie's arrival and we'd started to eat. "I've never had a salad made with a cream sauce. The apples and beets work well together."

"I can tell you what I did," Mamie said, flattered. "I don't have a recipe. I remember what my mother did, and taste along the way."

"Well, it's great," said Izzie, taking another bite. "Maybe I could watch you make it. I wish I'd done that with my mother's recipes. I didn't pay close enough attention. After she died I read cookbooks and tried to remember what I'd seen her doing. I wish I'd been older, and written everything down while she could still advise me."

"Did she cook Korean food or American?" asked Mom.

"Both," Izzie replied, taking another helping of the salmon mousse. "This has rice wine vinegar in it, right?"

Mamie nodded. "You have a sensitive palate."

"In culinary school, we had to be able to identify flavors." Izzie turned to Mom. "Dad didn't like Korean food, so Mom cooked lasagna and meatballs, hamburgers, and beef stew for him. When he was away, she cooked pulgogi, chop chae, and mandu. I grew up loving both cuisines."

"Before you leave, you'll have to cook something Korean for us," said Mamie. "I don't think I've ever tasted any."

"I'd love to," Izzie agreed.

"How long are you staying?" asked Mom.

Izzie hesitated.

"Izzie's welcome to stay as long as she wants to," I put in. "She's been a big help to me, and good company."

Izzie sent me a grateful smile. "Thank you, Anna. I haven't seen too much of Maine, but so far I love it."

"Mud and all?" Mom said skeptically.

"Mud and all," Izzie confirmed. "It's different from the world where I grew up. I can understand why my father and grandparents loved it."

No one said anything. I suspected Mom was wondering why they'd never come back to Quarry Island if they'd loved Maine so much.

"I'm going to drive Izzie around the island after lunch," I said. "She's only seen Island Road from the drawbridge to the center of town."

"Enjoy your drive," said Mamie, putting the apple and cranberry pudding on the table.

Izzie looked at it, questioningly. "I've never seen a pudding that looked like this."

"A lot of dishes used to be called puddings, in Quebec and in old Maine recipes, too," said Mamie. "Puddings could be sweet, the way people think of them today, or they could be a little spicy, with herbs. The French word for pudding is boudin, or little sausage. Maine's Indian pudding, which some people make with beef drippings or bits of meat, is a good example."

"I've never had Indian pudding either," said Izzie.

"Folks used to call cornmeal Indian meal," explained Mom. "Indian pudding has cornmeal and molasses in it. Very New Englandish. We'll have to make it one day soon."

"I look forward to that! And in the meantime, I look forward to tasting this pudding," said Izzie. We all watched as she tasted the cake and baked apple combination. Mamie had made it for me when I was growing up, especially when I'd been upset about something that happened in school, or when I had a cold. It was my idea of the perfect comfort food: soft and sweet, with the texture of the apples, the tartness of cranberries, and the crispness of the cake topping all melding together.

"Fantastic," said Izzie, looking at Mamie. "I'm already thinking of different combinations of fruit and cake that would work like this."

"My mother used to make it just with apples," Mamie said. "But I add cranberries. Makes it zestier."

"I agree," said Izzie. "Have you tried adding a little lemon?"

"Might work," said Mamie. "Not too much, though."

Izzie nodded. "It would be fun to experiment."

Mamie was clearly thrilled that a professional chef liked her food so much.

And Izzie was right. We should get Mamie's recipes written out while we could. How sad and frustrating it must have been for Izzie to try to replicate the dishes her mother had cooked.

Lunch ended all too soon, and Izzie and I went back to my house. A blueberry pie (from Cynthia Snowe) and a plate of whoopie pies (from Rose) were waiting for us on the porch. I wished we'd been there when they'd dropped off the food. I wanted to talk to both of them. They'd known Carl as a boyfriend. A different perspective than I had on his life.

I took the food into the kitchen and while Izzie put it away, I checked for messages on our landline. Cell phone service wasn't dependable on Quarry Island, so most of us kept our home phones, even if we'd upgraded to the twenty-first century and also had cells.

No messages on either. I suspected word had gotten around about Carl being murdered and no one knew what to say.

Sympathizing over a death was relatively simple. Murder was a whole other situation.

Where was Detective Preston now? His car was gone.

Carl had known people all over the island and on the mainland. Investigating his death could take the detective in a variety of different directions.

I hoped it would lead quickly to answers.

"Let's go for our drive now, Izzie," I said, pulling on a light jacket. Sea breezes were coming in. "If anyone wants us, they can call. Sitting at home will drive me crazy."

We climbed in the truck and headed for the other side of Quarry Island.

# Chapter Nineteen

"Most white or soft fish are best bloated, which is done by salting, peppering, and drying in the sun, and in a chimney; after thirty to forty hours drying, they are best broiled and moistened with butter."

—*American Cookery* by Amelia Simmons, 1796

Quarry Island was at the end of a coastal peninsula, surrounded on three sides by rivers or inlets and on the fourth by the ocean. On a map, Maine peninsulas look like fingers. Locals joke that those fingers point to warmer waters.

The older, more populated part of Quarry Island was, naturally, also the closest to the mainland and to the drawbridge.

"We're on the east side of the island," I explain to Izzie, who was confused. "So is the drawbridge and the town wharf. Island Road circles the island. I'll show you the rest of my world."

"World?" Izzie said, smiling at me teasingly. "The world is a big place."

"Outside of Quarry Island, it may be. All we islanders need is right here." Maybe that wasn't totally true, but it felt right.

We did leave the island to shop at supermarkets, hardware stores, and outlets, like the ones in Freeport. But on the island we had the school and church. Family and friends. Most people's jobs. We could buy basics like milk and hamburger at Martha Decker's general store. We had everything that was important.

We passed the small group of houses and the church and bookstore and store close to my house, and headed south. "That's the town hall, on your right," I pointed out. "The big Victorian house on your left is the library. They might have some of those cookbooks you were looking for. The Quarry Island Historical Society has a room there just devoted to the history of the island, the quarry, and genealogical information. They can trace what's happened on the island and who's lived here since the first European settlers arrived in about sixteen forty."

"What about Native Americans? Weren't they here then?" Izzie asked.

"In summer, to fish," I agreed. "And to dry those fish for the winter. In fall, when weather turned colder, they went up river. We'll get to the river soon."

I pulled into a small parking lot and pointed at Granite Point Lighthouse, above us, on a series of jagged ledges overlooking the end of the island and the ocean beyond. "Historical society docents give tours of the light and the keeper's house during the summer months."

"Does anyone live there now?" Izzie asked, looking at the connected buildings at the base of the light.

"Not in about fifty years," I said. "Maine lighthouses are automated now, but they're still protecting ships and boats that get too close to the rocky shore." I hesitated. "Burt found Carl's boat drifting off this point."

Izzie and I exchanged a look. Granite Point now had new significance.

"But what a beautiful place!" Izzie said, looking up at the lighthouse then out to the sea. "And maybe because I know Dad was here, and you're here . . . I almost feel as though I've come home. Like Anne Shirley seeing Green Gables for the first time? Being on an island is kind of magical."

Magical? "I'm not sure there are any Gilbert Blythes here," I said, referring to Anne's handsome true love, "but I'm glad you like it." And, of course, I'd found my true love here.

We left the parking lot and continued on Island Road. "The lighthouse marks the end of the eastern part of the island. Down there," I pointed to a weathered wooden staircase on the left side of the road, "is the community beach. We're on the south side of the island now. Any water you see between the trees on the left-hand side of the truck is ocean. Spain is somewhere over there."

"All I can see are trees and driveways," Izzie pointed out, craning her head to look.

"Those driveways lead to summer homes. Expensive ones. They have ocean views and ocean winds in winter. Year-round people, even when they can afford homes like those, usually choose to live on the more protected north or east sides of the island." I pointed to a high stone wall ahead on our left. "That's the Vandergriffs' estate. Newest and grandest on the island. Where Carl lived in the carriage house and was the caretaker."

"Carriage house?"

I slowed down so I could point it out. "What the Vandergriffs called a carriage house, anyone else would call a barn or a boat house."

Izzie stared at it. "Do you have a key to his apartment?"

I pulled the truck to the side of the road. "Carl gave Burt and me each one, in case of an emergency. Or if he lost his." I glanced down. It was still on my key ring.

"Let's go inside," Izzie suggested. "We haven't done anything to try to find his killer yet. Maybe there'll be clues there."

"The police were going to check. They've probably found anything important."

"They didn't know Carl. You did, and you know people on the island. You might notice important clues they didn't," Izzie pointed out."

I turned the truck into the Vandergriffs' driveway. "Let's do it. There's paper in the glove compartment."

"Got the pad," Izzie answered. "Pencils, too."

"Good. Because if we're going to do this, we need to be organized. I'll take notes."

Izzie didn't know I'd always gotten As in organization at school. That's how I'd managed to keep the books and talk to customers at Seth's business at the same time. Multitasking was second nature to me. Seth had been a good, dependable roofer, but his invoices hadn't gone out on time until I'd taken over his office. I'd also made sure bills were paid regularly and we always knew which of his guys would be working on what days.

Some people were creative. Other people made lists.

I made lists.

We were at the carriage house within a few minutes. "I

don't see any of that yellow crime scene tape police use," Izzie said.

"Carl wasn't killed here," I pointed out. "And the police must have left." That was good. I'd been worried we'd run into them.

The apartment had two entrances to meet fire regulations. One was a stairway from the first floor of what looked like a high-ceilinged barn, where the Vandergriffs stored their vehicles—cars in the summer and boats in the winter. The entrance Carl used, that I had a key to, was outside, up a set of stairs to the second floor.

Although Burt and Jake had visited Carl occasionally, I'd only been inside the apartment twice. Both times I'd wished for a pail of soapy water to scrub the floors and counters, and a large laundry basket to pile grungy clothes and towels in. Carl usually stuck his dirty clothes in a garbage bag and brought them to our house to wash while he was eating supper with us.

Today, after the police search, I expected even more than the usual mess. But I could hardly tell they'd been there.

"Nice place," Izzie commented.

She was right. Six months ago, Carl's only furnishings outside his bedroom had been two recliners, a large-screen television, and posters of Celtics and Red Sox players. Now his living room also contained a couch, several tables, a bookcase, and a large rug. Framed seascapes and hunting scenes were on the walls. Paperback mysteries were arranged in a small bookcase. All I ever remembered Carl reading was sports magazines and repair manuals.

Curtains hung at the windows.

While Izzie looked around, I walked into the bedroom.

Carl's king-sized bed was still there, with the comforter he'd bought to substitute for other bedding. Today, though, the bed was made, with sheets and a bedspread. His comforter was folded at the foot. The bureau was new, more pictures were on the walls, and the usual piles of dirty clothes were missing.

I was pretty sure the police hadn't taken his laundry.

Where had all this stuff come from? Burt and I'd chosen a few pieces of furniture from their parents' home after they'd died, but Carl hadn't wanted even one chair. And he'd been broke. These furnishings weren't expensive, but they hadn't been free.

His clothing was hung up neatly in the closet. The bathroom now even sported a toilet seat cover. *Carl* had a toilet seat cover?

"Did Carl do a lot of cooking?" Izzie called from the kitchen.

"Once in a while he'd grill hamburgers with Burt," I answered. "He was a typical bachelor. He usually managed to find himself at friends' homes at mealtimes, or ate takeout, or filled up on cereal or ice cream." I headed back into the living room.

"Really?" Izzie asked. "Because he has a fully equipped kitchen. He even has heavy copper and stainless steel pans. And the cookie jar is full of homemade molasses cookies."

Homemade? That was pretty much impossible. Maybe he'd bought them at a bakery.

"Are those pans good?" I asked.

"Very good." Izzie looked around. "The owners won't have to look far for a new caretaker. A lot of men or young couples would like this place, furnished the way it is."

I sat down on the new couch. "The apartment didn't come with these furnishings. Carl must have had the place decorated."

Izzie plopped onto one of the recliners. "You think he hired a decorator?"

"No. But I can't imagine Carl hanging curtains or buying pots and pans." Or making cookies.

"Maybe he was tired of living like a sloppy bachelor," Izzie suggested. "Or he was trying to impress some woman. Maybe that Rose I met down on the wharf Saturday?"

"I suppose that's possible," I said. "Or, some woman was trying to impress him."

"Did Rose live here, too?"

"No women's clothes are in the bedroom, and no cosmetics in the bathroom." I kept looking at the furnishings. "All this stuff had to cost more than Carl had. Or, at least, more than Carl said he had."

Had Carl told us the truth about having spent all his lottery winnings? What else hadn't Burt and I known about Carl?

"I can't imagine buying a guy furniture unless you planned to live with him," Izzie said.

"I agree." Had Carl been a lot more serious about Rose than he'd let on? Possibly. But surprising.

Izzie walked over to a series of framed photographs on the wall. "Is this you, Burt, and Carl?"

I joined her. "And Lucy and Dolan. The whole crew." We were all wearing swimsuits, down at the beach. "That was before Burt and I were married, so we must have been about sixteen. Carl and Lucy were the babies—they would have been about twelve or thirteen then." I smiled, remembering how young we'd been. Three years later, Burt and I were married and I had Jake, and fifteen-year-old Lucy was pregnant. We'd all grown up so fast. "I don't remember that picture."

"You all look so happy," said Izzie.

"We were." I kept looking at the photo. "It was a long time ago."

"And who're these people?" she asked, moving to another picture. "Wait—that's Lucy, right?"

The photo was of Carl and three girls. Typical. "Yes; that's Lucy. And Carl, of course. The other two are Rose and Cynthia Snowe."

"I wonder when that one was taken?" Izzie said.

"Must be from several years ago. Cynthia's hair was shorter then, and Rose has lost weight."

"I wonder why he has that picture up?"

"No clue," I said. "Or maybe to remind him of his girlfriends, past and present."

"If I'd were Rose I'd have wanted him to hang a picture of me. Just me. Not me with other girls. Especially other girls he'd dated."

I didn't disagree.

Izzie checked out the rest of the room. "I don't see a computer, or any kind of electronics other than the television."

"I'm pretty sure he had a laptop. But Detective Preston said they'd be checking it and his phone." Carl kept his phone in his pocket. Had the police found it on his boat? Or was it gone, beneath the waves?

"I wonder what else they might have taken? Besides his laptop." Izzie shrugged and plopped down on one of the chair. "There has to be something here that will help us figure out who killed him. All we know so far is that he cleaned his apartment and added some furnishings."

"You're right." I sat, too. "I thought I knew Carl well. But now I'm not as sure. And I have no idea why anyone would have killed him."

"He was shot, right?"

"Right."

"And he went hunting, so he must have had rifles here."

"Preston said the police took those. If anyone else used one of his guns, the crime lab could figure it out with fingerprints and bullets." I hoped. Didn't that happen on crime shows?

"Carl was on his boat when he was shot," Izzie continued.

She was reviewing what we knew. That was what we should do. But I still shivered when I imagined what had happened. "Blood was found on his *Fair Winds*, and Carl's body was in the water."

"So where could the shooter have been? On his boat? On another boat? On land? Wouldn't that be too far for someone to shoot accurately? A person isn't a big target, especially on a moving boat."

I shook my head. "I'm not a hunter, but a lot of folks around here are. Both men and women have long guns with scopes."

"Did Burt's have a scope?"

I nodded. "Sure."

"How far away could a shooter have been? To focus on someone on a boat?"

"Pretty far. Burt and Carl had both been setting traps close to shore. Someone on one of the ledges, say near the lighthouse, or on one of the private wharves would have been able to see the boat. With a scope, they could see a person on deck."

"They'd have to be a good shot, though," Izzie pointed out.

"Yes." I hesitated. "They would have to be a very good shot, even with a scope. And have a steady hand."

"Or someone on another boat could have gotten close enough to shoot him."

We sat, thinking. "Let's take the rest of our tour and go home," I finally said. "We're not going to discover anything more here."

I checked that I'd locked the door before we went down the steps to my truck. I might not lock my door at home, but Carl wouldn't be back soon.

"We haven't come up with any real motives, either," Izzie pointed out, looking at the blank pad of paper. "We don't even know anyone Carl was arguing with except Burt."

I winced. "Carl wasn't easy. I have to believe he had trouble with other people, too. But I don't know who. He was dating Rose. Either she decorated his apartment, or he did it for her. It also means he might have had more money than we'd thought. That's new information, but I don't see what it has to do with his murder."

We headed out on Island Road.

The cost of all that stuff in Carl's apartment bothered me. "Jake said Carl had asked Dolan for money. I hadn't known that." I said, almost to myself.

"Carl was tight with Lucy and Dolan, right?"

"Right."

"So why wouldn't he have asked them for money, since you and Burt turned him down?"

"I suppose it makes sense. But I hate that he got them involved. Dolan controls the money in that house. Lucy's never had a job. She once told me Dolan gives her an allowance for household expenses like groceries. She thought Carl still had his lottery earnings. She must not have known he'd asked her husband for help."

Izzie wrinkled her nose. "Lucy gets an allowance?"

"That's what she calls it." I looked at Izzie. "Every couple has to find their own way. Burt and I keep our money in an account that both of us can use, and both of us know what it's spent on."

Since I hadn't been working, that account hadn't been large. I hoped the inheritance Izzie and I would be getting would help that.

"We're almost to the west side of the island," I pointed out, getting back to our tour. "This time of year, you can see more of the ocean than in the summer. Leaves and bushes block views then, providing privacy for those that want it. In the eighteenth and early nineteenth centuries, there were only a few trees on the island. I've seen pictures in the historical society room at the library. Quarry Island looked very different then."

"Why weren't there trees?" Izzie asked as Island Road curved and we headed up the west side of the island.

"Trees were cut to build and heat homes, and lumber was sold and traded for food in Boston and Portland. Maine islands are rocky; the land isn't good for farming. Trees were seen as useful, not ornamental. It wasn't until late in the nineteenth century that people began to see them as decorative." I pointed out the window again. "We're no longer on the ocean. That's the Abenaki River you see through the trees. It's tidal, and flows inland about twenty miles. A lot of the houses in this area are seasonal. Many don't have central heating; they have fireplaces and stoves, like in the old days."

"Where's the quarry?" Izzie asked.

"In the center of the island, on the north side," I said. "During the nineteenth century, Maine had hundreds of active quarries. The small one here mined granite. Maine granite was shipped to New York where it was used to build Grant's Tomb, post offices, and other major buildings." Why had a tomb come to mind? Maine granite had been used for lots of buildings.

"What's the quarry like now?"

"A big, ugly hole," I said. "It's fenced off, although people find ways to explore it. And there's a gravel pit, where people practice shooting." I pointed to our left. "Used to be a big pier over there where stone was loaded into ships. The pier was falling down, and kids hung out there, so it was torn down when I was eight or nine."

The road made another slight turn, and the number of small houses and trailers on both sides of the car increased. "We're now on the north side of the island. That big building on the right that looks like a barn is the Windward Theatre. Actors from New York City come every summer and perform. Some board with locals, some live in the dormitories at the back of the theater. Over there," I pointed at a house painted bright blue with yellow shutters, "is where Burt and Carl grew up. The current owners painted it. Neighbors weren't too pleased about that."

Izzie grinned. "It doesn't quite fit in."

"Not really. But, of course, our end of the island has Willis' purple house. Over there's a small clinic for folks who want to see a doctor, but don't want to take the time or money to go to the mainland." I slowed down, wondering if Rose or Cynthia were working there today. Rose would probably know about Carl's apartment, and maybe more. I'd hoped we could drop in to see her. But the clinic parking lot was empty. "The school is across the street, so Dr. Neeson, who runs the clinic, is also the school doctor."

"That's the school where you and Burt went?" Classes were over for the day, and the two island school buses had left, but cars were still in the teachers' parking lot, and the three little Johnson girls were playing jump rope on the playground. They lived down the street and didn't take the bus.

"Right. And where Jake goes now. It could use some upgrades, but it still works. That big house next to it? That's the Quarry Island Inn. It was bought and fixed up a couple of years ago by two off-islanders. Nice folks. Didn't make waves and hired local. They'll open for the season in late May." I glanced at Izzie, who seemed to be enjoying the ride. "We're now back on the east side of the island. You can see the drawbridge up ahead."

"What's that building?" Izzie pointed. "The one near the water with the 'For Sale' sign on it."

"That used to be a small grill. A place where people bought lobster rolls and fried clams in July and August. The couple who owned it moved to Florida two or three years ago."

"Aren't there any restaurants on the island?" Izzie asked.

"The Island Inn serves breakfast to its guests," I said. "But, no. If you want to eat out, you have to go the mainland."

We passed the drawbridge and the town pier and pulled into my driveway.

"How much are they asking for that building?" Izzie asked, her eyes shining. "The one near the drawbridge?"

"I have no idea," I said.

"I'm going to find out," Izzie declared, as she climbed down from the truck. She wrote down something. "I have the number of the realtor. I'm going to call her."

"You're serious?" I asked as we walked in the kitchen door.

"Why not? Maybe there's a reason Dad decided to tell us we were sisters. Maybe he wanted me to come to Quarry Island."

# Chapter Twenty

"We cannot believe that any woman truly loves her husband who leaves all domestic matters to the cook or the housekeeper. What do they know of the husband's peculiar tastes, or, knowing, care? They do their part for hire; but a wife should do her part for love, and love is ever seeking some new mode of blessing its object."
—*Advice to Young Ladies on Their Duties and Conduct in Life* by T.S. Arthur. Philadelphia: J.W. Bradley 1860

Blue rubbed against my ankles and sniffed my shoes. Had I been near any other animals? I bent to stroke him.

"Anna!" Burt's voice came from upstairs. "Is that you?"

"Izzie and I just got in," I called back.

"About time!" He clumped down the steps from the second floor, still wearing his lobstering pants, although he'd left his slicker on the boat. He stopped in the door of the kitchen and ran his fingers through his hair. "You were right. My rifle's gone. And that Detective Preston's on his way here. I think we have a problem."

"Did you look everywhere?" I asked. "A gun doesn't just disappear."

"Don't I know that?" he said. "I've practically torn the house and barn apart looking for it."

"Is anything else missing?" asked Izzie.

"Nothing else," I assured her. "Besides—what would anyone want in our house?" Robberies weren't a problem on Quarry Island, although occasionally teenagers would break into a seasonal home to party. A few summer folks paid someone local to check their homes when they were away, although the Vandergriffs were the only ones who had a year-round caretaker.

Although, now they didn't.

"Where's Jake?" Burt asked.

"With Luc, at Maine Chance Books," I said. "At least, that's where he was headed this morning after Detective Preston interviewed him."

"I called Luc. Jake left there two hours ago," said Burt.

Jake had disappeared again? Burt was upset enough. I didn't tell him Jake had vanished for a while this morning.

"Izzie and I had lunch with Mom and Mamie, and then I took her on a tour of the island. Maybe Jake met Matt after school." I glanced at the clock over our stove. "It's almost four o'clock. Matt should be home by now."

"I checked. Neither of them are at the Martins," said Burt. "What's gotten into that boy? I know he's upset about Carl's death. We all are. But he can't just take off like this. Too much is happening. He's never done it before."

But he had. This morning. And he'd told the detective he'd been shooting out at the quarry last week when he'd told me he was at work.

"He might be at Mom's house."

Burt shook his head. "I checked there, too. And his bicycle's not in the barn."

"Maybe he needed to be on his own for a while," I said. Jake was usually with Matt, but he and Matt had argued yesterday. Had they resolved whatever their problem had been? I wished Burt and my problems were as simple as those of fourteen-year-olds. Years ago, he loved to ride all the way around the island. Island Road was close to twenty miles long. Biking around the island was an accomplishment.

"He's fourteen. And someone out there killed Carl. He shouldn't have left without telling us."

"You're right," I agreed, touching Burt's arm. "But he's probably fine. Have you had anything to eat besides the sandwiches I made this morning?"

"No," he said.

"You must be hungry," said Izzie. She moved toward the refrigerator.

"I don't need food!"

Izzie stopped.

Burt immediately realized his error. "It's all right, Izzie. Sorry. I'm fine. But why don't you make up a plate of the cookies and brownies and stuff people brought yesterday? We could offer them to Preston, when he gets here."

Izzie pulled out a plate and opened the boxes where she'd put the cookies.

"He called and said he was coming?" I asked.

"Carmela Heedles said he was. She called to give me a heads up that Preston had been at the sheriff's office, asking questions about all of us."

"He wants to know more about Carl," I said. "He told us he'd be asking questions of everyone we knew and checking Carl's apartment."

"Yeah. I remember. I can understand them talking to people. They probably think someone's going to tell them all of Carl's deep, dark secrets. But I doubt they'll hear anything we don't know. And what could they find in his apartment?"

Izzie put a plate of cookies and cake in the center of the table. Burt reached for an oatmeal raisin one.

"Maybe there was something helpful on Carl's computer," I suggested. Had there been? Only the police would know. They'd already taken the computer when Izzie and I were at the apartment. I didn't tell Burt we'd been there. "Snooping," he'd call it. He might not understand we were investigating. We were trying to help him.

"All Carl's computer had on it was games, most likely," said Burt. "Or engine schematics."

"I'm going upstairs to make a phone call," said Izzie. "Excuse me."

I nodded as she left Burt and me alone.

"Maybe something else was on his computer that we don't know about. E-mails. Or social media stuff." I suggested. "That's what the police were looking for."

"He was on Facebook, he told me once. I don't think he did that sort of thing a lot."

"The police are looking for people he was in contact with."

"The only person he's been close to recently besides us, the Martins, and Rob, was Rose. They've probably talked to her already."

"Maybe he'd joined one of those dating sites," I put in. "He mentioned one a couple of months ago. I thought he was kidding, but maybe he wasn't." Although something had changed in the past few months. Carl's apartment certainly had.

"Carl? Online dating? No way." Burt took a chocolate chip cookie and chewed it without seeming to taste it. "And even if he had, what would that have to do with his murder?" He sat back on the couch. "But who knows? He lived his own life. Everyone has secrets."

I squeezed Burt's shoulder lightly and went to put water on to boil for tea. That tablet Izzie had found in Jake's room was still on the kitchen counter, near Izzie's knife kit. If Burt had noticed it, he'd probably thought it was hers. Burt was worried about his missing rifle and his brother's murder. He didn't need to know how concerned I was about Jake.

But when Jake did show up, he and I were going to have a serious talk.

# Chapter Twenty-One

"New England rum, constantly used to wash the hair, keeps it very clean and free from disease, and promotes its growth a great deal more than Macassar oil. Brandy is very strengthening to the roots of the hair, but it has a hot, drying tendency which New England rum has not."

—*The Frugal Housewife: Dedicated to Those Who Are Not Ashamed of Economy* by Lydia Maria Child. Boston, 1833

Detective Preston arrived a few minutes later. Burt and I sat with him at the kitchen table. Preston didn't waste any time, either helping himself to a brownie, or getting to the point of his visit.

"Mr. Winslow, earlier today your son gave me his rifle, but your wife couldn't find yours. Would you get it for me now?"

Burt ran his hand through his hair. "I have no idea where

it is. I'm sure I put it away in the same place I always store it, but I looked as soon as I got home. It's not there. I don't know what to tell you."

"Who else knew where you kept your rifle?" Preston asked.

"My wife. My son. I may have mentioned it to someone else. Carl knew where it was. I've always kept it in my gun case, under our bed." Burt was getting tense. "I have no idea where it could have gone."

"Was your gun case locked?"

"I had no reason to lock it. My son knows how to use a rifle and has his own. My wife doesn't shoot. Carl had his own rifles."

Detective Preston nodded. "We found those at his apartment. So, no one else could have taken it?"

"I can't imagine who would have. And I don't know how long it's been missing. I haven't been hunting since last fall. I've had no reason to look for it since then."

"So, you last saw your rifle months ago."

"Right. But why does it matter?"

"Your brother Carl was shot with a rifle, Mr. Winslow. You'd argued with him that morning and so, far as we can tell, you were the last person to see him alive. If your rifle were available we could test it to see if it was the one that killed Carl. If it wasn't, you'd be cleared—or at least your gun would be cleared. We can't test a missing rifle."

Burt's face was getting redder. "You're accusing me of killing my own brother?"

"I'm saying we need to find the gun that killed him. You're not the only person who knew Carl Winslow and owned a rifle. But you and he had words, and family arguments can become violent. You need to find that missing rifle of yours. In the meantime, my team and I will be checking every rifle we find nearby, looking for the one that killed your brother."

"Did you find anything at Carl's apartment that would help you figure out who might have killed him?" I asked.

"Crime investigators are checking his computer in Augusta," said Detective Preston. "That's all I can say."

"On television crime shows they say a murderer has to have motive, opportunity, and means. Have you found anyone who has those things?"

Detective Preston almost laughed at my question. Instead, he stuffed another brownie into his mouth. "This isn't television. But finding the weapon that killed Carl Winslow would supply the means. It's a place to start. I can assure you, that rifle is not all we're checking into. I understand he was in a relationship with Rose Snowe," he said, looking at his notes. "I haven't been able to speak with her yet."

Neither had Izzie or I. But we'd only checked at the clinic. Rose was probably at work at the hospital, or at home. But, if so, why hadn't Preston been able to find her?

"Rose and Carl'd been together about a year," Burt confirmed. "He didn't tell any of us he was serious about Rose, but he'd seemed steadier recently. More focused. He was trying to be organized. Like, fixing the engine on his boat. Other years, he'd have sterned for other people until the money showed up." Burt looked over at me. "He'd never said anything directly. But he might have been serious about Rose."

That might explain the changes in his apartment. And Rose had certainly been upset about his death. I definitely needed to talk with her.

Preston nodded. "We'll be talking with Ms Snowe. All I can say now is that we're following several leads. All you need to worry about is that missing rifle, Mr. Winslow. Here in Maine not many rifles are registered, so we have to check any weapons that might have been used in a crime."

"Mine was registered!" Burt jumped up. "I have papers somewhere. I bought it at a store that sells guns across the country and requires customers to register their guns." He started rummaging through the kitchen drawer where we tossed receipts and appliance instructions.

"Don't worry about those papers now," said Detective Preston. "But I'm glad you told me. I can check that with the federal registry. If you do find your rifle, we can confirm it's yours. In the meantime," he stood, taking a brownie with him, "keep looking. I don't like it when a gun is missing in a murder investigation."

"I understand. Of course," said Burt. "I wish I knew where it was, too. I want it back. But I didn't kill my brother."

"Whoever did, we're going to find him," said Preston. "Or her."

He turned and walked out.

Burt collapsed into the chair he usually relaxed in at this time of day. "What am I supposed to do, Anna? Where can that rifle be? How could it have disappeared?"

I shook my head and went over to massage his shoulders. "I have no idea, Burt. But Preston's right. It doesn't look good. We need to find it."

"Ever since you called this afternoon, I've been trying to think where it could be. I've come up with nothing," Burt said. "I always clean the gun after I hunt, and put it away in the same place. I've been doing that since I was fifteen." He paused. "The gun case is still where I always put it, under our bed. All I can think is that someone took it."

"Who would take your gun? Most people we know have their own."

Burt's shoulders were tight. I kept massaging.

Izzie came down the steps from the second floor and glanced around. "Is that homicide guy gone?"

"He left a few minutes ago. No news. He's still asking about Burt's rifle, which seems to have disappeared."

Izzie shook her head in sympathy. "You guys have a lot on your minds. I'll take care of dinner. You have so much food, anyway. I'll heat the lasagna and make a salad."

"Sounds good, Izzie. Thanks for helping," said Burt, standing and stretching. "I'm going to lie down for an hour or two before supper and try to sleep a little. I didn't get much rest last night."

"Dinner will be ready whenever anyone's hungry," Izzie said.

"I hadn't even thought about food," I answered. "Thanks for taking over that job, at least for today."

Izzie headed for the kitchen, as Burt walked slowly upstairs. He looked twenty years older than he had Friday, before everything fell apart.

And Jake was still gone. Why wasn't he with Luc, shelving books and checking inventory? Keeping busy and not thinking about what happened to his uncle? Thank goodness he hadn't been here when Detective Preston came back. He didn't need to know his father was a possible suspect. Or at least his father's rifle was.

"So, did you make your phone call?" I asked Izzie.

She came into the living room and handed me a cup of tea. She'd even remembered I took it with a packet of sweetener and a little milk. "I did," she said. "I called the realtor listed on the 'For Sale' sign outside that building. I have an appointment to see it tomorrow morning."

"You do? You're serious?" I asked.

"I am," she smiled. "Why not look? I know you have tons on your mind, but could you tell me what that place used to look like? I love the location, right near the bridge with a view of the water, and I'm betting real estate here costs a lot less than it does in New York City."

"That property is on the water, but doesn't have an ocean view," I said. "Around here, the most expensive lots are on the ocean. Waterfront on the river is almost that pricey. Third most expensive is a view of the water, not frontage itself. The building you're interested in has waterfront, which is good, but it's on an inlet, not on the ocean or river."

"Makes sense," said Izzie. "Anything else I should know that everyone here takes for granted?"

"Fresh water," I said. "Some island houses have water piped over from a reservoir on the mainland, others have their own wells. Some have both, and switch back and forth."

"Which is better?" she asked. She leaned forward, listening intently. "Why have both?"

"Depends on whether you're going to be here all year or just summers. Town water's cut off in mid-October and pipes are drained so they won't freeze. They're not opened again until April. Summer folks and snowbirds heading for Florida or Arizona don't mind that. But if you're going to live here year-round, you have to have your own supply."

"That's what you have?"

"Absolutely. Every house in this area of the island does. Although some folks use town water in the summer, and switch to well water the rest of the year, to put less of a drain on their wells."

"So, I need to ask about water," she said.

"That place isn't big," I told her, trying to remember. "The couple who ran it had a take-out window for ice cream cones, lobster rolls, and such in the summer, and maybe a dozen small tables inside for those who wanted to sit."

"So, room for about forty people, depending on the size of the tables." Izzie was doing math in her head. "Was there a bar area?"

"I don't think so. They didn't serve liquor."

"Would it be hard to get a liquor license here?"

I was still focused on Carl's murder. But talking about restaurants was distracting, and distraction was good just now. "I guess you'd have to get approval from the town council."

"Will you go with me tomorrow morning to look at the place? I'd really like your opinion."

"I don't know anything about restaurants," I protested.

"Please? I'm already nervous. I don't want to go alone. I'm supposed to meet the realtor there at nine thirty."

"I'll go with you," I agreed. "But don't get too excited. That place hasn't been open in a while. It's probably a mess. They sold a lot of the equipment and chairs and tables. I remember seeing a truck picking up the stoves and refrigerators."

Izzie wasn't listening, or didn't want to. "I love the water view. It isn't the ocean, but the inlet is wide, and boats go by there, right?"

"Especially in summer. Sometimes they're lined up, waiting for the bridge to open."

Blue jumped into my lap, tapped my cheek with his paw, and then curled up for a nap.

"The parking area might have to be enlarged. And wouldn't it be great to have outdoor seating, so in warm weather people could sit outside and watch the boats? And a fireplace inside in winter."

I was beginning to be intrigued. "Fire regulations might be a problem for a fireplace. Plus, you'd have to have a lined chimney." We'd never used the fireplace in our house because it wasn't up to code. We hoped to change that someday. "And keeping a fire going would be time consuming, would require a lot of wood, and would be messy."

"Good points. Then a gas or propane fireplace," Izzie said. "One that would look real."

"A fire would be nice if your restaurant was open year-round," I admitted. Izzie's excitement was contagious.

"Would people come all year?"

"If prices weren't too high," I said. "And you were right about having a bar. A place people could stop after work or meet friends could be popular."

"Definitely a bar," she agreed. "Restaurants make more money on alcohol than on food. And a short menu, at least at first. Local ingredients, from farms and the sea." She winked. "Does anyone around here make raspberry cordial?"

I laugh at her reference to a scene in *Anne of Green Gables*. "I don't know! But there are local Maine wines, beers, and liquors." I'd never thought much about restaurants. Never even ate out often. One reason was price, of course. But there wasn't a convenient place to eat on Quarry Island. Maybe Izzie's dream had substance.

"Welcome home, Jake!" Izzie said, looking at the front door, behind me. "You're in time for dinner. It'll be warm soon."

"Okay," said Jake.

"Where have you been all day?" I asked.

"At Maine Chance. This morning you and that state trooper told me to go there."

"Your father tried to reach you there. Luc said you'd left a couple of hours ago."

"Why was he checking up on me? Don't you trust me? I had to talk to Matt about something. That's all. So, I left a little early. I'd been there for hours, anyway." He looked around. "Is Dad home?"

"So have you and Matt resolved whatever you were fighting about, then?"

"Not exactly. He's being an idiot about it all."

Izzie interrupted us. "Jake, is that your tablet?" She pointed at the counter. "Your mom and I were looking for you this morning and I saw it in your room."

"You were in my room? Can't I even have any privacy?" He looked around. "Where did you say Dad was?"

"He's lying down. I hope he's taking a nap. He didn't sleep well last night. What about the tablet, Jake?"

"It's not mine. It's Uncle Carl's. He loaned it to me so I could see a couple of movies. Uncle Carl trusted me. He didn't go through my things!"

I glanced at Izzie, who'd picked up the tablet. "We didn't go through your things. It was on your bed. You weren't home when I went to wake you up this morning. I was worried about you."

"You don't need to worry about me. I'm okay. I couldn't sleep, so I went for a walk down to the lighthouse."

"Next time you do that, leave me a note so I know where you are," I said. "Until whoever killed your uncle is arrested, I worry about all of us." I changed the subject. Jake was clearly not in the best mood, and I wasn't either. "Much homework tonight?"

"How should I know? That state trooper pulled me out of school this morning. I'll be behind in all my classes tomorrow."

He'd never worried about that before.

"Has that detective figured out who killed Uncle Carl yet?"

"No. But he's working on it. He was here half an hour ago to talk to your dad. Your dad's rifle is missing. Detective Preston and your dad are both concerned about that. Have you seen it anywhere?"

"That Preston is a pest. Mr. Burnham said he asked him a lot of questions, too."

"He's been asking questions all over the island. And the police searched Carl's apartment and took his computer and guns."

"That's stupid. They think Uncle Carl shot himself?"

I shook my head. "I don't think so. His computer was more important. They're trying to figure out who your uncle was close to, what trouble he might have been in, or who might have been angry with him."

Jake made a face. "All they're going to find on that computer are games and porn."

"Jake! What a thing to say."

"I'm right, though. I've used his computer."

Not exactly news I wanted to hear. What was Jake looking at on his own computer? I thought the school had fixed the software so the students couldn't get into trouble, but now I wasn't sure. I filed that question for the future.

And there was that tablet. That could be used for e-mail too, couldn't it? I'd never used one, but I'd seen them advertised.

"I'm going to take a shower. I had to unpack dusty old books today. Mr. Burnham has stacks of cartons of them. They stunk."

Blue jumped off my lap and went into the kitchen for a drink.

"Did you see any old recipe books or books on housekeeping?" Izzie asked.

"I was dusting them, not reading them." He turned to me. "Is the quiz over? Okay if I go upstairs now?"

"Go ahead," I agreed, and he stomped upstairs.

Jake was home and safe. That was really all I cared about. He'd just gone for a walk this morning. That was unusual for him, but these days everything was unusual. He'd gone to school, and he'd been working at the bookstore for a while. Maybe he needed privacy to grieve.

"Being fourteen isn't easy," Izzie said. She looked at the tablet. Carl's tablet.

"Being the mother of a fourteen-year-old isn't either," I said, joining her in the kitchen and starting to set the table for supper. "Do you know anything about those tablets? I don't."

"I have one." Izzie had stopped looking at food and was focused on the small screen in her hands.

"Jake said he was watching movies on it."

"Carl's got a couple of dozen movies on here. He must have used it for that."

"Movies won't help us."

"No. But e-mails might," Izzie said. "A lot of them are here. I don't know who most of them are from. A lot of them have screen names."

"He never wrote to me. And Burt didn't mention e-mails."

Izzie shrugged. "He probably called you or texted. Give me a little time. I need to read these to see if they're important. I can do that after dinner." She put down the tablet, took a knife from her kit, and started chopping apples and walnuts for the salad she'd planned.

"You do that so fast!" I said, watching her.

"Part of learning to be a chef," she said. "My knives are really sharp. If you ever borrow one, be careful. We were taught they're safer when they're sharper. They do what you want them to."

I shook my head. "I'll stick with the knives I have."

"Good decision," she agreed. "These can be tricky. Thanks for listening to me prattle on about my dream restaurant," she said as she added wine and water glasses to the table. "I'm excited about looking at that building tomorrow. But our other project is more immediate."

"Our other project?" I asked.

"We made a start today. But we still have to figure out who killed Carl," she said. "I know we can't talk much when Jake is around, and Burt is upset enough. But tonight, I'll check the e-mails and tomorrow morning, after we see the realtor, we'll ask questions."

She tucked the tablet in a drawer and added a dressing to the salad.

# Chapter Twenty-Two

"Egg Wine: Break a nice fresh egg into a tumbler and beat it until it is smooth and thick. Add a tablespoon of pulverized sugar and stir in a glass of the best Port wine. This is very strengthening for an invalid to take about the hour of noon, if the physician permits it. When wine is not allowed, a glass of new milk may be used instead."

—*Mrs. Seely's Cook-Book: A Manual of French and American Cookery, with Chapters on Domestic Servants, Their Rights and Duties, and Many Other Details of Household Management.* New York: 1902

Martha's lasagna was good, and after dinner we made a major dent in the brownies we'd been given. Burt and Jake covered theirs with ice cream. I was tempted, but Izzie resisted and I didn't want to look like the pig I sometimes was. I did manage to eat one of the chocolates in my stash when no one was looking.

My little sister was setting a good example for me. That was the first time I'd raided my chocolate hoard today.

Except for several brief condolence calls, including one from Reverend Beaman asking when we wanted to schedule Carl's funeral, the evening was quiet.

"Funeral! We don't even have Carl's body," Burt ranted after he got off the phone.

His rant didn't last long. We were all exhausted.

Jake was quieter than usual during dinner. He didn't ask about the tablet, and after dessert he put more ice on his swollen eye and headed up to his room. His uncle's death must be sinking in.

Izzie was restless. I could tell she was excited about her appointment with the realtor, but she didn't mention it to Jake or Burt. When the rest of us said we were tired, she borrowed one of my cookbooks to read in bed and took Carl's tablet with her up to her room.

I hoped she'd find something that would give us a clue to Carl's killer.

* * *

"So, was there anything important on that tablet?" I asked as soon as Izzie came downstairs the next morning. Jake and Burt had already left for the day, and I was drinking my second mug of coffee, with a brownie.

If you weren't supposed to eat brownies, why did people give them to you? We had several boxes full.

"I'm not sure," said Izzie, pouring herself a mug of coffee

and joining me at the kitchen table. "But Carl definitely had an active social life. He was writing, regularly, to more than one woman. Most of them had screen names, though, so I don't know who they were."

"Rose wouldn't be happy to know that."

"She was the only one whose identity I think I figured out. I'm guessing she's 'beachflower.' She always signed with love and kisses," Izzie wrinkled her nose. "Didn't you say there were beach roses on the island?"

"Definitely. In lots of places. By the lighthouse, and Mom has them on the trellis outside her house," I agreed. "People take the rose hips and make tea or jelly."

"Well, Carl and 'beachflower' exchanged a lot of messages during the winter. Most of them were long notes from her about his apartment. I think she was the one decorating it. Or she wanted to know what she should cook for dinner."

"That does sound like Rose," I agreed.

"But those messages stopped about a month ago. And the notes from people I assumed were other women, were different. Someone named 'Sincity' and Carl met sometimes, too. But while 'beachflower' wrote about furnishings and food, 'Sincity' wrote about sex." Izzie paused. "It sounded as though their meetings were basically for sex. They had cybersex, too." She wrinkled her nose. "Not fun to read."

"No love and kisses?"

"Not online."

I sighed. "Carl must have had different women for . . . different purposes."

"I only went back about six months. There were several people he wrote to once or twice, but not recently. I didn't think prices of bait would have led to him being shot. He'd written to several manufacturers of boat parts, too."

I nodded. "That makes sense. His boat's engine wasn't working right."

"There was one other person he wrote to often. Linus is a man's name, but the notes sounded too sweet to be from a man. Do you know anyone named 'Linus'?"

"No one."

"Another screen name, then. Or someone off-island. Anyway, Carl and Linus met pretty often, too—often late at night. Those messages were really short, sometimes just a time, like 'midnight,' but there were a lot of them. And a couple of references were to trips."

"Trips? Carl didn't travel."

"Maybe he was planning to. The messages never said when the trips would be or to where."

"Carl hasn't been farther than Portland in months, so far as I know. And we saw him almost every day. He certainly wasn't vacationing in the Bahamas. But it sounds as though he had a more exciting life than we'd assumed," I said, dryly. "Where's the tablet now?"

"I left it in my room, in a drawer. Maybe we should give it to the police."

"Maybe. But let's talk to Rose first. That first person you mentioned—'beachflower'—did sound like her. Maybe she knows more about what was happening with Carl."

"Or maybe she doesn't. Sounds as though he was hiding some of his life."

"True." I stood. "But maybe not from everyone. And I

haven't forgotten your appointment this morning. We need to get over to the café. After we do that, we'll try to talk to Rose."

Mrs. Evans, a realtor from the mainland, was waiting for us outside the deserted restaurant building.

"Good morning, Miss Jordan," she said, walking up to me. "So glad you called."

I stepped backward. "I'm Mrs. Winslow. My sister, Miss Jordan, was the one who called you." I pointed at Izzie.

Mrs. Evans' face froze for a second before she turned to Izzie. "Sorry for the mistake. And thank you for calling. This building's been on the market for a couple of years now. I haven't even shown it to anyone recently."

Izzie and I exchanged a glance. That meant the seller might be willing to bargain.

"I'm looking forward to seeing the inside," Izzie said. Her voice was high and breathy with excitement. I hoped she wouldn't be disappointed.

I needn't have worried. The building spoke for itself.

Izzie walked around the central area several times. The room where she might seat customers was empty, but I could see possibilities there. Its pine floor was scratched, but could be sanded and polyurethaned. The walls needed plaster and paint, and broken windows had to be fixed or replaced, but the structure seemed solid.

The kitchen was empty and its walls were stained with grease.

"Does the building get town water?" Izzie asked, glancing at me to show she remembered yesterday's conversation.

"Town water April to October. The couple who ran the last

restaurant here went to Florida in the off-season. But the business before theirs was year-round, so there is a well."

"What are the taxes?" she asked next.

"Five thousand dollars a year" Mrs. Evans focused on Izzie. "I assume you'd be making improvements. That would trigger a reassessment and taxes would probably go up then."

Izzie checked the one bathroom—a unisex facility.

"What do you have in mind for the building?" asked Mrs. Evans.

"A small restaurant," said Izzie. "A café." I could tell she was mentally measuring the space.

"I have a listing sheet that has the dimensions," said Mrs. Evans, handing it to Izzie. "And we don't have a Chinese restaurant anywhere near here."

"My restaurant wouldn't be Chinese."

Mrs. Evans had the grace to blush.

Izzie was looking at the listing sheet. "There's space for the parking lot to be enlarged then, and a patio for outside dining."

"You'd have to get zoning clearances from the town for changes like that, but, yes, I think there's enough property. Not all the land you see goes with the building. Near the bridge the land is owned by the state, and the neighbor on the other side owns several acres on both sides of the road."

"I'll have to do some calculations, but thank you for showing it to us."

"Perhaps you'd be more interested in a larger building, in better condition," said Mrs. Evans as she locked the door. "I have a listing for a restaurant in Pine Harbor, on the mainland. It's been operating for ten years, and the owners want to retire. The kitchen and dining room are in pristine shape."

"How many does it seat?" Izzie asked.

"About a hundred," said Mrs. Evans, looking through the pile of papers in the leather satchel she was carrying.

"That's larger than I have in mind."

Mrs. Evans handed Izzie a card. "Call me if you want to look at the place again, or have other questions."

"I will," said Izzie. She and I headed back to my truck as Mrs. Evans got into her car.

"What do you think?" asked Izzie.

"It needs a lot of work," I said.

"It does," Izzie agreed. "That's why it's perfect. Sweat equity could make it affordable." She raised her hand and mimed hammering. "How are you at painting and plastering?"

# Chapter Twenty-Three

"An appropriate dinner bill of fare in winter, not so varied as for a fashionable dinner, but enough to be elegant: (course 1) Mock-turtle soup (2) Baked salmon with sauce Hollandaise (3) Fried oysters with cold slaw (4) Lamb chops with tomato sauce (5) Roast turkey with oyster stuffing and Saratoga potatoes (6) Roman punch, in lemon-skins (7) Macaroni, with cheese (8) Pineapple Bavarian cream (9) Vanilla ice cream with little cakes (10) Fruits (11) coffee."

—*Old Doctor Carlin's Recipes: A Complete Collection of Recipes on Every Known Subject* by Doctor William Carlin. Boston, Massachusetts: The Locker Publishing Company, 1881

"I could hardly sleep last night," Izzie confided as we headed back home. "I stayed up late trying to figure out Carl's messages, and whether they could help us figure out who killed him. And when I stopped thinking about him, I thought about that building, wondering about it, imagining what it could look like. And what my menu might look like." She shook her head. "But the café can wait. I've seen the building. It definitely has possibilities. But first, we have to find out more about Carl. You'll call Rose and see if she's free?"

As I drove into our driveway, Detective Preston pulled his unmarked car in behind us. "Look who's here," I said. "I didn't expect to see him again so soon. This can't be good news." Izzie and I headed for the front porch. We got there before Preston did. A large casserole dish was in front of the door.

I opened the door and Izzie picked up the heavy dish and took it to the kitchen. "It's more baked beans," she called back to me. "A really, really big pot of baked beans."

"I called your husband. He's coming in and meeting us here," said Preston, brushing by me and following Izzie into the house. This time he sat in the living room.

"You have news, then?"

Izzie joined us. "I hope good news."

"I need to talk with Mr. Winslow," Preston repeated.

"He left several hours ago. If he's coming in, he'll have to tie up and walk from the wharf," I said.

What did he want to talk to Burt about? Preston looked serious. But then, he always looked serious.

I wanted chocolate. I told myself to stay calm. Stay in control. Treat a visit from a homicide detective as an ordinary event.

Blue meowed at me and then went and sat at his food dish. Everybody wanted something.

I filled his dish and changed his water.

My phone rang. I glanced down. Burt. Why was he calling?

He was supposed to be on his way home. I walked out the kitchen door before answering. I didn't want Preston to overhear me.

Burt was talking fast. "Something's wrong, Anna. I know it. Preston wouldn't wait until I'd finished my run today. He insisted on seeing me right away. I'm afraid he's found my rifle, and is ready to . . . Listen, you have to talk to Jake. That boy has to learn responsibility. If I'm arrested, it'll just be you and him here. He has to man up, and fast."

"You're not going to be arrested," I assured him, hoping that was true, and trying to calm him down. "You can't be arrested for something you didn't do." But, of course, once he *had* been arrested for something he hadn't done. Burt never forgot that. I wanted to tell him that Izzie and I were going to find Carl's killer, but why would he believe that? We weren't detectives. Right now, Burt needed to hear facts. "Stay strong. You're innocent."

"I am, Anna. I am. But you're not the police or the judge or jury."

I had to change the subject. "Carl loaned his tablet to Jake, and Izzie knows how to use those things. He was having relationships with at least two women, Burt—not just Rose. And maybe someone else. Maybe one of them found out about the others, and killed him. We're trying to figure it out. Even if Detective Preston is still asking you questions, he has to have other suspects. Suspects who have motives!"

Burt was silent. "Is he there now?"

"In the living room."

"I'll be home soon." Burt sounded out of breath. "I tied up the *Anna*. I'm walking as fast as I can." He paused again.

"I don't think any woman killed Carl. Whoever killed him, I think it had to do with money."

"Maybe you're right. Carl always did have had money problems," I agreed. "But we need to consider all possibilities."

"Is Izzie with you?"

"She's in the kitchen. I'm outside. I didn't want Preston to hear our conversation."

"Anna, she seems like a nice woman. And I know she's your sister by blood. But we don't know her. She doesn't know us. She comes from a different world. Maybe you should tell her to go home, come back and visit when life is simpler. Feels strange having another person in the house. And sounds like she's getting some strange ideas about Carl."

"I like having her here, Burt. She's company. And she makes me think about things outside the island. She's being a big help in trying to find out what happened to Carl. I'd like her to stay, at least for now."

"Up to you. But she's not like us, Anna, even if she is blood. Don't forget that." Burt hung up.

I walked back into the house, slowly. Burt was upset, but I wasn't going to ask Izzie to leave.

Right now, she was busying herself dividing baked beans into freezer containers.

I went into the living room. "Are you sure there's nothing I can help you with, Detective? Burt called. He'll be home in a few minutes."

He was staring at his telephone the way Jake did sometimes: as though his life depended on it. "No, thank you, Mrs. Winslow. I'll wait for your husband."

What did he need to see Burt about that he couldn't tell me? Was Burt right? Could Preston be here to arrest him?

I sat, hoping Detective Preston had come to tell us he'd solved the mystery. It had been an accident. Or he knew who'd killed Carl, and no one we knew was involved.

I'd begun looking at everyone with different eyes. I'd even considered locking my door when Izzie and I left the house.

It was only four minutes or so before Burt got home, but it seemed forever.

"I got here as fast as I could. It took time to bring the *Anna* in and tie her up," he said as he came in the door, breathing heavily. Burt was in pretty good shape, but he hadn't slept much in the past days.

He also hadn't taken the time to wash up. He stunk of bait and lobsters and seawater.

I'd never been so glad to see him. I didn't even say anything when he sat on one of the slipcovered chairs in his filthy clothes.

Detective Preston nodded. "Thanks for coming in early from your traps. I wanted to let you know in person."

"Yes?" Burt asked.

"We found your rifle. We checked the serial number on the federal registry after you told us it was registered."

"That's good news! Where was it?"

"One of my guys found it tangled in rockweed off Granite Point, below the lighthouse. It was banged up a bit. He took it to the lab in Augusta to test it."

Burt looked puzzled. "It's a good rifle. I hope it's all right. But how did it end up on Granite Point?"

"We don't know for sure. At the moment, we're working

with the assumption that whoever used it to kill your brother threw it there."

Burt held on to the arm of his chair as though it was a life raft. "Killed Carl? With my gun? You're sure?"

"Whoever shot him had to be near the Granite Point Lighthouse. Maybe they thought they'd gotten rid of the rifle by throwing it off the ledges into the water, but it washed ashore. Or they didn't throw it far enough, and it got caught on the rocks and seaweed and the tide didn't take it out."

"But, who?" asked Burt, looking dazed. "Who would have done that? And who would be a good enough shot to hit anyone out on a boat from that point?"

"Excellent questions, Mr. Winslow. Ones we're trying to find answers to. We thought you might be able to tell us. We don't know for sure that a shot from your rifle killed your brother. We'll know that for certain after we get the ballistics report. But you were the last person who saw him that day. And you'd argued. And your rifle was found close to where whoever shot Carl must have been."

"I told you, we argued all the time. And Carl was shot from Granite Point? I wasn't even on land when he was shot. I was out working my traps."

"Can you prove that, Mr. Winslow? I believe you went out that morning. But you could have returned, docked your boat, gone to Granite Point, shot your brother, tossed the rifle, and then returned to your boat."

"I didn't!"

"Plus, you and your brother didn't argue about him helping you that day or even, as your son suggested, about whether you should loan him moncy. You were right when you said you had nothing to loan him. You don't have any money because he'd already stolen it, hadn't he, Mr. Winslow?"

"What?" I blurted.

Preston ignored me. He focused on Burt, who'd turned pale under the permanent tan all lobstermen had.

"We checked your bank account, and your brother's."

"That was between Carl and me. It had nothing to do with his murder."

"Sounds like a motive to me," said Preston. "A month ago, you had over sixteen thousand dollars in your savings account."

"For emergencies," I put in. "And the future."

"Then maybe there was an emergency," said Preston, drily. "Because right now there's less than five hundred dollars in that account."

"What?" I blurted. "What happened to our money?" Burt and I had a joint account, but he took care of all our bills and, now that I wasn't earning a paycheck, our deposits, too. I used our debit card for groceries. I hadn't been near the bank in months.

Detective Preston glanced at his notes. "On February tenth, about six weeks ago, Carl Winslow deposited a check for over fifteen thousand dollars into his account."

"How do you know I didn't give him that money?" asked Burt. "He's my brother!"

"True enough. But if you gave him that money, why was the check from your account written in his handwriting?"

Burt sat, silent.

I stared at him, an empty feeling in my stomach.

"Carl forged a check from your account, didn't he?" asked

Detective Preston. "You knew about it, but clearly," he glanced at me, "your wife didn't. When you found out, you confronted him. I'm guessing he told you he needed the money and it wasn't doing any good sitting in the bank. He promised to pay you back."

Burt sat, silent, looking down at his hands.

The police had found a motive that implicated Burt. No wonder Burt had been so sure the police would arrest him. He'd known all along he had a motive.

I couldn't believe Burt had killed Carl. But why hadn't he told me about the money?

"I believe you were arguing about money on the day Carl was killed. But you weren't arguing about whether you'd give him a loan. You were arguing about when he'd pay back the money he'd stolen."

"That's right. But that was between Carl and me. What does it matter now?"

"It matters because your brother stole money you and your wife had saved for emergencies. You knew your brother didn't handle money well, and you didn't see any possibility he would pay you back." Detective Preston stood. "Burt Winslow, I'm arresting you on suspicion of killing your brother, Carl Winslow. You have the right to remain silent. Anything you say can and will be used against you in a court of law. You have the right to an attorney. If you cannot afford an attorney, one will be provided for you."

Burt stood slowly, as Preston handcuffed him.

"Anna, call Rob and ask him about a lawyer." Burt looked me straight in the eye. "I didn't kill Carl. I should have told you he took that money, but I was too embarrassed to admit my own brother had stolen from us. But I didn't kill him! And I don't know why my rifle was missing." He glanced at Preston. "Or how it ended up at Granite Point."

"Then I suggest you think of witnesses who can testify that you were out on your boat all of Saturday morning, until the time you found your brother's boat adrift," said Detective Preston. "Because right now, it's not looking good for you, Mr. Winslow."

"Don't say anything more, Burt," I cautioned him. "Not until you have a lawyer."

"I didn't do it," Burt repeated.

Burt had always taken care of me, protected me, tried to keep me from worrying. I'd seen him angry. I'd seen him sad. I'd never seen him cry.

Tears were in his eyes. I'd never seen him look so scared.

"I didn't kill him. I didn't kill anyone."

The door slammed behind the two men.

Burt needed me now, more than ever. He needed me to prove he was innocent.

# Chapter Twenty-Four

"If onions are sliced and kept in a sickroom, it is said they will absorb all the atmospheric poison. They should be changed every hour."

—*Peterson's Magazine*, August 1869

Our landline rang.

I was numb. I couldn't talk with anyone. Carl had stolen our money. Burt had been arrested for murder. How could I afford a lawyer when we had no money?

I heard Izzie picking up the phone in the kitchen. Good. She could handle whoever was calling.

But maybe not.

"Anna?" Izzie said softly, coming into the living room. "Sorry to disturb you. But a Mr. Flanagan is on the phone. He says he's the principal of the Quarry Island School, and he needs to talk with you. It's about Jake."

I followed Izzie into the kitchen and picked up the phone.

"Mrs. Winslow?"

"Yes."

"I'm sorry to bother you. I know you and your family are having a rough week. But I had to tell you. Jake's not at school."

"What? I'm sure he got on the school bus this morning."

"Oh, he was here this morning. But he disappeared sometime between his third period class and the end of lunch hour."

"Disappeared?"

"One of the other boys said Jake and Matt Martin were arguing behind the gym, and Jake took off. No one's seen him since." Mr. Flanagan paused. "He left his backpack here. Matt said he kept his cell phone in it. I have it in my office now."

"Have you looked for him? Jake's never left school in the middle of the day before."

"I know, Mrs. Winslow. Jake's a good kid. But he's having a difficult time right now. Several of the other boys said they saw him heading in the direction of the quarry. I've tried to talk with Matt, but he won't tell me what he and Jake were arguing about."

"They had a fight the other night."

"So I gathered. I saw Jake's eye, and Matt's arm is badly bruised."

I hadn't known Matt was hurt, too.

"Thank you for calling, Mr. Flanagan. If Jake comes back to school, would you call and let me know?"

"Certainly. I hope he does return. But I had to let you know."

Izzie looked at me as I put down the phone. "Jake had another argument with Matt, and took off. He left school." Could anything else in my life go wrong? I was being pulled under by a giant whirlpool. It took all my strength to keep my head above water.

"Where would he go?" asked Izzie.

"He headed toward the quarry." Usually I'd be furious. Right now, I didn't have the strength for anger.

"Oh, no! I'm sorry, Anna, but I was in the kitchen. I heard what happened. I can't believe they've arrested Burt. And now Jake decides to take off."

I couldn't talk about any of that. Not right this minute. I had to call Rob. "Jake's a teenager. He takes everything personally. He doesn't see the world the way we do." How would he react when I told him his father had been arrested?

"So, he's not in danger?" asked Izzie. "You're not worried about him? There's a murderer somewhere on the island!"

"Of course, I'm worried. Jake's alone at the quarry. My husband was just arrested for murder. I have to get him a lawyer, and I just found we're broke." I tried to take a deep breath.

"So, are you going to look for Jake?" Izzie asked.

"I'm going to give Jake a little time. He may even go back to school."

Izzie shook her head. "He could be in danger."

"He knows the quarry well," I assured her. "And he went there on his own. I have to believe he'll be okay for right now." Besides, maybe selfishly, I needed a few minutes to absorb what was happening before telling Jake his father had been arrested for murder. "I'll call Rob Erickson," I decided. "Then I'll go and find Jake."

Rob answered quickly. "Anna. Thank goodness you called. I was about to call you. Dad said he saw Detective Preston taking Burt out in handcuffs."

"He's been arrested, Rob. They think he killed Carl. His rifle was found over near the lighthouse, and it may be the murder weapon. And Carl stole money from Burt and me. Burt hadn't even told me. I didn't know until now."

"So that gives Burt a motive, and possible access to the murder weapon. I'm sorry, Anna."

"He didn't do, it, Rob. I'm certain he didn't. But you said you knew lawyers. Now we need one."

"I'll find him one. I promise. I'll get back to you as soon as I've confirmed I have someone who'll help."

I hung up, but stood frozen. It was all a nightmare.

Izzie kept talking, trying to pull me back from wherever I'd gone. "Despite what the police are saying, you don't believe Burt killed his brother."

"Of course not! Burt would never do that."

"Then first you have to get Jake, and then you and I have to figure out who took Burt's rifle and shot Carl. It had to be someone you know well, who knew where to find Burt's gun."

I knew that.

"The problem is, if Carl stole money from you, that gave Burt a motive."

"What about those women he was writing to? What if one of them found out about the others? What if one of them wanted more from Carl than he was willing to give? That could give one or several people a motive."

"True," said Izzie. "But right now you need to focus on Jake. I get that you think Quarry Island's a safe place, Anna. You've lived here all your life. And it isn't as though Jake's run away in the middle of New York City. But Carl's dead, and the police have focused on Burt. They're not looking for anyone else. Jake might be in danger!"

"You're right," I said, picking up my keys. "We need to go

and find him." I couldn't stand it if anything happened to Jake, too.

Izzie hesitated. "I'm still new to this family. I'm sorry you have to go through all this, but you should go to the quarry alone."

I turned toward her. "It's your family now, too, Izzie."

"It is," she agreed, giving me a quick hug. "But I think Jake would be more open with you if I weren't there. Now, you get going and find Jake before anyone else does. Rob's going to get Burt a terrific lawyer, and I'm going back to Maine Chance Books to talk with Luc Burnham. He's Jake's boss. He might know what Jake is thinking about, or what the problem is with Matt."

"All right. That makes sense. You might ask him about Carl, too. There were books in Carl's apartment. No other bookstores are nearby. Mr. Burnham might know who bought them." Someone did, and I wasn't convinced it was Carl.

"I'll ask him," Izzie agreed. "I'll be back as soon as I can." She looked at me again. "I'm sorry if I scared you. But something's happening on this island and until we find out what it is, you and Jake should be careful."

I shivered. Izzie was right. Could the rest of my family be in danger, too?

Until we knew who'd killed Carl, nothing was certain. The police had stopped looking for Carl's killer. They thought they'd found him. But they hadn't, I was sure. He—or she—was still here, somewhere on Quarry Island.

I had to find Jake before anyone else did. I had to bring him home.

# Chapter Twenty-Five

"There is something really so absurd and revolting in the idea of taking woman out of her present sphere, and her present high and holy uses in society, and placing her side by side with man in the world's rough arena, and in contest with him for honor, and fame, and wealth, that we cannot seriously argue against it. We have deemed it sufficient to show that, in the very nature of things, such can never be the case."

—*Advice to Young Ladies on Their Duties and Conduct in Life* by T. S. Arthur. Philadelphia: J.W. Bradley 1860

Was it only yesterday that I'd driven Izzie around Quarry Island? It seemed years ago.

The island was only six miles long and three miles wide. It didn't take me long to get to the quarry.

I pulled into the cleared area near the entrance. Rock

climbers parked there, and people used it as a turnaround. The rough dirt road leading to the quarry was blocked off, but anyone could duck under the heavy metal chain.

That's what Jake had probably done. That's what I did now.

The muddy road into the quarry curved slightly, heading up a newly wooded hill. When the quarry was active that hill had been barren. Trees had been cut so heavy galamanders, oxen-pulled wagons that hauled cut stone, had access. One road circled the top of the quarry; another road cut to the bottom, where granite was cut and loaded onto wagons and then taken to ships.

How many men and women in Philadelphia and other cities knew that when they walked their streets, they were walking on Maine granite?

In summer, the earth was packed down, hard. Today it was muddy.

And I wasn't the only person who'd been there. Several sets of footprints were clearly visible. Most headed up the hill. Was Jake alone in the quarry, or had he met someone there? Or been followed?

I listened. People came here to practice shooting. Jake had done that just last week. Today, I didn't hear anything. But that didn't mean no one was here. Or that whoever was here didn't have a gun.

Everyone who lived on the island knew the quarry. On summer days, rock climbers came here to practice. Amateur geologists prowled, hoping to find geodes or crystals or garnets. Teenagers went there for privacy. The deepest part of the quarry, now filled with water from rain and melting snow, attracted boys who swam there in July and August, challenging each other to ignore the silt and algae that filled the murky water. Despite the look of the water and the "No Trespassing" signs the town council had posted throughout the area, exploring the quarry and shucking your clothes to swim where you've been forbidden was part of a Quarry Island boy's childhood.

Today, the quarry was deserted. Except for whoever left those footprints.

I stopped, listening for voices. Or branches breaking. Or shots.

Two red squirrels chased each other across the road, and a crow cawed to announce that someone was nearby. Chickadees declared "dee-dee-dee" in the trees around me, and a cardinal called in the distance. I hugged myself. I was wearing my windbreaker, but I should have put on a heavier jacket. Early April might be mating season for the birds and animals who lived in or near the quarry, but the air was still chilly.

Had Jake grabbed his jacket when he'd left school?

My thoughts swirled, but they always came back to my husband and son. "Jake!" I called. "Jake?"

His name echoed faintly.

In another month, the trees and brush that had grown up around the working parts of the quarry would hide quarry visitors from each other. Today, the only green trees were a few pines and spruces, species some vacationers thought were the only ones in Maine, despite the maples and oaks and birches and poplars that covered more than half the state.

Why had Jake taken his gun up here to the gravel pit last week? With all that had been happening, I hadn't asked him. It probably wasn't important.

But right now, I didn't know what was important.

"Jake!" I called again. "Jake! Jake!" How far could he have gotten? Had he been running to get away from whatever had happened at school, or toward a place where he didn't have to deal with people asking too many questions?

Was anyone else in the quarry? Whose footprints had I seen?

I stood on one of the high points of the road above the quarry.

"Jake!"

Then I saw him. He was alone, standing on one of the ledges above the watery center. I realized I'd been holding my breath, hoping he was alone. He was. He was all right.

He looked up at me and waved.

"Time to come home, Jake!" I called.

He dodged up a path I couldn't see, but which he was seemed familiar with. "Meet you at the truck!" he yelled back. His voice echoed across the quarry.

"Right!" I answered, and headed back down the hill. Jake probably knew another way to the entrance. I didn't see anyone else. I hoped Jake wouldn't either.

Something glittered on the side of the rough, muddy road. A geode? A piece of quartz crystal? Others had found tiny garnets at the quarry. I bent over to see.

Several bullets were almost hidden under leaves.

Why here? I stuck them in the pocket of my windbreaker. Maybe they'd fit one of our rifles, and Jake or Burt could use them. Then, I remembered where those rifles were now.

I focused on positives. I had to believe Burt would be released very soon, Burt and Jake would get their rifles back, and Carl's murder would be solved quickly.

How could I tell Jake his father had been arrested?

Maybe he'd come here to the quarry to escape. Had Izzie come to Maine to escape the realities of her father's death? Our father's death, I mentally corrected myself. To someone from the city or suburbs, Maine might seem like a distant place. Those of us who lived here sometimes dreamed of living in a place where no one knew you or your past.

On Quarry Island, there was no place to go where you wouldn't be found.

I kept walking down the hill, back to my world. Back to where Jake would meet me.

# Chapter Twenty-Six

"To Dress Lobsters: When the lobster is boiled, rub it over with a little salad-oil, which wipe off again; separate the body from the tail, break off the great claws, and crack them at the joints, without injuring the meat; split the tail in halves, and arrange all neatly in a dish, with the body upright in the middle, and garnish with parsley."

—*Mrs. Beeton's Book of Household Management*
by Mrs. Isabella Beeton. London:
S.O. Beeton Publishing, 1861

"What happened in school?" I asked, trying to stay calm.

Jake looked out the window of the passenger seat as I drove. "Nothing."

"*Something* must have happened. You've never left school in the middle of the day before."

"Nothing happened. I just didn't want to be there anymore."

"Principal Flanagan said you and Matt were arguing."

"So? It's none of his business." Jake looked over at me. "Or yours. It's between Matt and me."

I didn't need this. "Jake, this has been an awful week, I know. But whatever's wrong between you and Matt, you can't let it mess up your whole life. Or your dad's and mine."

Jake sat, not saying a word. Then, finally, "You don't know what this is about. It's my problem, not yours. So leave me alone, okay?"

What had happened to Burt was more important than a boy's quarrel. "I need to talk to you about something else, too."

"I don't want to talk about anything!"

I turned the truck into our driveway. The ignition wasn't fully off when Jake jumped out and ran into the house.

The door to his room banged shut as I scraped the quarry mud off my shoes and walked into the living room. Jake hadn't stopped. His footsteps led across the room.

"Anna? Jake just raced through here as if a swarm of bees was after him." Izzie looked at the mud on the floor and then at me.

"He wouldn't tell me what was wrong."

"Did you tell him about his dad?"

"He ran off before I had a chance to. I'm hoping he'll calm down. I have to talk with him." At least Jake was home. Safe. For the moment that seemed enough, although I knew it wouldn't be for long.

"I talked to Luc Burnham."

"And?" I'd failed to get any information from Jake. Maybe Izzie'd heard something that might help.

"He didn't know a lot. Jake hasn't shown up a couple of times recently when Luc'd expected him to work, and Matt's been hanging around the store, especially when Jake was there. Luc figured Matt was looking for racy photos or books. He's been hiding out in the sections on families and looking through medical books."

"Sex?"

"Luc said he didn't mind. If Matt could find answers to his questions in books, it would be more accurate than whatever he heard from his friends or on some internet sites"

"Or maybe he just wanted to find pictures of nudes," I said, thinking of the old *Playboy* centerfold inside Jake's closet. I'd figured kids looked up stuff like that on the internet today, not at used bookstores. But I wasn't fourteen. "So Mr. Bouchard—Luc—didn't know what was wrong between Matt and Jake." I was glad Izzie'd tried to find out, but knowing the boys looked at pictures of naked women wasn't helpful. Or even important.

Izzie shook her head. "He did hear them talking about guns one day last week. He figured most kids around here have rifles, so it was no big deal. Jake went shooting at the gravel pit last week, right?"

"That's what he told the detective. Matt doesn't have a rifle." Lucy's dad had been a hunter, and he'd taught her how to shoot. She and Cynthia Snowe had practiced together at the gravel pit. That was when they'd become good friends, I remembered. But when Lucy was about the age Jake and Matt were now, her shoulder was hit by a hunter's stray bullet when she and her dad were out hunting. The shooting wasn't intentional, and it was a long time ago. She'd healed. But after that her dad swore off hunting and took Lucy's gun away. Lucy didn't talk about what had happened then, but I suspected that was why she hadn't wanted Matt to have a gun.

I'd overheard Jake bragging about his own gun a few times. It was something he had that his friend didn't.

"Jake could have loaned his gun to Matt. Or they took turns shooting," Izzie pointed out.

Jake wasn't supposed to loan his gun to anyone, or use anyone else's. Burt had told him that dozens—hundreds—of times. Told Jake he knew his own weapon, but he didn't know anyone else's. A week ago, I'd have been sure Jake hadn't done anything he wasn't supposed to. Now I wasn't sure about anything.

"What else did Luc say?"

"The books in Carl's apartment, those mysteries, might have come from Maine Chance. Carl'd been in there a few times, sometimes alone, and sometimes with Jake or Matt or with the Martins, but Luc didn't remember whether he'd ever bought anything. For the record, Carl's friend Rose and her sister Cynthia are regular customers, and they both read mysteries."

"That doesn't add much to what we know." I scratched Blue behind his ears. He purred a "thank you" before heading for his favorite chair in the living room. Blue had no problems.

"I'm afraid not. But Luc's a sweet old guy. I told him how much I loved the books I'd bought from him a couple of days ago, and he showed me three cartons of recipe books he'd just gotten in. When life is a little less frantic, I'll go back and look at them." She glanced up the stairs. "Does Jake even know the detectives found Burt's gun?"

"I didn't get a chance to tell him. He was in such a huff, and didn't want to talk on the way home, and I didn't want to blurt out the news."

"Better for you to tell him than for him to hear it from one of his friends."

"You're right. Those kids do nothing but text and . . . oh, darn."

"What is it?"

"I didn't stop at the school to get Jake's backpack. His cell phone is in it. So, he won't be hearing from any of his friends this afternoon."

"Want me to get it? If you call that Mr. Flanagan he'd probably let me pick it up."

"Would you? I don't want to leave Jake right now. I do need to talk with him."

"No problem," said Izzie, standing. "I'd like to stop at that building we looked at this morning and walk around it again, anyway. Going to the school first will give me an excuse to do that."

I handed her my keys. "Thank you. I'll call Principal Flanagan to let him know you're on your way. So, you're serious about that place?"

"I'm always serious," said Izzie, grinning at me. "Can't you tell?"

I didn't know whether she meant that or not, but right now it didn't matter. Only Burt and Jake mattered. They were my life.

I called the school as Izzie pulled out of the driveway.

I had to talk to Jake.

*That boy has to learn responsibility. If I'm arrested, or . . . convicted . . . it'll just be you and him here. He has to man up, and fast.* That's what Burt had said. But it wasn't what I'd say to Jake. That was too much pressure to put on a fourteen-year-old boy.

Even when his dad had just been arrested for murder.

# Chapter Twenty-Seven

"Bread made of wheat flour, when taken out of the oven, is unprepared for the stomach. It should go through a change, or ripen, before it is eaten. Young persons, or persons in the enjoyment of vigorous health, may eat bread immediately after being baked, without any sensible injury from it. Weakly and aged persons cannot without doing harm to the digestive organs."

—*The New England Economical Housekeeper, and Family Receipt Book* by Esther A. Howland. S.A. Howland, Worcester, Massachusetts, 1844

I knocked on Jake's door.

"I don't want to talk to you!" he yelled back through the wall.

"I won't ask any questions," I promised. "I just need to tell you a couple of things."

Silence from his room. Finally Jake came out, closing the door behind him.

"Are any of those cookies left? The ones people brought over Sunday?"

I smiled for the first time in hours. That was my Jake. No matter what the time or circumstance, he was hungry. "Let's check," I said, as we headed to the kitchen. "I'm pretty sure there's a fudge cake we haven't even cut into." I glanced at him, aware I was offering a bribe.

"Good," he said. "I missed lunch."

I put the cake and three plates on the table. I might as well have a little, too, and Izzie would be back soon. Jake cut himself a piece a third the size of the cake. He glanced at me. "So, I'm hungry."

"I didn't say a word," I said, cutting myself a piece considerably smaller. The chocolate layers were filled with raspberry jam, and the cake was topped with butter cream frosting.

I finished my piece and cut a second before either of us spoke.

Jake went first. "You had something to tell me?"

"Yes."

Before I had a chance to continue, Jake interrupted. "If you're going to tell me to call and get my homework assignments, I can't do that. I don't have my books or computer. I left my backpack at school," he said defiantly.

"Your aunt Izzie has gone to pick it up for you."

"You got her involved? Does she have to know everything?"

"She's staying with us. She volunteered to go."

Jake sighed. "Okay. So, what are these big things you want to tell me?"

"One, I just told you—Izzie's gone to reclaim your backpack and bring it home. The second, Detective Preston was here again late this morning."

"Yeah? What did he want?"

"The police found your dad's rifle."

Jake stopped chewing and stared at the unfinished cake on his plate.

"How? Where?"

"How? I don't know exactly. They were looking on Granite Point, overlooking where Uncle Carl's lobster traps were set. Near where his killer might have stood. They found the rifle on one of the ledges, near the water."

"How could it get there?"

"That's what the police are asking, Jake. But that's not all." I looked straight at Jake. "They arrested your father. They think his rifle was the one that killed Uncle Carl."

"What?" Jake looked at me in horror. "That Preston guy thinks Dad killed Uncle Carl?"

"Carl forged your dad's signature and stole money from us. I didn't know, but your dad did. Of course," I started to say, "he's innocent, and we're getting a lawyer, and . . ."

Before I could finish Jake dropped his fork and headed for the front door.

"Jake! Where are you going?" I followed him, but he was too fast for me. "Stop running away. We need to talk!"

He turned and yelled, "I don't know where I'm going. Away from here. I don't want to hear anything more about rifles, or about Uncle Carl! He wasn't a saint, but Dad's not a murderer!"

I watched as Jake ran down the street, this time not toward the quarry, but toward the lighthouse. The lighthouse above where Burt's rifle had been found. The lighthouse Jake had walked to before school. *He wasn't a saint?*

Carl had stolen our money. Maybe Jake was reacting to that. Or did he know something else about Carl? Or about Burt's rifle?

My chest felt tight.

Jake was a good boy. He couldn't have had anything to do with his uncle's murder. I refused to think that. But my gut told me he knew something he hadn't told anyone. I'd assumed whatever problem he had was with Matt. That it was some boyish disagreement. But what if Jake—or he and Matt—had seen something related to Carl's death?

No. That didn't make sense. Jake wouldn't keep anything secret that would free his father. I was sure of that. But Jake knew where his dad had kept his gun. It would have been easy for him to take it. Easier than for anyone else other than Burt or me.

I shivered, wishing that thought would disappear. Jake had no reason to hurt his uncle. Besides. When Carl was killed, Jake and Matt had been off-island at baseball practice.

If he knew something that would help bring his father home, then why wouldn't he tell me? How involved was Jake?

The nightmare of Carl's death kept getting darker.

# Chapter Twenty-Eight

"The man who desires to eat a good dinner every day, must be his cook's best friend."

—*The Epicure's Year Book and Table Companion* by Blanchard Jerrold, Bradbury and Evans, 1868

"Sorry I took so long." Izzie dropped Jake's backpack on the floor near the stairs to the second floor. "That Principal Flanagan wanted to talk about where he could find a good Chinese restaurant in Maine. I wasn't sure if he was flirting, or he thought that's what you talked about with an Asian-looking person." She rolled her eyes. "What is this thing Mainers have with Chinese restaurants? Flanagan's not bad looking, though. Has warm eyes. Then I stopped at a couple of places on my way home. What's happening here?"

"Jake freaked out when I told him about his father. He ran off again."

"Oh, Anna."

"Izzie, we have to figure out who killed Carl. Burt can't stay in jail!" How was he coping now? I hated thinking of what was happening to him. Could I visit him?

"I agree. We can't waste any time." Izzie paused. "That's why I stopped to talk to Rose Snowe on my way home."

"You did?"

"You told me she sometimes worked at that clinic near the school. When we drove by earlier there weren't any cars there. But when I came out of the school with Jake's backpack I saw Detective Preston leaving the clinic, and two cars were in the parking lot outside the clinic. I'd only met her that once, down at the pier, but I knew you were involved with Jake, and I decided to see if she'd talk with me."

"And?"

"She was alone at the clinic; the doctor was over at the school with boys on the baseball team. Rose was really shaken, since Preston had just been questioning her. She said she'd just kept repeating she didn't know anything about Carl's death. Then I told her Burt had been arrested and you were talking with Jake. She agreed Burt wouldn't have killed Carl. She wasn't sure anything she knew would be helpful, but she was willing to talk with me."

"I'm so glad! We need to talk with several people, but she was first on our list."

Izzie nodded. "We talked in that little reception room at the clinic. Since I didn't know her, I could ask questions you probably knew the answers to."

"Like?"

"She and Carl started dating last year. She even knew the date: March 18."

"Over a year then," I replied. "Did you ask her about his apartment?"

"She said she'd fixed it up; she thought that would prove how much she loved him, and how good a wife she'd be."

"Well, that confirmed what I'd thought."

"Rose was pretty emotional about it all, though. She said that all she'd done for Carl wasn't enough; that she thought he might be seeing someone else. For whatever reason, he broke up with her about a month ago, on their first-year anniversary. She'd made him a special dinner, and a cake."

"Ouch! That sounds awful. She must have been devastated." I'd suspected Rose had "set her cap" for Carl, as Mamie would have said. She hadn't made a secret of it. But I also knew Carl had never let any woman tie him down.

"I think she still is. She was crying about half the time I was talking with her."

"Carl didn't tell Burt or me that he and Rose weren't together anymore."

"I think she'd hoped he'd change his mind and come back to her. In fact, remember we saw her down at the wharf with everyone else, waiting for word? You invited her to come here for dinner."

"Right. I was worried about her. I didn't think she should be alone," I said.

"Well, guess what she did instead of coming here?"

I shook my head. I had no idea.

"She went to his apartment; she still had a key. She said she wanted Carl to come home to a place that showed him how important she was to his life. She cleaned the apartment and did his laundry and made those cookies we saw in his kitchen."

"Incredible," I said. That explained the condition of Carl's apartment.

"She was there when you called to tell her they'd found his body."

"I had no idea."

"I wanted to make her feel better. I said maybe he would have changed his mind. That he was lucky to have had her. But she said her sister Cynthia told her Carl wasn't the kind of man who'd ever settle down. He couldn't commit, she said."

Maybe Cynthia was right. But that probably didn't make Rose feel any better.

"It must have been a difficult conversation. Thank you so much for doing that, Izzie."

"It wasn't easy. You're right. Clearly, she loved Carl. But as she talked I kept thinking that also gave her a motive: anger, at his rejection, and jealousy, if he was seeing someone else. So, I asked Rose where she'd been the morning he was killed."

"I'll bet she didn't like that question."

"She freaked a little. Kept saying she couldn't have killed the man she loved. But she did say she and her sister were both hunters; they had rifles. So, even if one of them was guilty, they wouldn't have needed Burt's gun."

"So where was she Saturday morning?"

"At the hospital on the mainland, working a ten-hour shift, from six in the morning until four in the afternoon."

"That covers her. What about Cynthia? Where was she?"

"She was scheduled to be at the clinic most of that morning. Rose even looked through a log book they kept there to check. She said Cynthia had been there in the morning, but then had left. Dr. Neeson usually closed up about noon, but he came back in mid-afternoon. He was the one who called Cynthia and asked her to be available in case Carl needed medical care, and Cynthia called Rose to tell her what had happened."

I sat back. "So. That covers both Rose and Cynthia Snowe."

"They both have motives," Izzie pointed out. "Unrequited love."

"I suppose Cynthia could have left the clinic and gone to the lighthouse to shoot Carl."

"Her rifle could be the same model as Burt's. Although how would she have known where he'd be that day?" Izzie shook her head. "I think we can cross Rose off any suspect lists, but Cynthia is still a possibility.

"I agree. Rose didn't kill Carl. But love makes people do strange things," I said. "She wanted to help him. None of the rest of us even thought of his apartment."

"And now we know who decorated it," Izzie pointed out. "One mystery solved."

"But not the important one. I wish Jake would come home. I almost went to find him, but he knows so many paths on the island I might miss him. I just need to wait until he comes home. I'm hoping he'll have some more answers for us."

"While we're waiting, we should draw up a timeline. Maybe we're forgetting something. Or someone," Izzie suggested. "We need to know who was where, and when."

She was right. I retrieved the pad of paper we'd had in the car. We hadn't used it then. Now was the time. I needed to feel productive.

Izzie followed me to the kitchen. "You know everyone on the island. I don't. I only have first impressions. Why don't I write, while you talk?" Izzie sat at the pine table where we seemed to be spending a lot of time and I handed her the pad and a pen engraved "Agway."

"Fine. But your impressions could be important, too. I've known everyone for so long, I take them for granted. I may not notice something important."

"Motive, opportunity, and means." Izzie made a column on the paper. "We know now the police think Burt's rifle was the one that killed Carl. It might not be, but let's assume for now that they're right. It was missing for a while."

I winced. "I hate to start there. But, all right. So that's the means."

"So . . . who could have taken it?" Izzie posed her pencil, ready to take notes.

I counted on my fingers. "Burt, of course, and me, and Jake. We live here. Plus, our neighbors: Lucy, Dolan, and Matt. They're in and out all the time. Or Mom and Mamie. Or Carl."

Izzie wrote that down. "I doubt Mamie took the rifle. But we'll put her name down for now. We need to consider all possibilities. You don't lock your house door, right?"

I winced. "No one on the island does, except sometimes in summer when a lot of strangers are around."

"So, in theory, anyone on Quarry Island could have taken Burt's rifle any time since last fall."

"Except," I put in, "that I'm here most of the time, and nothing else is missing. I don't think it was a burglary. The gun case was under Burt's and my bed, for heaven's sakes, not out in plain sight."

"And you're sure no one else but you and the neighbors knew where it was? Could Burt have mentioned it to anyone else?"

"It's been under our bed for years. Who knows who he mentioned it to in all that time?" I paused. "When I first told Jake his dad's rifle was missing, he didn't say anything. But when I told him the police had found it and thought it was the murder weapon, he freaked and ran out of here. I suspect he knows something about it."

"Would he have taken the rifle and killed Carl?" Izzie asked bluntly, voicing my darkest fear.

"No way. He could have taken the rifle, of course—it was right here in the house. Why, I don't know, because he had his own rifle. But he was at baseball practice that morning, and then had lunch with Mom and Mamie. He couldn't have shot anyone. Besides, I can't believe he'd hurt his uncle."

"Anna, Jake is lucky to have you. I hope someday I'll be as good a mother as you are. But teenagers see the world differently." Izzie rolled her eyes. "After my mother died, I was convinced my life was over. I felt everyone was staring at me and feeling sorry for me, or hating me. I even planned my own funeral because I was sure I was going to die of cancer soon, too."

"You didn't!"

"Oh, believe me, I did. You've been trying to protect Jake from some of what's happening. But if there's even a slight chance he knows something about Carl's death—he saw something, or heard someone say something—you need to let him know it's all right to tell you what he knows. When someone's murdered, it's okay to tell secrets."

"I agree. At first, I hoped Carl's murder would be solved without Jake's having to get any more involved than he already is. Now he knows everything I know." I pointed at the plate of unfinished chocolate cake. "But he's still my little boy! He was just here, eating cake as though it was his last meal. Then he got up and ran."

"Would his friend Matt know where he was going?"

"Matt's still in school. Last week, before all this happened, I would have said if anyone knew about Jake, it was Matt. But not now." Tears stung my eyes. "Nothing's the way it should be." My world had fallen apart. Nothing made sense anymore. Izzie glanced at me, but continued with the time line.

"Jake went target shooting at the gravel pit last week. And according to Luc, he wasn't always at the bookstore when he told you he was working."

"Right." I dabbed at my eyes with a tissue and blew my nose.

"So, could he and Matt have gone somewhere together? Would Jake have borrowed his dad's rifle for Matt to use? As a favor for a best friend, if Matt pestered him?" Izzie pushed. "We have to think of any possibility."

"If he did that, Jake could be in the middle of this whole mess," I said, almost to myself.

I stood and went to the window. I didn't like the possibilities we were coming up with. I wanted to go back to the way life was a month ago—even a week ago—before all this happened. Although, a month ago the wheels leading us to today had already started turning. Carl had stolen our savings.

"I assume bullets fit different guns," Izzie continued. "And Jake shoots at the gravel pit by the quarry."

"He went there with Burt when he first got his rifle, a couple of years ago. And he was there last week."

"Maybe we could find casings from the bullets he'd shot. They'd tell us whether they came from Jake's .22 or Burt's Winchester."

"I'm not an expert on bullets," I said. "I suspect you're not either."

"No." Izzie looked intense. "But you have a friend who is. Your neighbor, Rob, is a retired homicide detective."

Izzie was right. And I *had* found bullets at the quarry. I'd been so focused on Jake I'd forgotten I had them.

"I found bullets when I was looking for Jake at the quarry. They're in my jacket pocket. I'll call Rob." It was a long shot, but any shot was worth taking.

# Chapter Twenty-Nine

> "Plum Pudding: Time, three hours. Six ounces of raisins, six ounces of currants, six ounces of bread-crumbs, six ounces of suet, half a nutmeg, a little lemon peel, five eggs, half a wineglass of brandy. Mix these ingredients together, put the pudding in a mold and boil it."
>
> —*Peterson's Magazine*, January 1869

We'd picked the right time to call Rob. "I'll be right over," he said as soon as I'd explained what Izzie and I wanted to ask him. "Dad's napping. I'll leave him a note. I'm waiting to hear back from two lawyers I respect, but I'll bring my phone with me."

"Thank you, Rob. We'll fill you in on the rest of the details on our way."

He came quickly. I'd just retrieved the bullets from my jacket pocket when he arrived. "Could these mean anything?" I put the bullets on our coffee table.

He looked puzzled. "Where did you get them?" Rob turned them over a couple of times.

"On the side of the dirt road in the quarry, before the turn-off to the gravel pit."

"Just like this?"

"Covered with leaves." I added. "I saw one through the leaves and uncovered the rest."

"They're new rifle cartridges," Rob said. "Not muddy, or rusted, or corroded. They couldn't have been outside long. I can't imagine why they'd be on the side of the road. If someone was on his way to the gravel pit to shoot, they should have been in his ammo case. And these are two very different types of shells."

"Yes," I agreed.

"The smaller one is for a .22 long rifle. The sort people use for small game, or target shooting. The other one is a serious .308, for a Winchester. That rifle could bring down a moose." He looked at me. "Or a person."

I flinched. "I don't know why those cartridges were on the side of the quarry road, or how they got there. But Jake has a .22, and Burt's rifle is a Winchester. And Jake was shooting at the gravel pit last week."

"The cartridges were from the same two rifles that were in this house?" Izzie shook her head.

"Right."

"Have you heard any other details from the police? Any confirmation on whether Burt's rifle killed Carl?" Rob asked. "It bothers me that they found his rifle on the ledges beneath the lighthouse. If someone was trying to get rid of the murder weapon I'd think they would have at least made sure it was in the water. Or taken it off-island and disposed of it somewhere else. Maybe even dropped it off the bridge. When I worked homicides in Portland I spent more time than I care to remember with crews looking for weapons tossed off boats or wharves or bridges into Casco Bay."

"We have bits and pieces of information. I keep hoping they'll fall into place and we'll know what happened. Jake told Preston he'd taken his rifle to the gravel pit last week." I glanced at Izzie. "The cartridges say Jake may have taken Burt's rifle, too."

Blue jumped up and settled himself in Izzie's lap. He'd accepted her presence.

"You think Jake shot Carl?" Rob cut to the chase.

"I never would have believed that. But now I don't know," I admitted.

"I do," Rob said bluntly. "Relax. Jake's .22 fired from near the lighthouse couldn't have killed Carl. A .22 isn't strong enough. Even a .22 long wouldn't do that. A Winchester with a scope might, if handled by an experienced user, but Jake certainly isn't that."

"As far as I know, he'd never used his dad's gun," I agreed. "Before this, anyway."

"If I were his father and he took my rifle without permission, I'd throttle him soundly," said Rob. "But even if Jake's taking it explained how Burt's rifle left your house, it doesn't explain how that same rifle got to Granite Point."

"No, it doesn't," I agreed. "But if we knew where Burt's rifle had been in the past week, it could lead us to Carl's killer."

"We need to get Jake to calm down," said Izzie. "He's run out of here, or disappeared from somewhere, several times in the past couple of days. Maybe he's running from having to tell you what he knows."

"I agree," said Rob. "Want me to talk to him? Man-to-man." He glanced out the window. "School bus just dropped kids off. He should be home soon."

"He's not on the bus. He left school in the middle of the day and went to the quarry. I picked him up there, but when I tried to talk to him he ran off again."

"Shall I try to find him?" asked Rob.

"Maybe Rob should try," Izzie said to me. "There's still a murderer out there. And we don't know where Jake is, or where he was going." She shuddered.

I hesitated. "I hear you that Jake could be in danger. But I can't believe he was mixed up in anything that got his uncle killed. Let's give him a little more time. I'd rather he came home on his own. Although Jake did well talking to Preston, he was nervous and scared. If he took Burt's riffle, he did something wrong. He's probably afraid to admit it."

"But this is a murder investigation. He may know what happened to it after he took it," Rob pointed out. "Whatever he knows may lead to another suspect."

"He could have given it to anyone," put in Izzie. "Or left it somewhere. Or . . . I don't know. We need to hear his story and advise him what to do, or not do, before the police put it all together."

"Izzie's right," Rob added. "If Jake's keeping any information secret that could help the state homicide police, he could be charged with obstructing justice, or being complicit in Carl's killing. You don't want that to happen."

"Of course not!" I agreed.

"I was once a fourteen-year-old boy. If I were in Jake's situation, I'd be scared to death. I don't think he killed his uncle, even accidentally. But if he knows where his dad's rifle was or who had it, he may think he knows who killed Carl, and he'd be a snitch if he told you or the police," Rob said quietly.

"This isn't a gang war in Chicago," I objected. "Jake wouldn't protect someone who'd killed his uncle!"

"Are you sure?" Rob asked. "Because from what you've said, the boy's involved in some way. For your sake, and his, let's hope he is protecting someone else, and not himself."

# Chapter Thirty

"(Advice to servants:) Don't upset the cook by telling her what the family says about her cooking. Leave that for the mistress. If there is any fault to be found, it is not so apt to cause trouble if it goes directly to the cook from her mistress."

—*Mrs. Seely's Cook-Book: A Manual of French and American Cookery, with Chapters on Domestic Servants, Their Rights and Duties, and Many Other Details of Household Management* by Lida Seely. New York: 1902

"Rob, thank you. I appreciate your advice. You've lived through nightmares like this before, with other families."

"Never with a close friend or neighbor," Rob said. "Carl was my friend, too. I wish I could add to what you already know about him. Whenever I saw him, he was either on his boat, at the wharf, or on his way in or out of your house or the Martins'. And, I assume, he was often over at the Snowes' to see Rose."

"Izzie and I started drawing a timeline for last week, but we didn't get very far. I've been trying to figure out where else Carl could have gone on a regular basis." I glanced at Izzie. "One possibility is that he was with another woman. Not Rose Snowe. Izzie talked with her, and Carl had broken up with her. But Carl loaned Jake his tablet, and Izzie looked at his e-mails. They sounded as though he was meeting one, or maybe two, other women. His life may have been more complicated than we knew."

"What about asking Jake?" Rob asked.

"Jake?" I asked

"He spent a lot of time with Carl, sometimes with Matt and sometimes just the two of them. Carl might have told him things he didn't tell you and Burt. Right?" Rob pressed.

"We're back to Jake again." I thought for a moment. "It's possible. I wish he and Matt would resolve whatever trouble they're having with each other, if that's why Jake is holding back."

"I agree that normally it would be better for Jake and Matt to settle their own problems. But, Anna, this is a murder investigation! Burt's been arrested! You need to know whatever Jake's dealing with. And he may be confused or scared, but I'm sure he'd want to help us find a murder suspect other than his dad." She looked down at the time line she'd made.

"You're both right," I agreed. "I was trying to protect Jake. But I was wrong. When he gets back here I'm going to have to find out what's been happening with him."

"Good plan," Rob agreed. "In the meantime, let's think about motives. Whoever killed Carl had to have a reason, but it might not be obvious, or even logical. I've worked cases where the motive was road rage, or a minor slight that happened years ago. What else do we know about Carl? Maybe we know something we don't realize is important."

"Carl was almost thirty. Single. Never married, no children.

Ex-girlfriends, but none too serious. We all thought Rose Snowe was the woman in his life, but they broke up a month ago, and based on the e-mails Izzie saw, there were other women. That's all we know about relationships. Of course, he also had money problems."

"The women could be an issue," Izzie pointed out, making a note. "Assuming Carl had synched up his tablet and computer, the police also saw the e-mails I read."

"You're right," I agreed. "Okay. But I keep going back to his financial situation. Carl squandered his small inheritance from his mother, and then after he won the lottery a couple of years ago, spent that money, too. He was struggling financially, asking Burt and me to loan him money. According to Jake, he'd also asked Dolan Martin to help him out." I paused. "He must have been desperate, because then he stole from Burt and me. He always said he needed money for a new engine for the *Fair Winds*. But he may have had other obligations. Several thousand dollars was spent on his apartment, even if the furniture and kitchen stuff came from auctions. Unless Rose bought everything."

"Auctions?" Izzie questioned.

"Auctions are big around here. If you want secondhand, antique, or 'vintage' as some people call used household items, you go to auctions. Dealers buy the real antiques, the good stuff, but you can get solid twentieth century furniture pretty cheap. That's where Burt and I got a lot of our furniture. Most of it was in pretty good shape."

"Your house looks cozy," said Izzie. "Do auctions sell old tables, chairs, china, and glasses, too?"

"Sure. Older folks moving into smaller places or estates

being settled consign household items. Auctions sell everything. Secondhand items go cheap. If I ever decide to get a good set of dishes I'm going to check auction previews."

"Cool," said Izzie. "I'll remember that."

I suspected she was thinking of equipping her restaurant, not of anything related to Carl's death.

I turned back to Rob. "Carl liked to hunt and fish. He liked the ladies. He couldn't cook, but he liked to eat. I can't believe any of those things would upset someone enough so they'd kill him. The worst thing he did was steal from Burt and me. That's the major reason they arrested Burt."

"Could he have borrowed money from someone else and not given it back? That could be a motive," Izzie speculated.

"It's possible. Someone he'd borrowed it from might be angry, might pressure him to return it. But why kill him? If Carl was dead they'd have no chance of getting their money back."

Izzie sat back. "Rob, why do people kill other people? I mean, really. Not like on television and in the movies."

"Crazy reasons, sometimes. Wrong time, wrong place. Those are the hardest cases to solve since there may be no connection, or no apparent connection, between the killer and the victim. I always hated those cases. More likely, people kill someone they know: often a family member or friend. They kill for love or money. They kill because they're jealous or angry. They kill to cover something up, or to hide secrets, or to protect someone else. Or themselves."

"Anything's possible. But nothing fits, yet," I agreed.

The front door banged open. In addition to Jake's black eye and swollen face, his fist was bleeding and he was crying.

# Chapter Thirty-One

"The food required by the body consists of gluten, fibrin, albumen, starch, fat, sugar, and saline matters. The first three are nutritive or flesh-forming; the last four are the heat givers. Men require daily five ounces of flesh-forming food and ten ounces of heat-giving or breath material."

—*Old Doctor Carlin's Recipes: A Complete Collection of Recipes on Every Known Subject* by Doctor William Carlin. Boston, Massachusetts: The Locker Publishing Company, 1881

I jumped up and went to Jake, reaching for his bleeding hand.

He looked from Izzie to Rob as though surprised they were there, and turned to me. "Mom? You said the police think Dad's rifle was the one that killed Uncle Carl."

I glanced at Rob. "Yes. What happened to your hand? Let me get it cleaned and bandaged."

"Forget my hand, Mom. It's okay. But nothing else is."

Rob raised his eyebrows at me and took over. "Come sit with us, Jake. A lot has happened in the past few days. It's important you understand what's going on."

"Are you helping Detective Preston?" Jake asked, sitting, but still holding his hand.

"I'm not a homicide detective anymore. I'm a friend. I'm just helping your family find out what happened."

"The police arrested Dad. They say he killed Uncle Carl." Tears ran down his cheeks.

Rob looked serious, but sympathetic. "What do you think, Jake? Do you believe your dad's guilty?"

Both of Jake's hands, even the one that was bleeding, were clenched. I wet a couple of paper towels in the kitchen and dabbed at the bleeding hand to see how bad the injury was. His knuckles were scraped and nasty-looking, but the cuts didn't look serious, thank goodness.

Jake took the towel from me and held it against his hand.

He still hadn't moved or said anything. But he hadn't left. That was major.

"Of course not. Dad didn't kill Uncle Carl," he blurted.

"We don't think so either," I agreed.

"You knew your uncle pretty well, didn't you, Jake," said Rob.

"He was a good guy. At least, most of the time. Some people thought he was messed up, but I got along with him fine. He wasn't just my uncle. He was my friend."

"Izzie, Rob, and I are trying to figure out what happened to him. We could use your help." I said.

Jake perched on the arm of one of our chairs. He'd joined

us, but was posed to take off at any minute. "Dad didn't kill Uncle Carl. He didn't have his rifle on Saturday. I took it," he said quickly, as though trying to get the words out before he regretted telling us. He glanced around quickly to see our reactions. "I borrowed it. I was going to put it back."

Rob gave me a look that said "down, Mom." "When did you borrow it, Jake?"

"About a week ago. Last Wednesday."

"What happened then?"

"Matt's been really upset and angry. He doesn't want his mom and dad to get divorced. I was trying to do something that would make him happy again."

Matt thought Lucy and Dolan were getting divorced? Where'd he gotten that idea? I had a dozen questions. But I let Rob take the lead. Rob wasn't a father, but he sounded as though he'd had a lot of experience asking teenagers questions.

"You wanted to help your friend," Rob said.

"Right. I figured Matt'd calm down if he could do something he really wanted. So, I told him I'd teach him how to shoot. His mom and dad won't let him learn. He's old enough, Mom. And he promised to be wicked careful."

"With your dad's rifle?" I asked.

"No, Mom. I'm not stupid! I figured he could use my rifle. It's for beginners. I borrowed Dad's to use myself." He stood, as though to get further away from my anger, which I was having trouble containing. "Dad promised when I saved enough money I could buy my own Winchester. He thought I could handle one."

Burt had said that. Knowing how expensive rifles were, I

was also sure he hadn't counted on Jake's saving that money any time soon.

"So, you took both the rifles," said Rob, sending me another "keep cool" look and continuing to question Jake.

"And Uncle Carl drove Matt and me to the gravel pit."

"Carl! When did he get involved?" I asked.

"Matt and I couldn't ride our bikes and carry rifles, too. Besides, someone might have seen us."

"True," I said, hoping my voice sounded calmer than I felt.

"They might have stopped us, or told you or Dad," Jake explained, with teenaged logic. "Uncle Carl hung around while I showed Matt how to load and shoot. He did pretty well, too, for a first-timer."

So, they hadn't been alone at the gravel pit. Carl had been with them, thank goodness, in case anything had gone wrong.

"And then Carl drove you both home?"

"Yeah. Only, Dad was out front loading traps onto the truck. We couldn't bring the rifles in, you know, because he'd see us."

"Right," I said. It all made perfect sense from Jake's perspective.

"Uncle Carl told us not to worry. He'd take care of the rifles until we could get them back into the house."

"So, your uncle took the rifles, Jake?" Rob asked.

Izzie and I exchanged glances. Where was this story heading?

"He left them in his truck and went home, to his apartment."

"What did you and Matt do?"

Jake looked as though Rob's question was dumb. "It was time for supper and we had homework to do. We went home."

"When did you get your rifle back?"

"The next day. Thursday after school. No one was home—you were over at Mamie's house, Mom, and our truck wasn't in the drive, so I figured Dad was at the wharf. I called Uncle Carl and he brought my rifle over, and I put it away."

"What about your dad's rifle?" I asked.

"That's when it got weird. Uncle Carl couldn't find Dad's rifle. He said he'd left our guns in his truck overnight, and Dad's was gone in the morning. I told him I had to have it back. I was going to get in big trouble if Dad found out I'd borrowed it. If it was lost, he'd never forgive me."

"Did Carl have any idea where it was?"

"He said he hadn't touched the rifles. So, I asked him if the truck had been at his place all night."

Jake dropped the bloody towel he'd been holding, but didn't seem to notice. "He fussed around a bit, but then he told me he'd been home for a while and then had come back over this way later that night, before he went home to bed."

I thought for a second. "I don't remember Carl's stopping in Wednesday night."

"He wasn't visiting *us*," Jake mumbled.

"Who was he visiting?" Rob asked.

"Someone at the Martins' house, probably. That's what he usually did," Jake muttered.

*What he usually did?* I knew Carl and the Martins were friends. But Jake's tone was strange.

"So?" Rob prompted.

"So, I figured out what happened to the rifle. Whenever he was over this way at night, Uncle Carl parked behind the church. Matt knew that, and he was the only other person who knew the rifle was in the truck. I figured he had to have taken it."

Izzie and I exchanged glances. "Did you ask Matt whether he had?"

"Sure! As soon as I figured out it must be him, I texted him. At first, he said he hadn't done it. But then he said, yeah, he'd borrowed it in case he needed it."

"In case he needed it?" Rob asked. "Why would he need it?"

"He wouldn't say. He was pissed—sorry, Mom—he was wicked angry at his mom and dad. I told him I had to put the rifle back. Then he said he'd give it to me, but he wanted to keep it for a couple of days just to look at it and hold it." Jake paused. "Matt's a little crazy about rifles. I wish his mom and dad would let him have his own."

"Weird," Izzie said softly.

"It wasn't weird! It was wicked scary!" said Jake. "Matt's just wanting to hold the rifle? And I knew he was mad at his mom. And then Uncle Carl drowned, or we thought he'd drowned, and I forgot about Dad's gun. Sunday, I remembered it and that's why Matt and I had a fight then. I wanted the rifle back, and he wouldn't give it to me. He kept saying he didn't have it any more."

"That's when you got your black eye," said Izzie.

"Yeah. Got the black eye. Didn't get the rifle. Then, when that detective asked me about my rifle on Monday, I got scared. I thought maybe Matt lied. That he did know where Dad's rifle was, and he'd killed Uncle Carl. And I was the one who showed him how to shoot and didn't get Dad's rifle back, so it was all my fault. I didn't know what to do. I didn't know for sure. And I had no proof." Jake looked relieved. "So, that's all I know.

And now those detectives are saying Dad killed Uncle Carl. He couldn't have! Like I said, he didn't have his rifle on Saturday."

Jake rubbed the tears off his face with his shirt sleeve.

"Thank you for telling us," said Rob. "That wasn't easy. But you've been a big help."

"So, can Dad get out of jail now?"

"Not right away," Rob assured him. "We still need answers to other questions. We need to know for sure who had that rifle Saturday morning."

"So, that's why you've been fighting with Matt?" I asked.

Jake nodded.

"When did Matt first tell you he didn't have the rifle?" asked Rob.

"He told me on Friday, but he was lying."

"Are you sure, Jake?" I asked him.

"I stayed over at the Martins' house Friday night, remember, Mom? I asked him for the rifle—again. He said he didn't have it. I figured he'd hidden it, so I wouldn't find it and take it back. But he kept saying it had disappeared." Jake looked at Rob, and then at me. "I'm not stupid. I know rifles don't disappear. So, I didn't believe him. I called him a liar. And worse."

# Chapter Thirty-Two

"Roasting meats: The first preparation for roasting is to take care that the spit be properly cleaned with sand and water; nothing else. When it has been well scoured with this, dry it with a clean cloth."

—*The New England Economical Housekeeper, and Family Receipt Book* by Esther A. Howland. Worcester, Massachusetts: S.A. Howland, 1844

Just then, Rob's phone rang. Jake bolted. "I've said enough," he said. "I don't know anything more. I've got homework to do." He grabbed his backpack from where Izzie had left it at the bottom of the staircase and took the stairs to his room two at a time.

Rob shook his head, but answered his phone. "Yes. I've been trying to reach you. I have a friend on the mid-coast who needs a lawyer." He paused. "Murder. He's been charged with murder."

I didn't want to hear the rest of the call. Rob would tell us if his friend could help Burt. I gestured to Izzie to follow me into the kitchen.

"Wow. That was some story," said Izzie. "Thank goodness Jake finally told us he'd taken the rifle, and what happened to it. That should get Burt off the hook, shouldn't it? He didn't have his rifle when Carl was shot."

I hesitated. "I don't know what the police will think. Sure, Burt said he didn't have his rifle, and Jake's story seemed to back that up. But we don't have any proof Matt—or anyone else—was the killer, and no motive. Plus, Matt and Jake were on the mainland at baseball practice Saturday morning when Carl was shot. We need to find out who had it Saturday morning."

"Jake filled in some details on our timeline, but not enough," she agreed, as Rob joined us in the kitchen.

"I have a lawyer—a good defense attorney—who says he'll take Burt on as a client. But he's asking for a four thousand dollar retainer. Can you manage that, Anna?"

Four thousand dollars. Yesterday, I would have said "yes." Yesterday, I didn't know Carl had taken our savings.

We had some money in our checking account, and maybe Mom or Mamie could loan me a little. I had to get the best lawyer for Burt.

"You're sure he's good?" I asked.

"I've seen him handle some challenging cases. Handle them well," Rob assured me.

"Then tell him we'll hire him. When does he need the money?"

"I'll find out." Rob went back to his phone.

I turned to Izzie. "You said we'd be getting money from our father's estate. Any idea how soon that would be?"

Izzie shook her head. "Not exactly. This morning I called the lawyer who's making arrangements. He's already filed the will and the general inventory of the estate, and there's been a bid on Dad's house. The couple who're interested have cash. If that sale goes through, the estate could be settled quickly."

"But not in the next week."

"Not in the next week," Izzie agreed. "Some estates take six months to a year to settle, although this one shouldn't take as long. Dad had his papers in order. But he also left a life insurance policy made out to both of us. We should be getting that money any day. His lawyer said life insurance policies come through quickly. He expected our checks to arrive next week. He's going to send both of ours here."

"Life insurance?" Had Izzie mentioned that before? "How much will that come to?"

"The company Dad worked for had a hundred thousand dollar policy on him. Fifty thousand for each of us."

"Fifty thousand dollars?" I repeated, stunned. "Just from life insurance?"

"So I understand," said Izzie. "That's why I wasn't totally crazy looking at that building yesterday. And you should have enough for a lawyer for Burt."

"What a relief. All we need to do is find out where that gun was Saturday morning. That should solve the case, so Burt can come home." There was hope. And even if freeing Burt took longer than I hoped, I'd have enough to support Jake and me for a while.

"Your lawyer's on board," said Rob, coming back into the kitchen. "He says if you're a friend of mine he won't need the retainer for a week or so."

"I can handle it," I said, with a lot more confidence than I'd felt a few minutes before.

"Jake told us a lot," Rob said. "But I wouldn't advise you to share any of what he said with Preston. Not until we know for sure who had that rifle on Saturday. The police have a suspect they like for the murder right now. They won't listen to anything else until we know for sure what happened. Information from the suspect's family playing detective won't hold a lot of water with law enforcement."

"We can figure out the rest," Izzie said confidently.

"The rifle was at the Martins' house Thursday, or Jake thought it was. Friday night Matt told him it was missing," I reminded him.

"But did Matt tell him the truth?" Izzie asked.

"Good question," said Rob. "I'm not sure."

"If the rifle was at the Martins', then Lucy or Dolan could have taken it," I pointed out. "They didn't want Matt to have a rifle. But wouldn't they have returned it to us?"

"If they'd known it was Burt's," Rob pointed out. "If Matt wouldn't tell them where he got it, they might not have known."

"But why did Matt tell Jake it was missing?"

"Maybe he didn't want Jake to know his parents had found it," said Rob.

We were all quiet for a moment.

"On a lighter note, I overheard you saying you looked at a building yesterday, Izzie. Thinking of moving to Maine?" Rob asked. "What building were you looking at?"

"That small, old grill on the other side of the bridge," Izzie explained. "I'd like to open a restaurant here on Quarry Island."

"A restaurant! Terrific! Quarry Island could use one. Although it'd take a lot to buy that place and put it back in business," Rob pointed out.

"It would," Izzie agreed. "But if I had a partner," she added, looking straight at me, "and we could get a mortgage, it might be possible."

I stared at her. Go into business with Izzie? My mind, already confused by what Jake had said and what Burt was facing, flooded with questions.

And excitement.

"What do you mean, 'partners'?" I asked.

"Simple. I can cook, and I've had courses in restaurant management. You ran your stepfather's business, you're organized, and you know the community and the way things are done here. Plus, we're each going to have money. I'll bet if together we put fifty thousand dollars down we could buy that property. That would still leave us cash to fix the place up, even if you used part of yours to pay Burt's lawyer. Burt's a priority, of course. But you said furniture and dishes could be bought at auctions. We could go for a country casual style . . . buy sturdy wooden furniture and paint it bright colors. I'll bet you know people who could help with putting in a patio and awning. We'd have to buy kitchen equipment, but sometimes you can find that used, if another restaurant closes. Together, we could do it, Anna."

Izzie's dream. I could help her make it happen. I could make it my dream, too.

"Sounds exciting," Rob said. "Put me down as your first

volunteer. I'm pretty handy with home repairs and a paint-brush. And, after you open, you could use a bartender."

"A bartender?" I asked. I loved the idea of opening a restaurant with Izzie, but this was all happening too fast.

"What a great idea," said Izzie. "Rob, that would be wonderful! You could be our first employee! But we have to get that insurance money, and some of the money our father left us, first."

"Even before that, we have to get Burt cleared," I said. "Until he's home and we know who killed Carl, I can't think about opening a business, Izzie. With you or with anyone."

Part of me was as excited as she was. But what if Burt was in jail, and his legal bills mounted up? What if the restaurant failed? Izzie and I hadn't even known each other a week. Could we work together, long hours, in a small place?

"We don't have to decide right now," Izzie assured me. "But I've been bursting with ideas, and I had to share them."

"Maybe after this situation with Carl's murder is solved we can plan for a future," I said, cautiously.

"You're right. I'm ahead of myself. That happens when I get excited. We don't have to decide about the restaurant tonight. First, we have to find out who killed Carl."

"A lot has happened today," said Rob. "You both should take a little time." He glanced at his phone. "I have to check in with Dad and get him some supper."

"Let me give you some of the lasagna we had left over from the other night," said Izzie. "There's plenty for you and your dad and for the three of us."

The three of us, I repeated to myself as Izzie pulled out the lasagna and two heavy paper plates. Tonight Burt would be eating in jail, and I'd be alone in our bed.

I held onto the back of one of the kitchen chairs.

"Thanks, both of you," said Rob, accepting the lasagna. "If I can help with anything else, you know where I am." He headed for the door. "And, Izzie, don't hire anyone else to be your bartender. I make a great champagne cocktail!"

Izzie's enthusiasm and energy were contagious. Maybe she really would have a restaurant someday. Or . . . we would.

"Shall I get you a cup of tea, Anna?" asked Izzie. "I'm sorry if I just blurted all that out. I couldn't hold it in any longer."

"I could use a glass of wine."

"Good idea. I'll join you." Izzie opened the cabinet with the wine glasses. "And then I'll heat the rest of the lasagna for our dinner. After the three of us eat, you and I can get back to working on our timeline."

I sipped the wine she handed me.

I was certain we were close to an answer about Burt's killer.

And I had a major decision to make. What would it be like to go into business with my sister and own half a restaurant on Quarry Island?

# Chapter Thirty-Three

"Confectionary, and bad food, and bad drinks, and uncontrolled passions, and misplaced affections—all of which might be banished, were housekeeping restored to its primitive dignity—are the prolific source of half the licentiousness with which our earth is afflicted, and changed from an Eden to a scene of mourning, lamentation, and woe."

—*The Young Housekeeper or Thoughts on Food and Cookery* by William A. Alcott.
Boston: George W. Light, 1838

Jake didn't need to be prompted to go to his room after dinner to work on the homework Izzie had brought home for him.

Izzie and I cleaned the kitchen, and then got to work.

"Back to our timeline," I started. "To Saturday. We need to know where Carl and Burt were that day. And the Martins, too, since the rifle was in their house Thursday night."

"Okay," said Izzie, getting out the pad we'd been working on earlier. "What do you know happened? In order."

"Saturday morning Burt and I talked about your arrival, so he left the house later than usual, about six. He saw Carl at the wharf and they argued. He told me later he'd left the wharf at about seven thirty. Carl was still on the dock then."

"So, assuming it took Carl a little time to organize his gear and traps on a boat he hadn't used in a while, and make sure the engine was still working, Carl probably left the wharf a little after that," confirmed Izzie.

"Right. He was going to set traps near the lighthouse. Burt's rifle was found over at Granite Point, below the light, so we can assume Carl did what he'd said he do. He was shot while he was working traps in that area. Burt found Carl's boat adrift about noon, called 911, and began towing the *Fair Winds* in."

"We don't have anyone confirming where either Burt or Carl were between seven o'clock and noon," Izzie pointed out.

"There may have been other men on the wharf," I agreed. "But most set out at first light, so they wouldn't have been there as late as Burt and Carl."

"Okay," said Izzie. "We know Burt was out on the *Anna* when he found the *Fair Winds,* about noon."

"And Carl was out on the *Fair Winds* sometime after seven thirty, until he was shot, before noon."

"So—where was everyone else?" Izzie asked, turning to a fresh page.

"Matt and Jake had baseball practice from eight thirty until eleven Saturday morning, over on the mainland. Lucy took them and brought them back, since I was heading to Portland to meet you," I explained.

"When did you leave home?"

"I had a couple of errands to do, and I wanted to be at the terminal in plenty of time in case your bus came in early." I didn't mention how nervous I'd been about driving to Portland on my own. "I left here about eleven thirty." Not long before Burt was discovering the *Fair Winds* adrift, I was heading off-island, excited at meeting my sister for the first time. "Jake had spent the night at the Martins', so I didn't see him or anyone other than Burt that morning. No, I did! I waved at Willis Tarbox as I left. He was picking up his mail."

"I don't think you shot Carl, Anna, so we don't need to check with Willis." She thought a minute. "Unless he saw someone else."

"Right," I agreed, making a note. Maybe we should talk with Willis.

"Jake and Matt weren't even on Quarry Island that morning," Izzie said, frowning. "Why would Jake think Matt had possibly shot Carl? Wasn't he with Matt at the time Carl was shot?"

"It doesn't make much sense, does it? The boys were back on the island by noon, because they had lunch at Mamie's and Mom's." I glanced at the clock on my phone. "It's too late to call them tonight. They go to bed early over there. But we can check with Mom tomorrow about the exact time. I know the boys ate there. Burt told me they were on their way to Maine Chance when they heard about Carl. They went directly to the wharf and went out with Burt, searching."

"That doesn't leave a big window for Matt or Jake, for that matter, to excuse themselves, walk to the light house . . . how long would that take?"

"Ten minutes. It isn't far."

"But if Matt was at practice until eleven, Lucy probably wouldn't have him back on the island until almost eleven thirty, right? Would Matt have had time to get the rifle, go to the lighthouse, wait for Carl to come close to shore, shoot him, and be back by noon for lunch at your mom's?" Izzie shook her head. "Sounds unlikely."

"And Jake or Lucy would have seen him doing something odd. "Plus, we're talking about about using Burt's gun and sight. Matt had just learned to use a rifle. He would have had to be very lucky to hit Carl," I pointed out.

"Or Carl was very unlucky," Izzie nodded. "I don't know who shot Carl, but it doesn't sound as though Jake or Matt did."

"Thank goodness," I agreed.

"But we know Matt had the rifle a couple of days before that. So," Izzie glanced at me, "we have to consider all possibilities. Lucy and Dolan would also have had access to the rifle. If they knew it was in their house."

"What motive would either of them have?" I said. "Besides, Lucy was chauffeuring the boys to practice and Dolan was probably out on his boat."

"You don't know for sure?"

"He was out searching in the afternoon, but I didn't ask anyone if he'd gone out in the morning. I just assumed he was working on the waters. Most days he does."

"Tomorrow, why don't we check with Lucy about when she took the boys and brought them home, and with your mom about when the boys ate lunch. Lucy would also know about Dolan."

I wrinkled my nose. "Nothing like asking your best friends

where they were when someone was murdered. Or, if they knew that the possible murder weapon was in their house a day or two before it was used."

"I suspect Detective Preston has already asked them some of those questions," said Izzie.

"You're right," I sighed. "But that doesn't make it easier."

"Is there anyone else who had access to that rifle?" Izzie asked.

"Not unless Matt loaned it to someone else while he had it." I shook my head. "Nothing makes sense. Of course, they haven't confirmed Burt's rifle was the murder weapon. He probably wasn't the only one on the island who owned that model." I pushed my chair back from the table. I was exhausted. "But before we give up for the night, what about your restaurant idea? Were you serious?"

"Absolutely. I stopped and looked at the café again on my way home from talking to Rose." Izzie counted on her fingers. "Quarry Island doesn't have a restaurant. The building we saw could be one. I'm a chef. You've managed an office and the books for a business. And we're going to come into some money soon. A restaurant is an investment."

"A risky investment," I put in. "A lot of restaurants close."

"True," said Izzie. "But maybe the people running them didn't work as hard as you and I would."

I shook my head and smiled at her.

She added, "I need to find a job or start a business, and I have no obligations to anyone anywhere right now. And you don't have a job either."

I winced at her last point, but she was right.

"It's an intriguing idea," I agreed. "But—we hardly know

each other. Running a business together would mean we'd be in each other's space twenty-four seven. Could we make it work?"

"What do you think?" she asked

"I don't know," I admitted. "And I'd need to talk to Burt and Jake. Working at our restaurant would mean I'd be away from home a lot."

"You were away from home when you worked for Seth," Izzie reminded me. "And the restaurant will only be a few minutes down the road. Assuming Burt is cleared, he'll be out lobstering, and Jake will be at school. And we'd start out small—small menu, small staff. No patio or extra parking spaces at first. We'd figure it out slowly."

My mind was racing. Planning a new venture—a new life—was much more fun than solving a murder.

"I could manage the kitchen on my own at first with a limited menu."

"We'd have to get approved, right?" I asked. "Board of Health regulations and such."

"We would. I don't know what those regulations are in Maine, but I'm sure there are some. And Rob was right. We should get a liquor license."

I didn't know a lot about restaurants, but I suspected I was going to learn a lot. Soon. "I have to focus on Burt's situation now," I said, tentatively. "But, assuming Carl's killer is found and we can put together financial figures that would show it's possible . . . I think I'm in."

Izzie jumped up and gave me a hug. "How do you like the name 'Quarry Island Café'?" she said.

I thought for a minute. "I may have a better idea."

"What?"

"What about 'Kindred Spirits'?" I ventured.

"I love that!" Izzie almost squealed. "I can already see the sign."

I laughed. "But tomorrow, first priority is answering the questions we have on the timeline, and getting Burt out of jail."

Kindred Spirits. It had a good ring to it.

But before we had a restaurant we had a murder to solve.

# Chapter Thirty-Four

"Diet has a marked influence upon personal beauty. Generous living is favorable to good looks, as it tends to fill out and give color and sleekness to the skin. A gross and excessive indulgence, however, in eating and drinking, is fatal to female charms, especially when there is a great tendency to 'making flesh'."

—*Peterson's Magazine*, March 1871

I wasn't used to sleeping alone. I'd dozed restlessly through the night. When I'd managed to sleep, my dreams were full of people with rifles in a kitchen where Lucy was handing out beers to a group of kindergartners, and I kept looking for Burt. I woke in a cold sweat, my heart pounding.

It was still pounding.

All I could think about was Burt, in jail. I needed to see him.

Jake took his usual one-minute shower and raced downstairs,

his wet hair sprinkling me as he grabbed his sandwiches and gave me a quick hug. "Thanks for listening last night, Mom. I feel a lot better now. See you later!"

I was relieved that he felt (and acted) more himself, but his confession hadn't solved the mystery of who'd killed Carl. Burt was still the police's prime suspect.

Izzie joined me in the kitchen about eight and handed me a book on restaurant management. "Take a look at this when you get a chance. And could we get lobsters for the café directly from Burt?"

I put the book on the counter. "Burt sells his lobsters to a wholesaler. But probably we could make some arrangement with him." *If he isn't in jail*, I added to myself.

"We need a patisserie on this island," Izzie declared. "I love evil pastry."

"Let's work on getting Burt home first," I said. "Then we can talk about the restaurant, or a patisserie, or whatever you'd like. I had cinnamon toast earlier. I've had my share of evil for the morning." At least edible evil.

"That sounds good," said Izzie, sipping her coffee. "I haven't had cinnamon toast in years. And cinnamon is good for your heart."

"When it's mixed with white sugar?" I commented skeptically.

She put two pieces of oatmeal bread into the toaster. "Have you decided what we should do first today?"

"I'm going to see Burt. I need to know how he's doing, and let him know I've hired a lawyer and we're doing all we can to prove that he's innocent, and get him home."

Izzie nodded. "Of course."

I picked up the telephone and called Rob.

"Good morning! I'm going to see Burt. What's the name of the lawyer you talked to yesterday? I didn't write it down. And do you know if he's seen Burt?"

"Morning, Anna. The lawyer's name is Isaac Kimble. He's from Damariscotta. He told me he'd see Burt today."

"Thank you, Rob. If Burt hasn't seen Kimble yet, I'll let him know. Thanks again for your help contacting him. And for talking to Jake yesterday."

"No problem. If you think of anything else I can help with, just let me know."

I turned back to Izzie. "After I see Burt, let's go to see Mom and Mamie, and Lucy, too. They can confirm a lot on our timeline for last Saturday."

Izzie nodded. "I'll stay around here, do some laundry . . . and some thinking. Should we ask Lucy whether she knew Burt's rifle was in her house last week?"

I thought a minute. "I'm not sure. I do want to ask her if anyone else was at their house Thursday, Friday, or Saturday. If Jake was the only one there after the night Matt took the rifle from Carl's truck, then we have only three suspects: the three Martins. Getting more detail on our timelines should help with that."

"Give Burt my best wishes. Tell him everyone's thinking about him," Izzie said, as I picked up my bag and headed for the door.

The morning was dark and rainy. April showers? More like an April downpour. The world looked soggy and dank as I headed across the drawbridge, away from the island. When would Burt be able to come home?

It was up to me. Sitting in a cell, Burt couldn't do anything to help himself.

Muddy water splashed onto the truck as I drove through puddles. Carl had been proud of his shiny, new truck. He'd have hosed it down after a day like this. Was it still at the wharf? Or maybe the police had taken it. A little more mud wouldn't make much difference to our truck.

I blinked and stared at the road ahead. Was the road blurry because of the rain, or because of the tears I couldn't keep from flowing?

Burt and I'd been through a lot. An early wedding. Jake's birth. Buying and fixing up a house. The deaths of both his parents. Financial struggles. Now, Carl's death. Together, we'd get through this, too.

I gripped the steering wheel harder. I had to be strong for Burt. That was my job right now.

The county jail was in back of the courthouse. I'd only been at the jail once before, when I'd bailed out one of Seth's roofers who'd had a few too many beers on a wintery night and slammed his four-wheeler into a tree. I'd never thought I'd be back at the jail to see Burt.

I turned into the parking lot shared by the jail and the courthouse. The buildings were attached: convenient for lawyers and judges and guards, especially in bad weather. Prisoners had no chance of breathing fresh air until they were released, or were taken to the state prison.

But Burt would be released. Soon, I told myself. I just hadn't figured out exactly how.

I straightened my shoulders. By the time I'd reached the

door, my sweater and jeans were dripping. I should have worn a jacket. But rain wasn't my major concern today.

"May I help you?" asked the officer at the desk.

"I'm Anna Winslow. I'd like to see my husband, Burt Winslow. He was arrested yesterday." It hurt to say those words.

The officer checked my ID and nodded. "Leave your bag with me." He handed me a receipt. "And sign in. Here's the visitor's log."

I wrote down my name and address, the prisoner's name, and my relationship to the prisoner. My hand was shaking and wet with rain. My name in the log smudged. The guard didn't seem to notice.

He handed me a pass. "Clip this to your sweater and have a seat. You'll be called when you can see the prisoner."

I joined several other people—all women, and all wearing visitors' passes like brands—sitting on a long bench with their backs to the wall.

A young blonde, barely out of her teens, was called first. Then it was my turn. I followed the guard through a passageway to an open space where several men in jumpsuits were sitting at tables. One of them was Burt.

"No touching," the guard warned me.

All I wanted was to hold Burt, and have him hold me. I blocked out my longing and the presence of other prisoners and the guards and sat on the other side of the table from the man I'd always loved.

"Anna! I'm so glad you came." He said, trying to smile. "You're wet."

"It's raining. How're they treating you?"

Burt's voice was low. I realized all the other prisoners and their guests were also talking quietly. It was the only way to get any privacy. "I'm okay, for someone in jail."

I nodded. "Rob found you a lawyer. His name is Isaac Kimble. He's coming to see you today."

"Thank Rob for me. But how're we going to pay a lawyer?"

"Izzie says I'll be getting some of my father's life insurance, soon. And there'll be more, once his estate is settled. We'll have enough."

He nodded. "That's good news. I've been worried about the expense of a lawyer. How's Jake?"

"He's at school. He's coping. Burt, last night he told me he was the one who took your rifle."

"What? Why would he do a stupid thing like that?" Burt made a fist. A guard stepped toward us. Burt saw him and consciously relaxed.

"He wanted to use his rifle to teach Matt how to shoot. He used your rifle himself. Carl went with them to the gravel pit."

"Carl let those boys get away with that? Did he throw my rifle down on the ledges, too?"

"No! Of course not. According to Jake, Carl had your rifle in his truck one night, and then Matt had it. We don't know what happened to it after that. Izzie and I are trying to find out."

"You and Izzie? That should be the job of the police."

"Yes. But we want you out of here. Fast. Anything we find out can help." I desperately wanted to reach my hand out to touch him. Comfort him. Assure him. "Burt, try not to worry. You didn't kill Carl, and somehow I'm going to prove it."

Burt almost smiled. "Anna, you're not a detective."

"No. But I ask a lot of questions. And Rob and Izzie are helping, too. Believe me, Burt. We're going to bring you home."

"I want to believe that, Anna. More than you know."

The rain had let up some as I climbed into the truck and headed back to the island.

I was sure of one thing. I couldn't let Burt down. He was the man I loved. The man I'd believed in since I was a teenager. This time, he had to believe in me.

# Chapter Thirty-Five

"A pig, when prepared for baking, should have its ears and tail covered with buttered paper properly fastened on, and a bit of butter tied up in a piece of linen to baste the back with, otherwise it will be apt to blister. With a proper share of attention from the cook, I consider this way equal to a roasted one."

—*The New England Economical Housekeeper, and Family Receipt Book* by Esther A. Howland. Worcester: S.A. Howland, 1844

Izzie was sitting at the kitchen table, making notes.

"How did Burt seem?"

"Physically, he's all right," I said. I didn't tell her how I felt, seeing him sitting alone at the table in a jumpsuit. "He's coping. But we have to get him out of there."

"I'm working on lists of who was where, especially on

Saturday morning," said Izzie. "We need to confirm a lot of this, though. Are you okay to visit your mom and Mamie now?"

"I'm ready."

The rain had stopped, but it had left deep puddles and mud. Once we arrived at Mom's house, we pulled off our shoes and left them by the door.

Mom was working at her quilting frame in the corner of the dining room, her hair pinned out of the way so she could concentrate on her stitching. Mamie was reading the sports section in today's *Portland Press Herald*, probably checking to see when the Celtics played their next game. I hoped the paper hadn't reported Burt's arrest.

"Ladies! Lovely to see you. Any news?" Mamie was as enthusiastic as usual. "Tea? Coffee?"

"No, thanks, Mamie. We can't stay long."

"That Detective Preston was here the other day, just as you said he might be. I don't think we were much help to him. I see you're still with us, Izzie."

"I am," Izzie agreed. "Anna's a great hostess. I'm happy to be here. I'm getting to know Quarry Island. It's a special place."

"It is, indeed," said Mamie. "And we're glad you're here. Any particular reason you both stopped in now? Anna, I can tell something's on your mind."

Mamie and Mom knew me better than anyone, even Burt. They could tell immediately when I was troubled or depressed or hiding something. When I was a little girl, I'd thought they could read my mind. Thank goodness I'd been wrong.

"Actually," I glanced from Izzie to the others. "Yes. We have some good news and some bad news."

"Bad news first, then," said Mom. "Better to get whatever it is out in the open."

"Burt's been arrested for Carl's murder," I said quickly. It was hard to get the words out.

"No!" said Mom, leaving her frame and coming over to hug me.

"Why?" asked Mamie.

I untangled myself from Mom's sympathetic arms. "Burt's rifle was found on the rocks below the lighthouse on Granite Point. The police say it was the murder weapon. Plus, Carl had stolen money from Burt and me, so Burt had a motive."

"Stolen money?" Mom leaned forward. "When did that happen? And Burt would never have killed Carl, even then!"

"Carl forged a check a couple of months ago and took our savings." I still felt nauseated about that. "Burt knew about it, but hadn't told me. Of course, Burt wouldn't have killed Carl. I saw him this morning at the county jail. He's holding up all right. I've hired him a lawyer, and Izzie and I are trying to figure out what really happened last Saturday."

"If the police haven't been able to figure out what happened, how can you girls?" asked Mamie.

"We know some details the police don't have yet," I said, ignoring her calling Izzie and me "girls." To Mamie, anyone under fifty was a girl. "It turns out Jake had borrowed his dad's rifle."

"I hope you gave that boy a talking to," said Mamie. "He did that? And fighting with Matt? He's going wild all of a sudden. That isn't like him."

"I agree," I said. "But he and Matt argued because Matt took the rifle."

"Strange," said Mom. "Matt? I can't believe he'd kill Carl either. How are you coping, Anna? Truthfully. With Burt being accused and arrested, and now Jake somehow involved."

"It's not easy." For a moment, I wished I were twelve years old again, and my biggest problem was wanting a Barbie doll dress we couldn't afford. In those days, Mom and Mamie would bake my favorite cookies and make me cocoa and I'd feel better. Today's problems couldn't be solved by food. Not even the pieces of chocolate I'd tucked in my bag this morning.

"How could Matt take the rifle out of Carl's truck?" asked Mamie. "And why?"

"Carl had parked over behind the church," I said. "And Jake told us Matt's always wanted a rifle."

"So, he took Burt's?" Mom shook her head. "That doesn't make sense."

"I can see that parking lot from the window where I sit and read when I can't sleep," said Mamie. "I'm an old lady. I don't sleep much. I get up and listen to the spring peepers, and I see things. Carl parked there some nights. Days, too, when he was visiting the Martins."

"I need to know where that rifle was Saturday morning when Carl was shot. If I figure that out, then I hope Burt will be cleared, and can come home. Izzie and I've made up a timeline for Saturday. Mamie, were you here all morning?"

"I was. Cooking and cleaning and such."

"Mom, were you here, too?"

"Do you think I shot Carl?"

"We're just trying to find out what everyone knows, Mrs. Chase," Izzie assured her.

"Saturday morning, I drove over to the food bank on the

mainland to help out. On my way home, I stopped at the island clinic to get a new prescription for my cholesterol, and got back here about eleven thirty."

"Did you see Cynthia at the clinic?" Izzie asked, looking at our notes.

"No. Just Dr. Neeson," said Mom.

Izzie and I exchanged looks. Where had Cynthia been?

"When were you at the clinic?"

"Maybe eleven o'clock? Matt and Jake arrived for lunch pretty close to noon. They gobbled their food as usual, said their thanks, and told us they were heading to Maine Chance Books. That was before we knew Carl was missing, of course."

"Thank you. That's exactly what we wanted to know," Izzie wrote something down.

"All right. That's the bad news. What's the good news? Sounds like we could use some," said Mamie.

"Izzie and I've been thinking about buying that old grill near the drawbridge, and opening a restaurant," I blurted. After all this talk of murder, I was taking a ninety-degree turn.

"You're doing what?" asked Mom.

"Going into business together," Izzie confirmed, putting her notes away. "We'll call the restaurant 'Kindred Spirits,' like in *Anne of Green Gables*. And because we want to have a bar, and liquor and wine are distilled spirits. Of course, nothing's definite yet."

"But we wanted to get your thoughts," I added. I'd never made a major decision without letting Mom and Mamie know. I'd be much more comfortable with my decision if they were cheering me on.

Mamie clapped her hands. "How exciting!"

"We've looked at the building," Izzie said. "And we have some ideas. But we haven't put a bid in yet, and it would need a lot of work, especially if we tried to open before summer visitors arrive."

"How would you come up with the money for this restaurant?" asked Mom.

"The down payment would come from Dad's life insurance. He left it to both of us," answered Izzie. "And there may be some money from his estate for rehabbing the place later. We want to do most of the work ourselves." She smiled at me. "With a little help from our friends."

"So . . . sh! For now, okay? I want to get Burt home first. We'll let you know what happens, and what we decide," I said.

"Peter left you that much money?" said Mom. "After ignoring you all these years?"

"We don't know how much it will come to." I glanced at Izzie, hoping she wouldn't quote any of the large sums she'd mentioned to me. Peter Jordan hadn't given Mom more than a few pennies for all my upbringing, and that had been before I was born.

"And you'd take this money and invest it in a restaurant? You don't know anything about running a restaurant. And after Carl took all the savings you'd managed to put away? You should save any pennies you inherit." Mom had always played it safe with relationships and money. She wasn't comfortable with risks—maybe because she'd taken one with my dad, and been hurt.

"Izzie's a chef, she's studied restaurants and worked in some. And I ran Seth's office, Mom. You know I'm good with numbers and people. The restaurant would be an investment," I tried to reassure her.

"I still think a bank would be a better place to put your money," Mom advised. "But, of course, it's your decision. Just don't bite off more than you can chew."

"We won't, Mrs. Chase," said Izzie. She glanced at me. "Anna and I are both hard workers, and we're excited about this."

"So I can see," said Mom. "I hope you're both right. I'm still digesting the whole idea. I'll admit it does sound exciting."

"It's wonderful," added Mamie. "It's about time Quarry Island had a decent restaurant. Count on me to be one of your first customers."

"Good! Because I'm also going to ask you to help me with several of your Quebecois recipes. They'd be great for the café—a little French, and a little Maine. Especially recipes that involve seafood," Izzie said, smiling.

"I'll help. But remember, young lady, you promised to cook something Korean for us, too," Mamie said.

"I haven't forgotten. I'll do that," said Izzie. "But first, we need to make sure Carl's murder is solved and Burt is home again."

I added a silent "amen" to that.

# Chapter Thirty-Six

"Basic Wine Sauce, for puddings: Cream one-half cup butter and add, gradually, while beating constantly, one cup brown sugar, four tablespoons milk or cream, and one and one-half tablespoons sherry wine."

—*The Modern Priscilla*, November 1905

Lucy was vacuuming her living room when Izzie and I knocked on her front door. She'd once told me she washed her kitchen floor every day. I liked a clean house, but that was a bit much for me.

As at Mom's house, we left our shoes at the door and walked in.

"Good morning," Lucy said, turning off the roar of the vacuum. "Anna? Izzie? I've been thinking about you both." She shook her head. "Thanks for warning me the other day about Detective Preston wanting to question me. He did, although

I'm not sure I was able to tell him much. He came back later and talked with Dolan, too."

Lucy was my best friend. I was blunt. "We've being seeing a lot of Detective Preston, too. Yesterday he arrested Burt."

"What?" Lucy stared from one of us to the other. "Why?"

"The police believe Burt killed Carl," I explained. "Rob recommended a lawyer, but right now Burt's in jail."

"No!" Lucy sat. "I can't believe it. I still can't believe Carl's gone. And how can anyone believe Burt killed him? That's not right." She plumped the pillows on her couch and gestured that Izzie and I should sit. "How are you managing, Anna?"

"I'm coping," I said, as I'd told Mom. "I hope the police find the real killer soon."

Lucy nodded. "Of course. And life has to go on. But, poor Burt!"

"I wanted to check with you about Jake and Matt," I asked, making myself comfortable on the couch. Izzie sat on one of the armchairs across from me.

Lucy looked relieved that I'd changed the subject. "Those boys! They've been at each other for a week now. I have no idea what's wrong between them. They seemed fine last Friday night, when Jake spent the night here. Although, not surprisingly, I didn't see them much. They stayed in Matt's room most of the time playing those video games they love so much."

"So, you didn't sense any problems then."

At least for now, I didn't want to ask Lucy about the argument that Jake told me had happened last Friday night when he tried to get Burt's rifle back. Probably Lucy didn't know anything about that anyway.

"They were fine," she continued. "And, like I told the detective, that was the last time I saw Carl."

"Carl was here Friday night?" Hadn't Carl told Burt he'd been working on his boat's engine Friday night? Maybe he'd stopped at the Martins' house before or after that. I glanced at Izzie. Did we have that on our timeline?

"He was here pretty late, I'll admit. I was getting ready for bed, and Dolan was already asleep. Carl was only here briefly."

"Why did he come over?" I wouldn't normally ask a question like that. But today I was a detective. I wanted to know everything I could about Carl.

"No special reason. He just stopped to chat. I think he gets lonely, living by himself in that apartment."

"Did he talk with the boys?"

"No, just to me. It was late. I'd told the boys to get to bed. They had practice in the morning."

Right. I was sure two fourteen-year-old boys had gone to sleep at ten o'clock on a Friday night.

"Thank you for taking Jake Friday night and then driving the boys back-and-forth to practice Saturday morning."

"No problem," said Lucy. "But didn't Jake tell you? Baseball practice was canceled. Coach had the flu. He called about seven thirty Saturday morning. I told him Jake was here, so he probably didn't bother to call you."

"So, both boys were here all morning?"

"I let them sleep in, and made them breakfast. They said it was such a nice day they were going for a walk, and they'd eat lunch at your mom's. They left here about nine."

"A walk?" I questioned.

"They headed toward the wharf."

"No one would have been at the wharf then. Dolan and Carl and Burt went out much earlier."

"True. But maybe some of the other fishermen were there, or they just wanted to hang out. Who knows? Matt's been keeping an eye on Lim Simon's boat. His son is trying to sell it, to help pay for Lim's assisted living bills. Matt keeps hinting that Dolan and I should buy him a boat of his own. Of course, we can't afford to do that. But Matt keeps hoping."

"Lim's boat is in pretty rough condition," I noted. "But Matt's always talked about lobstering. It's not surprising he's paying attention when a boat comes on the market."

"True enough," said Lucy. "Here, I haven't even offered you a cup of coffee!" She started to get up.

"No problem. We've had our share of caffeine this morning," I said, and Izzie shook her head. "I just wondered if you knew what the boys were fighting about."

"I have no clue," said Lucy. "Honestly, Matt hasn't even spoken to me in the past couple of days. He was shaken by Carl's death. He and Carl were close."

"Carl liked hanging out with Jake and Matt. It's too bad he never had boys of his own." I hesitated. Lucy would be furious if she knew Matt had used a rifle. But I needed to know. "Burt's rifle's been missing for about a week. You haven't seen it, have you?"

She frowned. "How would I know where Burt's rifle was? I don't allow firearms in this house. They make me nervous. I made Dolan get rid of his guns years ago. I didn't want them tempting Matt. You know how some teenage boys are with guns."

"I do."

What more was there to ask?

Izzie walked over to look at a photograph on the mantle. "What a great picture! You were a cheerleader, Lucy?"

"In junior high," she confirmed. "I loved cheering! If I'd stayed in school longer I might have been on the high school squad. I was better at cheering than Cynthia, and she became head cheerleader." For a moment she looked wistful. "But life didn't work out that way. Those were happy days, though. Happiest in my life."

Lucy's happiest days were in junior high school? What about her wedding to Dolan? Giving birth to Matt? Buying this house? Not to mention all the celebrations and holidays and festive occasions we'd shared along the way.

Izzie smiled. "At least you have the picture. And the memories."

"I do," Lucy agreed.

"We have to go; we have errands to do," I said, excusing ourselves. "I was worried about the boys and wanted to ask if you knew anything. They've been close friends for so many years. It's strange they don't seem to be getting along now, when they both need support."

"I never know what's in their heads," agreed Lucy. "Matt hardly speaks to me anymore even on good days, and I have no clue why. Maybe it's puberty. I keep hoping one morning he'll wake up and be back to normal."

"I hope so," I said, as Izzie and I headed out.

"So, the boys weren't off-island Saturday morning," Izzie said.

I noted she'd used the phrase "off-island" as though she were a native.

"And they were wandering around. They could have seen something important."

"Matt may not be talking to Lucy," I confirmed, "But Jake trusted us yesterday. Maybe he knows more than he told us then."

"And Carl was at the Martins' late Friday night," Izzie added. "That's new information, too, to add to our timeline."

"Lucy didn't really tell us why he was there—just that Dolan and the boys were asleep." I shook my head. "That would have been pretty late. Dolan probably goes to bed early. Fishermen do. When those boys spend the night at my house they quiet down after I yell at them, but they don't go to sleep. They use headphones on their games and hope I don't check on them. I'd guess they did the same when they were next door."

"I remember slumber parties when I was their age, or younger," said Izzie. "Part of the fun was staying up as late as we could."

"So, Jake and Matt might have been awake when Carl stopped in," I said. "Could they have overheard anything that would explain a late-night visit?"

"Mamie said Carl parked his car behind the church at night when he visited the Dolans," said Izzie. "Did he visit late at night regularly?"

"Good question," I agreed. "We have to talk to Jake again after school today. He may have the key to everything."

# Chapter Thirty-Seven

"As a rule, the tasks given to girls, especially girls between twelve and seventeen, are too severe. The brain, in consequence, is over-tasked just at that period of life when the strain does most harm. Parents forget that if the physical system breaks down and the daughter becomes a tenant of the invalid's sofa, accomplishments go for nothing."

—*Peterson's Magazine*, November 1871

Within minutes we were back at the kitchen table, making changes to our timeline. What we'd found out had changed some of our earlier assumptions.

Blue ignored us as he gave himself a thorough bath in a spot of sunshine near the kitchen door. I wished I could be as relaxed as he was.

"I keep telling myself the key to who killed Carl is in this timeline," I said, puzzling over the list of people we were keeping track of.

"What're you doing?" Jake asked, as he walked in. School was over for the day.

"Trying to figure out who was where in the twenty-four hours before your uncle's body was found," I said.

"Dad couldn't have killed him," Jake said. "He didn't have his rifle then."

"I know. But to convince the police, we have to find at least one other suspect who was angry at Carl, had a reason to kill him, and could have had that rifle. Or the same model."

Jake pulled the list toward his seat at the table. "Why are there question marks here?" He pointed. "Like, it says Uncle Carl was at the Martins' house late Friday night, but then you have a question mark." He looked at me. "How did you know he was there?"

"Matt's mom told us."

Jake laughed a low, almost nasty laugh. Not his normal, happy laugh. "Did she tell you why he was there?"

"She said he'd stopped in to chat for a few minutes after you and Matt and Dolan were asleep."

Jake pushed the pad of paper away, into the middle of the table. "She's lying through her teeth. She lies all the time."

Izzie glanced at me.

"She lies all the time?" I repeated.

"That's why Matt hates her," said Jake.

Her son hated her? I'd never sensed that. "What is she lying about?" I asked in the calmest voice I could muster. Lucy'd never lied to me that I'd noticed, although everyone had secrets.

I was desperate. She was a close friend, but I had to hear anything that might head the police away from Burt.

Jake hesitated. "She's been sleeping with Uncle Carl. She has been for a long time."

"What?"

"Matt's been wicked mad at her ever since he first saw them together and figured out what was happening."

"How does he know? I mean, Lucy and Carl have been good friends for years. Ever since they were younger than you and Matt."

"See? I figured you wouldn't believe it. But Matt's seen them kissing, and getting into Carl's truck in the middle of the night. Then, two weeks ago, he was supposed to go lobstering with his dad, but he and his dad forgot their lunch. His dad sent him home to get it. And . . . he saw his mom and Uncle Carl. They had their clothes off and . . . Mom, you know what I mean. They were there, in his living room." Jake didn't usually blush, but he'd turned red as a boiled lobster.

"Did they know Matt saw them?" *Keep calm*, I told myself. *Just keep calm.*

"Nah. Matt took one look and ran. He told his dad she'd forgotten to make their lunches that day."

"So, he didn't tell his dad."

"No! That would've been wicked dumb. If his dad knew, his mom and dad would get divorced. Matt didn't want that. Even though he's PO'd at his mom." Jake sighed. "I'm going to get in big trouble with Matt for telling you all this. But it's my dad they've arrested! And he's innocent!"

"What else do you know, Jake?"

"Matt kept saying he was going to kill his mom, because she was ruining his life and his dad's. He wasn't really going to hurt her. He was just mad. But that's why since February he's been bugging me to teach him how to shoot. He wanted to show his mom he could do what he wanted to . . . he didn't need her permission. Anyway, he kept at me about shooting, so finally, I borrowed Dad's rifle like I told you, and got mine, too, and went to the gravel pit. Uncle Carl took us and brought us back, and I just showed Matt how to load and shoot. Real basic stuff. We didn't stay a long time. Only thing I didn't tell you yesterday was how wicked mad Matt was that I got Uncle Carl involved. He wasn't one of Matt's favorite people anymore, either. And I wasn't sure you'd believe me about Uncle Carl and Mrs. Martin."

"I believe you, Jake." I glanced at Izzie. The story he was telling me was horrible, but I realized it was possible. I'd known Lucy and Carl were close. Maybe I hadn't allowed myself to know *how* close. Had Dolan known? "Matt took the rifle out of your uncle Carl's truck, so you assumed he had it Friday night."

"Only he said he didn't. I was so mad at him. I'd done everything he wanted me to. He had no reason to lie to me."

"What happened then?"

"At first, Matt and I argued. I told him I needed the rifle back. Matt kept saying he didn't know where it was. I didn't believe him, but after a while I gave up. I didn't see the gun anywhere in Matt's room, and Matt wouldn't tell me anything. So, we were started playing video games, the way we always do. His mom came in and told us to go to bed, so we just put on headphones and turned off our lights and kept playing."

I nodded. That, I believed.

"We were sitting in the dark room playing and we saw headlights across the street, maybe about midnight. It was Uncle Carl. We snuck out into the hallway and heard him and Mrs. Martin downstairs in the living room. They were being all gross and mushy. Matt was wicked angry, and he went and got Dad's rifle. I'd been right—he *had* lied to me. He'd known where it was all along. He'd hidden it in their spare room. He kept saying he was going to shoot Uncle Carl and his mom."

"No!"

"I was really scared," Jake admitted. "I didn't know if Matt would really do it. So I woke Mr. Martin up, and he came out, like, in his underwear. He saw Matt with the rifle and Mrs. Martin and Uncle Carl, and they all had this humungous fight."

"What happened to the rifle?"

"Mr. Martin took it. Matt was wicked mad at me for getting his dad involved, though. I don't think he would really have shot his mom or Uncle Carl. But he said he was going to."

"You did the right thing, Jake." What if Matt *had* killed Carl or his mother? His life would have been ruined along with theirs.

"So, like I said, Mr. and Mrs. Martin and Uncle Carl were downstairs, and they were all screaming at each other. At first Matt and I stood on the stairs and watched, but then they yelled at us to go back to bed." Jake grimaced. "It was awful. Right after that, we heard the front door slam. Uncle Carl drove away, fast. Mrs. Martin was crying downstairs and Mr. Martin was yelling, but then everything got quiet. I don't know what they did, but Matt and I went to bed."

"And the next morning?"

"Mrs. Martin acted like nothing happened. She was all cool and calm, you know? So, we didn't say anything. She told us baseball practice was canceled, so we got out of the house. Matt wanted to talk to his dad and see what he was going to do about what happened Friday night. We figured he was out lobstering, but Matt wanted to check anyway. Plus, there's this boat at the wharf he's been looking at."

"So?"

"We went to the wharf. Mr. Martin's boat was at the dock, but we didn't see him. Uncle Carl's boat was out, and so was Dad's. Matt stayed and fooled around with the boat he hoped he could talk his dad into buying for him, but I left. I thought I'd go back to his house and see if I could find Dad's rifle. I knew Dad was out on the *Anna* and you were going to Portland to get Izzie, so I figured maybe I could find the rifle and put it back in Dad's gun case. No one was at the Martins', but I couldn't find Dad's rifle. Then it was getting late, so I started down to the wharf, to get Matt for lunch. He was on his way back, and we went to Mamie's and Mamie's, like we'd told Mrs. Martin we were going to. After we ate we were going to the bookstore, but Mr. Erickson stopped and told us Dad had found Uncle Carl's boat. He'd heard about it on that special radio he has. We ran down to the wharf. Dad was there, and he took us out with him to look for Uncle Carl." Jake was out of breath. "That's what happened. The last time I saw Dad's rifle was Friday night when Mr. Martin took it away from Matt. Maybe Mr. Martin killed Uncle Carl."

# Chapter Thirty-Eight

"The crudest form of bread is a simple mixture of flour and water, worked to a stiff paste, spread thin, and baked hard. Under the name of navy-bread or hard-tack, this constitutes the nutritious but homely fare of the sailor and the soldier. Between this rude, though effective, means of sustaining life, and the light, fragrant, and delicious loaf, resting beneath the snowy napkin, beside the ball of golden butter, around which the family gather at their evening meal, there is a contrast as wide as between the roughness and hardships of the camp and the forecastle and the sanctity, the purity, the taste, and the rest of home."

—*The Philosophy of Housekeeping: A Scientific and Practical Manual* by Joseph B. Lyman and Laura E. Lyman. Hartford, Connecticut: S.M. Betts & Company, 1859

"Did you see Mr. Martin at all on Saturday?" asked Izzie.

"Sure. When we got to the wharf the second time he was getting his boat ready to go out to look for Uncle Carl. He asked Matt to go with him, but Matt didn't want to talk about what happened Friday night, so he went with Dad and me."

I went over and hugged Jake. "Thank you, Jake. I know that was hard. Matt and the Martins are our good friends. But it was important you tell us all that."

"How could Mrs. Martin and Uncle Carl do that?

"I don't know, Jake. I don't."

"I could tell Detective Preston that I took Dad's rifle, that Matt and I had it, and then Mr. Martin confiscated it. Wouldn't they have to let Dad out of jail then?"

"I think that's a big start. But your dad still has a motive. Uncle Carl stole money from him. And we don't know what happened to that rifle between late Friday night and when the police found it over on the ledges."

Jake looked exasperated. "I told you. Mr. Martin had it. And he had a motive, too. Mrs. Martin was sleeping with Uncle Carl."

Jake was right.

"You once said you thought Matt might have shot your Uncle," said Izzie, looking at the notes she and I'd made. "Why did you say that?"

Jake looked down. "I thought maybe Matt knew where his dad had hidden the rifle Friday night. And maybe he'd gone down to the lighthouse while I was searching for the gun in his house. He was awfully mad at Uncle Carl. When I went to look for him after that he wasn't at the wharf. He was only a little bit down the road."

"So, you thought he might have had time to get past you, get to his house, find the rifle, go to the lighthouse cliffs, shoot Carl, and then go back toward the wharf?" Izzie sounded skeptical.

Jake shrugged. "I thought maybe. He wouldn't have needed to take the road to his house, like I did. We know shortcuts through the woods between here and the shore."

Jake and Matt knew this part of the island as well, or better, than anyone else. They'd been wandering and playing here since they were little. But for Matt to have done *all* that would have taken more time than I suspected Jake had figured. What he was saying now—that maybe Dolan Martin had shot Carl—made more sense.

"Would you like some cake, Jake? Your Mom and I are going to have to figure out what we should do next." Izzie's solution to problems was food. It wasn't a bad idea.

"Is there any of that chocolate cake we had yesterday left? That was the best."

"I'll find you some," promised Izzie, getting up.

I didn't even mention Jake ruining his dinner. I was proud of him. Truth wasn't simple.

But—Lucy and Carl? I was still stunned. They'd been my friends for years. They'd been childhood sweethearts. I hadn't a hint they were anything more.

Jake went to wash his hands before eating his cake.

Izzie said softly. "So, Carl was having relationships with both Rose and Lucy at the same time. I wonder if he was any more serious about Lucy than he was with Rose. And there was a third woman, I'm pretty sure."

"He'd broken up with Rose, we know. And he'd known

Lucy all his life. I wonder how long they'd been lovers. And what would have happened to Dolan and Matt if Carl *was* serious about her?" I whispered back.

Not to speak of what others in the town would have thought, or the awkwardness of the whole situation. How could Lucy and Carl have betrayed all of us?

And—still—who'd killed Carl? Was Jake right? Was it Dolan Martin?

Jake took his cake and went to his room. Izzie looked at the sheet of paper with the timeline (she'd been taking notes as Jake talked) and motives. "We've gone from no one having a motive to kill Carl, to Burt having one, along with Rose, and maybe Cynthia. Now we can add Dolan and Matt."

"I don't think it was Matt. Even though Jake wasn't with him all morning, he didn't have enough time. He may have been hurt and angry at his mother and Carl, but I can't believe he'd kill anyone. Besides—he'd only used a rifle once before. He wouldn't have been able to shoot someone on the deck of a boat, even a boat just offshore."

"That leaves Dolan. He found out about Carl and his wife Friday night. He must have been furious. He was the last person we know of who had Burt's rifle. And when the boys went to the town wharf after breakfast at the Martins', his boat was still there. He hadn't gone out early, like Burt and Carl, as he usually did."

"I'll admit, I can't get my head around any of this. Dolan wasn't violent. He'd even given up hunting."

"Because Lucy was against it, right?"

"Partially, I'm sure. He did everything for Lucy and Matt."

"You should call Detective Preston. Tell him he has other suspects," said Izzie.

"But it's all based on what Jake's said. Preston could say Jake invented it all, to get his father out of jail." I kept thinking of years before, when Burt had been arrested for stealing the boat a friend had loaned him. The police hadn't believed him then. And right now, his rifle was probably the murder weapon . . . and he had a motive. Why would they believe him now? Before we called the police, I wanted to tie up all the ends.

"Jake didn't make all that up," said Izzie.

"I agree."

Jake could be back at any moment. He didn't need to hear this. "An hour or two won't make a difference. After supper, I'll call Rob and get his advice. If Dolan is guilty, I don't want to mess up any evidence.

"I don't think you should wait much longer. Dolan might figure out Jake talked."

I got up and stretched. My whole body had tightened while I'd been talking with Jake. "I just want to be sure before we accuse anyone. It's after four in the afternoon. Wine? And then an early supper."

"Definitely," she agreed.

Someday Izzie and I might have a restaurant. Today we didn't need a bartender to serve us.

# Chapter Thirty-Nine

"Lettuce, greens, and celery, though much eaten, are worse than cabbage, being equally indigestible without the addition of condiments. Besides, the lettuce contains narcotic properties."

—*The Young Housekeeper: Thoughts on Food and Cookery* by William A. Alcott. Boston: George W. Light, 1838

Supper was a quiet meal. We were all too aware of what was happening.

Izzie tried to chat about the weather and the island. Jake was silent. I tried to respond to Izzie, but was too conscious of the empty place at the table, and the bed I'd sleep alone in again later that night.

Burt and I had only been separated a few nights since we'd been married. When I'd given birth to Jake he'd stayed with me at the hospital. That was the only night I'd been away from home. Two or three times Burt had headed with Carl or Dolan up to the county to hunt, and stayed there overnight. But they hadn't done that in years.

The house was empty without him.

No matter what Izzie or Jake said, I kept seeing how Burt had looked in jail: discouraged and alone.

Normally, if I had a problem I'd talk to Lucy. But I didn't know what was happening next door. I didn't want to barge in on the Martins.

And I wasn't ready to talk to Mom or Mamie, or accuse people we all knew so well. Years ago, when I'd found out I was pregnant, I'd told my mother before I told Burt. Mom had asked me, "What's the worst that could happen?"

I'd told her, "I would lose the baby. Or find out Burt doesn't love me."

"Then what will you do?"

I remembered saying, "If I lose the baby, I'll cry. And then I'll marry Burt. If Burt doesn't love me, I'll cry more. Could I stay with you, Mamie, and Seth if I had a baby on my own?"

"This will always be your home," she'd said. "Remember, no matter what happens: imagine the worst possibility, and decide how you'll cope with that. If you're prepared for the worst, you'll be strong enough to handle anything."

Tonight, I didn't feel strong. The worst that could happen would be Burt being convicted and spending the rest of his life in prison.

But, on the other hand, I was going to inherit money that would pay for a lawyer. And if Izzie and I found the person who really killed Carl, Burt could come home. Everything—well, almost everything—would be back to normal.

Izzie's dream might come true, and she and I would become partners in a restaurant.

And no matter what happened, Burt and I would love each other and believe in each other, and Jake would be all right. I sometimes had doubts about my own strength, but together, our family would survive.

"I'm going to see Rob now," I told Izzie as soon as Jake had gone to his room on the usual homework premise. Who knew? He might actually be doing it.

"I'll clean the kitchen. Don't worry about anything here," she said.

Izzie had been part of my life for only a week, and I already trusted her to do what was right. She'd clean the kitchen and watch television or read one of her recipe books. She'd answer the telephone and not give away any secrets or say anything stupid. She'd be there if Jake came downstairs and needed anything.

I walked over to her and gave her a hug. "Thank you, Izzie. I'm really glad you're here."

"I am too. No matter what."

As I got to the Ericksons' house, I realized I should have called first. Maybe Rob was taking care of his dad. Or Gus wasn't having a good day. Or . . .

But the door opened before I'd a chance to consider any other possibilities.

"Anna! Come on in," said Rob. "I was about to call you."

I followed him into the small living room his mother had decorated in pastels and flowered fabrics years ago. Now, only men lived there, but it was still her house. Rob was a little over six feet tall. He dwarfed the furnishings.

"Dad's watching the sports channel in his room. Red Sox are playing."

"This early?"

"Pre-season game," Rob explained. "Coffee? Tea?"

"No, thank you," I said, sitting on one of the yellow sprigged slipcovers.

"Wine?"

"Thank you," I agreed. "Just half a glass." A little more wine might help me relax. More than that and I might lose my courage.

Rob was back in a few minutes with glasses for both of us. "To Burt," he said, as he handed mine to me.

"Do you know if the lawyer has seen Burt yet?"

"He planned to see him this afternoon."

"Then I won't worry about that right now. But I have another problem I need help with."

"At your service," said Rob, stretching his long legs so they reached under the coffee table to the other side. "What's happening?"

"I've found another suspect in Carl's murder," I said. "And I don't know what to do about it."

Rob sat up. "What did you find out? Who is it?"

"One of the reasons I came here is it sounds impossible. But all I know points to one person."

"Who is?"

"Dolan Martin."

I saw Rob shake his head slightly.

"I know. Everyone likes Dolan. You and me both. He's been one of Burt's and Carl's best friends for years. And your neighbor. But hear me out."

"I'm listening."

"You know Jake took Burt's rifle."

"Yes."

"Matt used it, and it was in Carl's truck. They didn't want Burt or me to know they'd borrowed it, so they left it in the truck. Later that night, Matt went and got it."

"Okay," said Rob, listening intently.

"Jake spent the night at the Martins' Friday night. He and Matt saw Carl coming into the house to see Lucy after she thought everyone else was asleep. Seems Matt knew Lucy and Dolan were having an affair."

Rob grimaced, and put his glass down. "That explains why I've seen his truck parked behind the church so often when I get up to help Dad to the bathroom in the middle of the night."

"I guess it's been going on a while. Jake says Matt's been upset, and angry at his mom. But, of course, he never said anything to anyone but Jake."

"I sense that changed." Rob leaned forward, listening intently.

I nodded. "Friday night. Carl arrived at the Martins' late, when he and Lucy assumed the boys and Dolan were asleep. The boys weren't. Matt threatened Carl and his mother with Burt's rifle, and Jake was scared he'd hurt someone, so he woke Dolan and told him what was happening. Dolan took the rifle, told the boys to go to bed, and he and Carl and Lucy had a major argument."

"So, Dolan had the murder weapon Friday night."

"Exactly. But no one was hurt then. Carl left. Saturday morning baseball practice was canceled, so Jake and Matt went to the wharf. Dolan's boat was there. He hadn't gone out."

"He was still on the island? With Burt's rifle?"

I nodded. "So it seems."

"Did the boys see him that morning?"

"Not until after Carl's boat was found adrift. They had lunch at Mom's house and were on their way to Luc's bookstore when you saw them and told them Carl was missing."

He nodded. "I was going to offer them a ride, but they looked at each other, and both took off, running toward the wharf."

"And ended up going out with Burt to look for Carl. They said Dolan was at the wharf then, too, but neither of them wanted to go with him."

"So, you're saying Dolan Martin had a motive—his wife was having an affair with Carl—and he had the murder weapon—and he wasn't out fishing the morning Carl was killed."

"Right. So, should I call Detective Preston?"

"You heard all this from Jake?"

"Yes."

Rob sat for a few minutes. "Testimony from the suspect's son isn't perfect. We need proof of what happened."

"That's what I thought. You saw Carl's truck parked nearby sometimes."

"True. But that wouldn't convict anyone. I didn't see Carl's truck Friday night. And I did hear Carl and Burt arguing Saturday morning." Rob thought for a minute. "Assuming he was the killer, Dolan got rid of the rifle he used. But he probably has other guns."

"I don't think so," I said. "Lucy told me she made him get rid of his guns."

"If Dolan had killed Carl Friday night, that might be seen

as an act of passion. But if he waited until the next day, took a rifle, and went to a spot near where he knew Carl would be setting traps, that's premeditation." Rob shook his head in disbelief. "Dolan's a good guy. It's hard to believe he'd kill Carl. But if he was stressed and angry . . . If he did kill Carl, he's probably nervous and wicked scared now."

I nodded.

"And I'll bet he's still angry with the two of them, unless he's convinced himself Carl seduced Lucy and it wasn't her fault."

"No way," I blurted. "Lucy's known what she was doing since she was a kid."

"Husbands sometimes see their marriages differently than do people outside it," Rob pointed out. "Has Dolan ever hurt Lucy?"

"Not that I've heard of. Or seen. And Lucy and I've been friends for years."

"Good. And if there aren't guns in their house, better. I'd hate for anyone else to be hurt."

"Do you think Lucy's in danger now? Or Matt?"

"I don't think so. I hope not."

We both sat for a few minutes.

"So right now, Dolan doesn't know anyone suspects him."

I winced a little. Dolan and Burt were close friends. How could Dolan relax knowing his friend had been arrested for something he'd done?

"I know Dolan pretty well. Or, at least I thought I did," said Rob. "I'd like to give him a chance to turn himself in."

"But why would he do that if everyone believes Burt killed Carl?"

"Because you and I are going to confront him," said Rob. "He doesn't have a weapon. But I do, if necessary."

"Are you sure we shouldn't call Detective Preston?" I asked. "Jake wanted us to do that this afternoon."

"Right now, let's not tell him anything," said Rob.

I looked at Rob doubtfully. "You were a homicide detective. Is this the way cases are usually run?"

"No. But not every suspect is a good friend. It's worth a try. If it doesn't work, then," he held up his phone. "I have Preston on speed dial." He looked at me carefully. "Are you okay with this? Are you nervous? Afraid?"

"Yes. Yes. And . . . yes," I said. But my husband was in jail and my brother-in-law was dead. I believed Jake's story. I could do this. I had to. "But I want to do it as soon as possible, before Dolan figures out we suspect him. I want Burt to come home."

"We'll do it tonight, then," said Rob. "We don't know how Dolan's going to react when we confront him with what you've found out. But I'll record everything that's said. Is that okay with you?"

"Isn't that illegal?"

"Not in Maine," he said. "We'll both be there. If I do the recording, and you and I've agreed it's all right, the other parties don't have to know. The recording would stand in court. Are you still okay with this?"

"Whatever we have to do to prove Burt isn't guilty."

I could do this.

"Why don't I call Lucy and Dolan and invite them to my house? I'll tell them we have desserts left over from all the food people gave us, and that I'd like company. I'll send Jake over to see Matt. Despite their problems, the boys will do that, and I don't want them around to hear whatever happens. Lucy will convince Dolan to come. It won't seem unusual: we often get together for an evening."

"That works for me," Rob agreed. "Give me fifteen minutes to get Dad settled."

I could be as brave as anyone if it meant bringing my husband home.

# Chapter Forty

"Oysters and clams are scattered along our coasts—usually in the neighborhood of some miserable barren soil. Perhaps they are in part designed to afford a temporary sustenance to the miserable mariner who has been wrecked, where there is nothing better for his support."

—*The Young Housekeeper: Thoughts on Food and Cookery* by William A. Alcott. Boston: George W. Light, 1838

Izzie was watching the news in our living room when I got back. "How did it go?" she asked, switching it off. "What did Rob say?"

I spoke quietly, so Jake wouldn't overhear. "Rob thinks we should confront Dolan and see if he'll confess. I'm going to invite Lucy and Dolan here for desserts and coffee. Rob will be here, too."

"What about the boys?" Izzie asked.

"I'm hoping Lucy and Dolan will agree Jake can go to their

house to play videos or talk with Matt. I don't want either of the boys to hear whatever happens here."

"You make the call. I'll check the desserts." She gave me a quick hug on her way to the kitchen. "You can do this, Anna. You can."

"Do I look that scared?" I asked her.

"Petrified," she nodded. "But in control."

I gave her a thumbs up and called the Martins.

"Lucy? It's me. I know it's short notice, but nights are long with Burt in jail, and I'd love you and Dolan to come over and share some of the desserts people left for us after church Sunday. We have more food than Izzie and Jake and I can eat. I'd hate for it to spoil. Frankly, I'd really like to have company and see friends. Rob's stopping by, too."

Lucy didn't answer immediately. Then, "We'd planned to make an early night of it. But, sure, we could stop over for a short time."

"Would you mind if I sent Jake over to your house? He and Matt could finish their homework together. They should have some time to solve whatever problems they've been having."

"Or play games. Sure, that's fine. Give Dolan and me a few minutes, and we'll be over. Jake's always welcome here."

"All set," I called to Izzie, who was busy arranging a buffet of cakes, pies, cookies, and brownies that could have fed twenty. "Looks like there's enough to make a plate for Jake and Matt." I took two pieces of fudge for myself. Tonight I'd need all the help I could get.

"Doing that now," she replied, pulling out my stock of disposable tableware.

I knocked on Jake's door.

"What?" he yelled back.

"I invited the Martins over to talk," I said through the closed door. "They've said you can spend the evening with Matt at their house."

Jake opened the door. "You're trying to get rid of me?"

"You and Matt should have time together. Izzie's making a plate of sweets for you to take with you. I think there are whoopie pies."

Jake's eyes lit up at the possibility of whoopie pies. He loved them, and although many women on the island made them, I never had. Then he turned serious. "Why are the Martins coming here?" he asked suspiciously.

"Izzie and I need to fill out that timeline we were working on," I told him. "And, honestly, I thought they might speak more freely if you and Matt weren't around."

Jake didn't say anything.

"I'm trying to get your dad home," I explained. "And Rob Erickson will be here. He agreed that what you told me explained a lot, but wasn't quite enough to take to the police and get your dad released."

Jake nodded. "I want Dad home. If you need me or Matt, we can be here in a few minutes."

"I know. And this won't take long." *I hope*, I added to myself. "Have you finished your homework?"

He shrugged. "Sure."

Not reassuring. But with all that was happening today, homework wasn't the priority it usually was.

"Get your jacket, then. Izzie has your food in the kitchen."

I heard Rob's voice from downstairs. He'd arrived sooner than I'd thought. The evening had begun.

# Chapter Forty-One

"To stop bleeding at the nose—Chew a piece of paper; or take two or three pinches of dried salt beef, grated fine, and use as snuff; or raise the left arm and keep it up some time; or bathe the back of the head and neck in cold water."

—*The Philosophy of Housekeeping: A Scientific and Practical* Manual by Joseph B. Lyman and Laura E. Lyman. Hartford, Connecticut: S.M. Betts & Company, 1859

At first, it seemed like a normal neighborhood gathering, with everyone playing familiar roles. But we all felt Burt's and Carl's absences. No one ate much, and the stress in the room was obvious. Lucy and Rob chatted about the weather, while Dolan drank three cups of coffee quickly. I wished I could serve wine, but I wanted all of us to have our wits about us.

"So, does Burt have a lawyer yet?" Lucy finally asked. The elephant in the room was out.

"Thanks to Rob, he does," I answered. "Rob knows several defense attorneys."

"Then he should be fine," Dolan said, as though having a lawyer would solve all of Burt's problems. "How are you and Jake coping?"

"We're doing the best we can," I answered. "Izzie and I've taken on a couple of projects that are keeping us busy."

"Oh?" Lucy asked.

"Anna and I may open a small restaurant here on Quarry Island," Izzie explained. "We've looked at that property near the bridge that used to be a grill."

"That place that used to sell over-priced lobster rolls and ice cream cones?" Dolan asked.

"Right," I agreed.

"That place is a mess," he declared.

"True. We'll have a lot of work to fix it up," Izzie acknowledged. "And we haven't made an official decision. But we're thinking about it, like Anna said."

I couldn't stand putting off the real reason for this gathering any longer. "We've also been drawing up a timeline of where everyone was Saturday morning. We're trying to figure out who, other than Burt, might have killed Carl."

The room chilled.

Dolan and Lucy didn't look at each other.

"Of course, the police are also doing that," Rob put in. "But Izzie and Anna have come up with a few details the police don't have yet. We hoped the two of you could add some more."

"We've both already talked with the police," said Dolan. "There's nothing we can add to that." He got up, as though he was going to leave.

"Dolan, Jake told us what happened Friday night," I said, deciding to come straight to the point. "You found out Lucy and Carl were having an affair, and you had Burt's rifle. You must have been furious at Carl. He was one of your closest friends, and he'd betrayed you. He was breaking up your marriage, your life. That your son found out before you did, must have made it even harder."

"I told you one of the boys would talk," Dolan said, glancing sidewise at Lucy, and then turning to me. "I had no idea about Carl and Lucy. I was so angry I didn't want to talk about it. After Carl left Friday night, I couldn't think straight. I hid the gun in the closet of our extra bedroom and I slept in there. I didn't want to see Lucy, or talk to her, or deal with the boys. I was going crazy, and I didn't know what I'd say or do."

"Where were you Saturday morning?"

"I left early, like I always do. That way I didn't have to talk with anyone at our house."

"But Jake and Matt said you didn't take your boat out."

"I didn't. Not right away." Dolan suddenly stared at me. "Wait a minute, Anna. You think *I* killed Carl? Sure, I was wicked angry at him. And, yes, I had the rifle Friday night. I was going to give it back to Burt on Saturday. You know Lucy doesn't like guns in the house. Saturday morning, I was still furious and hurt. My life had been turned upside down. But there was no way I'd kill Carl! Or anyone else, for that matter." He glanced at Lucy. "I wasn't *that* crazy! Just angry, and scared, and disappointed. Confused about what I should do. I didn't want to lose my wife."

"So, on Saturday morning when Carl was shot, you weren't out on your boat."

"Once in a while I take a day off. Saturday, I had a lot on my mind."

Lucy looked the other way.

Dolan kept talking. "I was up at first light, as usual, but then I drove over to the mainland to do errands. I wanted an excuse to get off-island, fill time. I bought some groceries and got paint at the hardware store. I'm going to paint the back of our house this year, and I figured I'd get the supplies I'd need."

Dolan, like some other Mainers who lived near the harsh cold and salt air that was rough on house paint, repainted one side of his house every year, dividing the time and expense by four years and keeping his house looking good. I wished Burt did that. Our house—all four sides of it and our barn—could use a paint job.

"When did you get back?" Rob asked.

"About eleven," said Dolan. "I dropped the stuff I'd bought off at home, and went to the wharf. By the time I got there, Burt had towed in Carl's boat, the marine patrol folks were there, and the wharf was chaotic. I took the *Harbor Princess* out to look for Carl, like everyone else took their boats." He paused. "Sure, I was mad at Carl. But I didn't want him dead!"

"Lucy, did Dolan stop at your house about eleven, the way he said?" Izzie asked.

"Lucy wouldn't know that," Dolan put in. "She wasn't home when I got there. She was at baseball practice with the boys over on the mainland."

Lucy didn't say anything.

"Baseball practice was canceled Saturday morning," I said quietly, turning to Lucy. "Lucy was on the island."

Dolan stared at his wife.

"When you were home about eleven in the morning did you check to see if Burt's rifle was still in the closet where you'd put it?" Rob asked.

"I didn't even think to look for the rifle until that evening, after we got home from eating supper here," Dolan said. "We all had a lot on our minds that day. I knew I could give that gun back to Burt any time."

"And was it there Saturday evening?" I asked.

"No," Dolan admitted. "At first, I thought Matt had taken it back. He was the one who'd brought it into the house in the first place. I was exhausted and angry, and I gave him a real talking to. But he kept saying he didn't have it and he didn't know where it was, that he hadn't seen it since Friday night."

"Did you believe him?" I asked.

"After I calmed down, yes. Matt doesn't always volunteer information. Honestly, during the past few months he's hardly spoken to his mom or me at all. We didn't know why." Dolan glanced at Lucy. "Although, I'm pretty sure we do now. But one thing I know for sure. Matt never lies. He sometimes avoids the truth, but he doesn't lie. So, yes, I believed him Saturday night."

"What did you suspect had happened to the rifle?" Izzie asked.

"I figured Lucy had found it," Dolan said, softly. "She'd taken it back to your house. Or thrown it away. I was worried about how I'd explain to Burt that she'd tossed his expensive rifle."

"Did you ask Lucy if she'd taken it?" Rob asked.

"I didn't." He glanced at his wife again. "Frankly, I didn't want to bring it up again. We hadn't talked much since our fight the night before, and she'd been all weepy at your house. Carl was gone. Lucy and I would have to make peace with each other, but it was too soon. Too much had happened. After I talked to Matt about the rifle, I went to bed. Alone. I figured I'd talk to Lucy about the rifle in the morning, when we were all calmer."

"The police found Burt's rifle on one of the ledges below the lighthouse, at low tide. Whoever killed Carl must have shot from the light or one of the higher ledges, and then tossed the rifle, thinking the tide would take it out," I pointed out.

"It wasn't in my house Saturday night." Dolan said. "How did it get from the closet in our spare bedroom on Friday night to Granite Point?" He looked at his wife. "Matt was out with Jake. Lucy, you were the only other person who could have guessed where that rifle was. I had guns when we were first married and I always kept them in my closet. If you wanted to get rid of that rifle there are a lot better ways than throwing it off a ledge at Granite Point. Lucy, you knew it was Burt's. Why didn't you just take it back to the Winslows' house?"

I'd been so sure Dolan had killed Carl. Motive, opportunity, means. He had them all. But his story seemed to hang together. Lucy had been alone after the boys had their breakfast Saturday morning. She'd been the only one who'd known where Dolan might have stashed the rifle.

"Lucy. You were the one. You killed Carl," I said, turning to her. "You took Burt's rifle. You knew how to shoot years ago. On Friday night, Carl probably told you he'd fixed his engine, and where he'd be working Saturday. You went to Granite Point and shot him."

Lucy's face was frozen. She didn't move. She stared at me. "You don't understand," she said, too quietly. She stood, and looked around the room. "None of you understand. I couldn't take it any longer."

Rob stood, too. He moved between Lucy and the front door.

"You and Carl were lovers," I said stepping toward Lucy and trying to stay calm. "Why would you want to hurt him?"

"Carl was a liar and a blackmailer," she spat. "Your dear brother-in-law told me he had money. He promised to take me away from this horrible island where no one has any privacy, and there's nothing to do but talk about everyone else. And then Dolan told me Carl had asked him for money. He'd had the audacity to ask my husband to loan him the money we'd need to leave!"

And that was probably after Carl had already stolen money from Burt and me. I hadn't known much about a man I'd known my whole life.

Lucy kept talking, as though everything she'd held inside for months, or years, was spilling out. "I loved Carl! I've loved him since we were in grade school." She turned to me. "You know what that's like, Anna. You and Burt loved each other from before you knew what love was. It was all doves and Valentines for you two."

Dolan went white under the permanent leathery tan he had from being on the water.

"So, your affair wasn't new," I probed, hesitantly. Lucy's answer could hurt Dolan even more.

"Hell, no! We'd been together off and on since I was thirteen. It had gotten more . . . intense . . . in the past few months.

I was restless. I wanted to leave the island. But I had no money. Carl promised he'd take care of us. He got rid of that simpering Rose Snowe, and he was saving for our life together."

I swallowed, hard.

Lucy started to pace between the living room and the kitchen. "He said we'd have a life together, wherever I wanted to go. He talked about Arizona, North Carolina, Paris! All sorts of places. But it was all a lie. When I confronted him about the money, he said he was still working on that, but I could move in with him any time. Move in with him? Move into an apartment on Quarry Island? I needed to escape!" She shook her head. "I was furious. I told him if he loved me he'd find the money we needed. Fast. We needed at least fifty thousand dollars to start a new life together. Maybe more. I'd been going crazy for years. A few more weeks, or even months wouldn't make a difference."

"And then?"

"Then Matt and Jake heard us . . . saw us . . . Friday night. I'd thought they were in bed, asleep. Dolan and Matt always sleep hard. Carl had come over late lots of nights, or I'd left to go to his apartment. No one had ever woken up. But Friday night, everything was different. I nearly had a heart attack when Matt said he was going to shoot both of us. And then Jake was there, and thank goodness Dolan got the rifle away from Matt. It was like a horrible dream. A nightmare."

"So, you and Dolan," I glanced at him. He'd sat back in his armchair as though he'd been pushed back. Pushed aside. "You and Dolan argued. And Carl left."

"Sure. He left. He waited until the house was quiet again, and then he texted me and came back. I met him across the street, so no one at the house could see us. He wanted me to go away with him right away, now that Dolan and Matt knew and there was no reason to keep our love secret. We could live together in that apartment of his."

Rob stepped toward the front door, blocking it. Lucy didn't seem to notice.

"Can you believe it? He really thought I'd be happy living down the street from Dolan and Matt, and never leaving this island!"

"So, you told him no." I put in.

"Darned right I did. And that's when it got bad."

"What could get worse?" asked Izzie. She'd kept still until now, but she'd been listening intently.

"A lot could get worse! Carl said he was tired of waiting around. That he could make me come with him, and that he'd take Matt, too. All he had to do was tell Dolan . . ."

"Tell Dolan what?" asked Dolan, getting up quickly. He was about a foot taller than Lucy. He looked down at her. "Just what didn't Dolan know already that would make a difference? I already knew you were sleeping with one of my best friends. You've said it'd been going on for years. What could be worse than that?"

Lucy jumped up, ran into the kitchen, grabbed a knife from Izzie's knife kit and held it in front of her. "A lot could be worse than that, Dolan Martin. Carl knew you well. He knew it would freak you out to know what he and I'd known for years. Just a little secret between us. I couldn't let him tell you. That's why I had to kill him."

Rob and I moved toward the two of them. I headed toward the kitchen door, in case Lucy tried to run.

Izzie's knife blade glittered in the kitchen lights.

"What secret, Lucy?" Dolan reached for Lucy and she spun around, still holding the knife. I blocked her way, and she moved to push me aside. I felt a sharp pain as the knife's blade pierced my shoulder.

Her eyes stared coldly into mine. "Why couldn't you leave us alone? Why couldn't you just let Dolan and I solve our own problems?"

"What secret?" Dolan demanded grabbing Lucy by the shoulders and turning her to face him. The knife clattered to the floor.

Blood was gushing through my sweater.

"Matt's not your son," Lucy hissed. "He's Carl's. Carl wouldn't drop out of school to marry me, so I settled for second best. You never knew."

Dolan looked stricken.

Rob moved between Dolan and Lucy and pulled her arms behind her back to handcuff her. "I can't arrest you, Lucy, but I can darn well make sure you'll stay right here until someone comes who can," he said. "And, for the record, I have everything said in this room tonight on tape."

Izzie was already dialing 911. "We need an ambulance, immediately," she said to the County Emergency Office. "Someone's been stabbed. And we need police, too. The Winslow home on Island Road, Quarry Island. Across from the church."

# Chapter Forty-Two

"To keep meat fresh in hot weather, place it in a clean porcelain bowl and pour very hot water over it so as to cover it; then pour oil on the water. The air is thus excluded and the meat preserved."

—*The Hearthstone; or, Life At Home. A Household Manual.* By Laura C. Holloway. Philadelphia: L.P. Miller & Co., 1888

Two weeks later, Izzie and I had lunch with Mom and Mamie, this time at my house. My shoulder was still sore, and I couldn't lift anything, but the doctors assured me it would heal. Time healed almost everything.

"These are delicious, Izzie," said Mamie, eating her third Korean shrimp and scallion pancake.

Izzie beamed. "Do you think Mainers would like them? I'm thinking of putting them on our menu."

"This Mainer does," said Mom, approvingly. "They're

delicious. One could be an appetizer, or more could be a whole dinner, maybe with a salad."

I loved that Mom was now having ideas about Kindred Spirits.

"I still can't believe Lucy killed Carl, but it all seems to be working out now that Burt's home again. What a horrible time we've had this spring," Mamie said. "And thank goodness you're healing, Anna."

My shoulder was bandaged and my arm was in a sling, but every day it felt better.

Izzie grimaced. "When I told you my knives were sharp, I never imagined someone would use one as a weapon."

"And Burt's dealing with it all?" asked Mom

"He is," said Burt, coming in the kitchen door. "Finished up with the traps a little early today and figured I might know where some good food could be found." He came over and kissed the top of my head and smiled at Izzie. "How're my two personal private eyes doing today?"

"We're just glad you're home. Get yourself a plate and pull up a chair. Izzie's made a delicious lunch."

"I'm not surprised," he agreed. "This new sister-in-law of mine is a darn good cook. Although, it sounds like soon I'll have to go down the street to get some of her cooking."

"We're hoping to close on the restaurant building in another ten days or so," Izzie explained. "The life insurance company came through with cash, and the owner was so happy to sell that we got a good price and a speedy closing."

Mom shook her head. "It's incredible. You two are really going to have a restaurant. Everything's happened so fast!"

"We're going to an auction this weekend to see if we can pick up some old wooden tables and chairs," I said.

"We're going to paint them bright enamel colors," Izzie said. "We'll look for old dishes and silverware, too. We've decided to feature furniture and fixtures that don't match."

"We think that would look happy: bright for the summer, and warm for the winter," I put in. "Jake's going to help us scrape walls and paint after school and weekends, and he's excited about busing tables this summer and helping out."

"If we can get the restaurant up and running and blessed by the health department and the town council by then," Izzie put in.

"Yesterday we ordered two signs, one for outside and one for inside. KINDRED SPIRITS. I can hardly wait to hang them," I said. "We're going to design and print our own menus on my computer."

"That way we can change menus every day, depending on what fresh local food is available," Izzie explained.

"And, Mom? We're hoping you can make simple quilted placemats for us. And stitch up some napkins? Plain bright colors would be perfect for those. We'll credit you on the menu, of course. It might even bring you some new orders. Maybe you could loan us a quilt to hang on the wall, too? We're going to ask Willis if he'd like to hang a couple of his paintings in the café, too."

"You've got it," said Mom. "I was hoping I could help with something."

"We'll probably think of more things we could use help with as we get closer to opening," Izzie said. "Mamie, I need to sit with you and figure out Quebecois recipes we can use. Each day, I'm hoping to have a Korean dish on the menu, since China isn't the only Asian country with a cuisine, and a French recipe, in honor of Maine's ties to Quebec."

"Plus, of course, we'll serve lobster every day, at least in the summer," I put in. "Vacationers expect that. And at least one traditional Maine recipe, like Indian pudding, or haddock chowder. Izzie's found some great historical recipe sources, and we'll include a little cooking history on the menus, too."

Izzie and I grinned at each other.

"We're optimistic. I don't expect anyone else will be killed on Quarry Island in the next couple of months, so we should be up and running by the Fourth of July."

"At the latest," said Izzie.

"If you two can solve a murder, you can get through Maine's regulations for restaurants," said Mamie. "Remember, I'm planning on being your very first customer."

"It's like a miracle," said Izzie. "Anna and I didn't even know each other a month ago. And now we're going into business together." She glanced toward the ceiling. "I hope Dad knows. It was his will and the money we've inherited that's making it all possible."

"I saw his picture on your refrigerator," said Mom. "He was a handsome man."

"He wasn't a perfect father," said Izzie. "Even to me, and certainly not to Anna. But he brought us together, and gave us the means to dream together. That has to count for something."

Mom nodded. "More than something. I'm getting used to him being back in our lives, in a good way."

"You did a wonderful job raising me. If it weren't for all I learned from you and Seth I couldn't help Izzie live her dream. And now it's my dream, too. I love being Burt's wife and Jake's mom and your daughter. But if we can make Kindred Spirits work—that will be something I did on my own." I smiled at Izzie. "With my sister, of course."

"I'm so glad you're part of our family now, Izzie. And, Anna, I've never seen you as excited and happy. Kindred Spirits, indeed." Mamie pulled two small boxes out of the large pocketbook she carried everywhere. "These are for the two of you, for luck. There's an old superstition that a gift of coral brings strength and perseverance."

Izzie and I looked at each other and opened the boxes.

My gift was a pair of coral earrings. Izzie's was a coral bracelet.

"Thank you, Mamie," Izzie said, giving her a hug. "They're beautiful!"

I squeezed Mamie's hand. "Absolutely. Where did you get them?"

"My great-grandfather worked on a clipper ship out of Quebec City in the late nineteenth century. He brought several pieces of coral jewelry back from the Far East for my great-grandmother. I inherited these from her. I've been saving them to pass down to the right person. And my two granddaughters already have a lot of strength and perseverance, but times, like the seas, can get rough. Maybe these will help you both through them."

Izzie and I both had tears in our eyes as we put on the jewelry.

No matter what happened in the future, I didn't need earrings to remind me of the strength of the women I was descended from. And I loved Mamie even more because she'd included Izzie in the family.

Two sisters. Very different. But very much the same.

Kindred Spirits, for sure.

# Mamie's Quebecois Apple/Cranberry Pudding

Note: In the early seventeenth century, North American puddings or duffs—as they were sometimes called—were basic parts of almost every meal. Ingredients were put in a cloth bag and hung inside or above a pot being used to cook other food, and cooked for four to five hours. After stoves came into common usage in the middle of the nineteenth century, puddings were baked and usually served as desserts with lemon, wine, or brandy sauces. New Englanders used molasses or maple syrup as sweetener instead of sugar. Similar classic apple puddings are called pandowdies, slumps, cobblers, or grunts in different parts of the United States and Canada. Mamie has added cranberries to her basic recipe.

## Ingredients

5 medium-sized Granny Smith (or other tart) apples, sliced as you would for apple pie. You may peel or not peel; Mamie prefers them unpeeled
1 cup brown sugar
1 cup dried sweetened cranberries
4 tablespoons butter, softened
1 cup white sugar
2 eggs
1 cup flour
1 teaspoon baking powder

Preheat oven to 350°F. Butter rectangular pan (approximately 7 × 12 inches.) Mix apple slices and cranberries, spread evenly in pan, and sprinkle with brown sugar. In medium-sized mixing bowl, cream butter and sugar, then add eggs. Mix well. Add flour and baking powder; mix thoroughly. Drop large spoonfuls of batter on top of apples. Bake at 350°F for 45 minutes, or until toothpick inserted in middle of pudding comes away clean. Serve warm or at room temperature. Mamie prefers it warm, topped with whipped cream or vanilla ice cream.

Yield: 6 servings

# Izzie's Glazed Lemon Nut Bread or Muffins

## Ingredients

4 tablespoons butter
¾ cup sugar
5 teaspoons grated lemon peel
2 cups flour
1½ teaspoons baking powder
1 teaspoon salt
¾ cup milk
1 cup sliced almonds (or chopped walnuts or pecans—whichever you prefer)

For glaze: 6 teaspoons lemon juice & 6 teaspoons sugar

Preheat oven to 350°F. Cream together butter and sugar until light and fluffy. Add eggs and lemon peel. Beat well. Mix together flour, baking powder, and salt; add to creamed mixture, alternating with milk. Beat smooth. Mix in nuts. Pour into either greased loaf pan (8½ × 4½ × 2½ inches) or 12-serving cupcake/muffin pan. Bake until inserted toothpick comes out clean; 50–55 minutes for bread loaf; 18–20 minutes for muffins. Cool in pan for 10 minutes, then remove. Combine sugar and lemon juice for glaze and spoon over top. Freezes well.

Yield: 12 muffins or one loaf

# Mamie's Maine Seafood Chowder

This is a flexible recipe, since fishermen don't always know what they'll be bringing home. Feel free to eliminate the shrimp or lobster and substitute more white fish, or to add more potatoes or onions. Calorie counters might substitute milk for the light cream.

The best broth for this chowder is made from boiling the shells of lobsters. Second best is clam broth, which can be bought in bottles, or chicken or fish bouillon. Lacking any of the above, water will do fine.

Chowder is best when made hours, or even a day, in advance and then reheated. Great when you're expecting company, but don't want to be tied to the kitchen when guests arrive!

## Ingredients

3–5 strips of bacon, cut in small pieces
½ yellow onion per person, sliced and diced
3 garlic cloves, or more if you love garlic
2 cups of broth (see above) per person
2 medium white potatoes per person, pared and cut in 1-inch pieces
½ teaspoon salt
1 teaspoon black pepper
2–3 teaspoons Tabasco sauce, to taste
½ pound of fish (preferably haddock) per person, cut in ¾-inch pieces

½ pound of shrimp or lobster meat per person, also cut in ¾-inch pieces
½ cup light cream per person
2 tablespoons fresh chopped parsley per person
Oyster crackers or French bread

Heat bacon in a 5-quart saucepan (or larger, depending on how many you're feeding). Add the diced onion and garlic, and stir over medium heat until you can see through the pieces of onion. Pour in the broth and add the potatoes (if the broth doesn't cover the potatoes, add more broth or water until it does so). Add salt, black pepper, and Tabasco sauce. Bring to boil. Reduce heat and simmer for about 10 minutes, or until you can stick a fork easily through a piece of the potato. Add the fish and shellfish. Cook another 5 to 10 minutes, until all is cooked. Then add light cream and heat until hot. Add parsley, stir, and serve with plain chowder, or oyster crackers, or with French bread.

Yield: at least six servings, depending on amount of ingredients.

# Izzie's Spicy Korean Shrimp and Scallion Pancakes

## Ingredients

¾ cup white flour
3 large garlic cloves
¾ teaspoon salt
¾ cup cold water (put in refrigerator while you're preparing other ingredients)
2 large eggs, beaten
1 tablespoon sesame oil
½ teaspoon cayenne
8 scallions, cut finely lengthwise and crosswise (scissors help!)
½ red bell pepper, cut in small pieces like scallions
1 pound raw, peeled shrimp, halved lengthwise and cut in 1-inch pieces
¼ cup olive oil

Mince and mash garlic with salt. Mix together garlic mixture, cayenne, water, eggs, and sesame oil. Add flour, and stir until smooth. Stir in scallions, bell pepper, and shrimp. Fry in skillet or frying pan at medium hot temperature (about 350°F if you have an electric frying pan) in about 2 tablespoons olive oil. Cook as you would other pancakes, pressing down with spatula to flatten. Cook until golden, 3–5 minutes each side. Drain on paper towels, put on baking sheet, and keep warm in low (200°F) oven until all pancakes are cooked. If pancakes are large, cut into triangles. If small, serve whole. A great appetizer or buffet or brunch dish. Serve with Soy & Scallion Dipping Sauce (below.)

Yields: 18 three-inch diameter pancakes.

## Soy & Scallion Dipping Sauce

### Ingredients

½ cup soy sauce, preferably low-sodium
3 tablespoons dark sesame oil
¼ cup scallions chopped into small pieces.

Mix together all ingredients. Left over sauce can be stored for 3 days in refrigerator.

Yield: enough sauce for pancakes above

# Mamie's Salmon Mousse

<u>Note</u>: If you're serving this as part of a buffet, or as an appetizer on its own, Mamie suggests you double it. It's that good!

## Ingredients

1 large can red salmon (15 ounce or 2 cups cooked salmon)
½ tablespoon salt
½ tablespoon sugar
½ tablespoon flour
1 teaspoon dry mustard
½ teaspoon cayenne
2 egg yolks
1½ Tablespoons melted butter
¾ cup milk
⅓ cup rice wine vinegar

1 envelope granulated gelatin dissolved in 2 tablespoons cold water. Clean & flake salmon and put it in a thin bowl or mold. Mix dry ingredients in the top of a double boiler (or small pan you can cook over another pan). Add egg yolks, butter, milk, vinegar. Cook over boiling water, stirring almost constantly, until the mixture thickens enough to stick to your spoon. Add the gelatin and stir until the gelatin dissolves. Pour mixture over salmon; mix gently. Chill in refrigerator (not freezer) overnight. To remove from mold, put bottom of mold in hot water to loosen; be gentle as you turn mold upside down. Then replace

in refrigerator for at least 2 hours to ensure mousse will maintain its shape. Serve with crackers, thin slices of French bread, cucumbers, olives . . . whatever you choose. Especially good on a hot day.

Yield: as an appetizer, enough for 6–8

# Marnie's Anadama Bread

½ cup cornmeal
½ cup molasses
2 tablespoons butter
2 teaspoon salt
1 envelope or cake of dry yeast
2¼ cup water
5 cups of flour (approximately)

Boil 2 cups water. Add cornmeal and stir, slowly, a minute or two. Add molasses, salt, and butter. Cook and stir together until well mixed. Put mixture in large bowl and cool. Mix yeast in ½ cup warm water. When mixture in bowl is lukewarm, add dry yeast. Stir. Now add the flour, 1 cup at a time. When dough is stiff, put on floured surface and knead. Add a little more flour if you need to. Continue kneading until you have a ball of dough that is smooth and shiny and bounces back when you push it down. This takes about 5–8 minutes. Put ball of dough in large buttered mixing bowl in a warm place. Cover with light dish-cloth and allow the dough to rise until it doubles in size. This could take 30–90 minutes. After it has doubled, push dough down in the bowl once or twice. Then remove it from the bowl and let it sit 5 minutes. Divide it in half, shape it into loaves, and place the loaves in greased loaf pans. Cover pans with towel and again let dough rise until it doubles in size (it should rise until it is just slightly higher than the side of the pans).

Bake for 15 minutes at 400°F, then reduce heat and bake at 350°F for another 20–25 minutes, or until the loaf tops are slightly brown. Turn the loaves out of pans & cool on racks. One loaf may be frozen for later use.

Yield: 2 loaves

# Acknowledgments

With bows and applause to Anne Brewer of Crooked Lane Books, and my agent, John Talbot, who made Anna, Izzie, and this new series possible.

To Jen Donovan, who did an initial edit; Jenny Chen, who had my back with marketing and cover art; Russ Sirois, who tried to keep my maritime information correct; retired homicide detective Bruce Coffin, who did the same for guns and jails; and Jean Kerrigan and Rick Hirsch, owners of my favorite restaurant, Damariscotta River Grill, who advised me about opening a restaurant.

All remaining errors are mine.

To Nancy Cantwell, Anne Marie Nolin, Bob Adler, and my husband, Bob Thomas, my first readers.

To my writing friends, all wonderful writers, listeners, and kibitzers. And to my fellow mystery writers at www.mainecrimewriters.com.

To my daughters, Caroline, Ali, Becky, and Liz, who watched the *Anne of Green Gables* movies so many times we wore out our VHS (and then DVD) copy.

To my husband, Bob Thomas. Every day we have together

I'm thankful for his support and love, and for the life of words and art we've created together on the coast of Maine.

To my neighbors, JD and Barbara Neeson, who listen to plot rants, taste test recipes, and are wonderful porch sitters and Patriots watchers, and, most of all, care.

To mystery fan Carmela Heedles, who loaned her name to a detective, courtesy of her daughter-in-law, Mo Heedles.

To every one of my readers who are surely "kindred spirits," especially those who've followed me from one series to another . . . and now to a new name. Your support, enthusiasm, recommendations, and reviews have made this book possible.

And a special thank you to the grandmother I never knew, Cornelia Kidd Wait, who was killed in 1911 when a train hit her car stalled on a railroad track, and whose name I've borrowed for this series, in memory.

If you've enjoyed *Death and a Pot of Chowder*, please like my Lea Wait / Cornelia Kidd page on Facebook, friend me on Goodreads, and, to hear about the next book in this series, write to me at corneliakiddmaine@gmail.com so I can add you to my mailing list.

Read on!

Cornelia Kidd / Lea Wait